AFFAIRS OF STEAK

AFFAIRS OF STEAK

Julie Hyzy

CHIVERS

British Library Cataloguing in Publication Data available

This Large Print edition published by AudioGO Ltd, Bath, 2013.
Published by arrangement with the Berkley Publishing Group, a division of Penguin Group (USA) Inc.

U.K. Hardcover   ISBN   978 1 4713 2782 7
U.K. Softcover   ISBN   978 1 4713 2783 4

Copyright © 2012 by Tekno Books
A White House Chef Mystery

Printed and bound in Grea
TJ International Limited

Though belated, this dedication
is no less heartfelt.
For Dean and Kris

ACKNOWLEDGMENTS

As always, thank you to my wonderful editor, Natalee Rosenstein, as well as to Robin Barletta, Kaitlyn Kennedy, and Erica Rose at Berkley Prime Crime. Thanks also to the folks at Tekno, especially Marty Greenberg — who will be missed — and John Helfers.

Ollie and I owe a major debt of gratitude to Denise Little, whose inventive recipes are always a hit. Thank you, Denise!

Thanks, too, to reader Patrick Smith, who sent me three beautiful Secret Service medallions I now treasure, as well as a marvelous book on life at the White House. Patrick always cheerfully points me in the direction of great research resources, and I can't thank him enough.

At the time I wrote this book, a section of New York Avenue Northwest in Washington, D.C., was under construction. In order to create the scene where Ollie meets Milton for the first time, I took a little liberty with the landscape and described a city block crafted entirely from my imagination.

Thanks to Mystery Writers of America, Sisters in Crime, and Thriller Writers of America for camaraderie and support.

Lastly, but most important, thank you to my fabulous family. Love you guys.

CHAPTER 1

Peter Everett Sargeant and I walked east on H Street as fast as our short legs would carry us. Though the cold April day was overcast and damp, it wasn't the threat of sleet that kept us moving briskly on our trek through the heart of Washington, D.C. What spurred us on was our unspoken agreement. We both wanted to put this morning's task behind us as quickly as possible.

The First Lady intended to throw a lavish birthday party for Secretary of State Gerald Quinones. That was unusual enough, but having the executive chef — me — and the sensitivity director — Sargeant — visit potential venues together to choose the best site for the event was even stranger.

"How much farther, Ms. Paras?" Sargeant asked me. He knew the answer as well as I did, but he never missed the opportunity to throw a zinger my way. I knew this was his attempt to chastise me for suggesting we walk from one location to the next.

He huffed as he strove to keep up. "I still don't understand," he said for at least the fifteenth time since we'd left the White House, "why on earth Mrs. Hyden insisted you and I work together on this."

At this point I didn't care if my exasperation showed. I turned to him long enough to roll my eyes. He missed it. The collar of his Burberry trench coat was turned up against the chill, and his cheeks were pink from exertion. As for me, my dark hair was flying free in the wind. I wished I'd worn a hat.

"Peter," I said to the little man, "I don't know what great insight you might be expecting, but we won't learn anything new until we meet with Patty at Lexington Place."

Patty Woodruff, the First Lady's newest assistant, had engineered this unique collaboration. I'd have to remember to thank her personally.

Sargeant's grimace deepened. "I am the White House sensitivity director," he said unnecessarily. "I should not be required to traipse all over the city to look at available meeting spaces for a party. What's wrong with holding it at the White House?"

I didn't bother to acknowledge him. He'd

ranted on this topic from the moment we'd set out this morning. So far, we'd visited three prestigious banquet halls, all within easy walking distance. The fourth and final venue, a brand-new standalone location in a refurbished building just a few blocks farther, promised a gorgeous space, LEED-certified efficiency, and plenty of room for all of the invited guests.

Patty had made it clear that this was Mrs. Hyden's front-runner, which is why it was the final visit on our agenda today. Patty wanted our approval, but I wondered how much impact our opinions would really have. Unless something drastic happened, it was Lexington Place's gig to lose.

I didn't know what had prompted Patty to put the two of us together on this project. Anyone else on staff would have known better.

Even though the First Lady was hosting the event, this party was not considered an official function. That was another reason I hadn't expected to be included. At the White House, I was in charge of the menu and all food preparation. As the first female in the role of executive chef, all State and official dinners were my responsibility. I was proud of my position and my accomplishments — even those that had resulted from me poking my nose in where it didn't belong. Still, I was surprised that Mrs. Hyden had asked me to oversee the food preparation for the Quinones party. After all, she'd brought on a family personal chef, Virgil Ballantine, shortly after they'd moved in. He was a thorn in my side, and would have jumped at the opportunity to one-up me.

"We've entertained thousands of guests on-site before," Sargeant continued. "Why should this be any different? Why can't we set up tents on the South Lawn like we did for the Easter Egg Roll last week?"

I pointed skyward. "Patty's worried about rain. There's no guarantee the weather will be any better for the party than it is today. We can get away with using tents for the Easter Egg Roll because it's a casual event. Plus, the weather cooperated." I thought about the gorgeous spring day last week, with sunny blue skies and temperatures in the seventies. Where was that great weather today? "This event is black-tie. For more than a thousand guests. We can't fit half that many in the residence. And what happens if it rains all next month? I can't imagine the president and Mrs. Hyden squishing across saturated grass in their finest clothes."

"How many of that thousand-plus are

coming for dinner?"

Hadn't he read the update? "One hundred and ten for dinner. One thousand four hundred and twenty-two for the entertainment."

"Protocol nightmare," he said.

I didn't say a word.

"I thought President Hyden and Quinones were sworn political enemies," he said. "I was surprised enough when he appointed someone from a different political party to the position of secretary of state, but to throw a birthday bash for him?" Sargeant fixed me with a look that made me believe he'd just sucked on a lemon. "I don't understand that at all."

Not only did Sargeant not read the memos, but he apparently didn't pay attention to White House scuttlebutt. "It's an olive branch. You do know what that is, don't you?"

"Of course I do."

Might be nice if you offered me one once in a while, I thought. But what I said was, "Secretary of State Quinones has had some early successes in his position. There's a tenuous truce between both political parties right now. An event like this could help cement that."

"Doubtful."

Glancing at Sargeant, I noticed perspiration breaking out over his angry brow and I slowed to accommodate him. I was at least fifteen years younger than my companion and clearly in better physical condition. Rather than appreciate my efforts, however, he tapped his watch. "No dawdling. Let's just get this over with."

"Fine," I said, resuming my former pace. We were at least twenty minutes ahead of schedule. There was no need to rush.

"I still don't know why we didn't take a cab," he said.

Though the comment was clearly rhetorical, I answered him anyway. "It's less than six blocks from our last stop. Plus, it's healthier, not to mention greener, to walk."

"Green, maybe. Colder, definitely." He tugged his collar tight around his neck. "Hmph."

We walked in silence for a short while up New York Avenue, passing the National Museum of Women in the Arts, among other notable spots in the city. "Not much farther," I said.

At the next intersection, Sargeant slowed his pace. "Let's cross here."

I pointed. "But Lexington Place is on this side. Next block, in fact."

"Have it your way." He pulled his collar

up higher and hunched his shoulders as he started walking again, this time even faster. "Let's keep moving."

We passed a couple of stores and restaurants, their bright lights cheery beacons in the cold gloom. I glanced inside as we passed Tous le Monde — one of *the* places to see and be seen in D.C. For his part, Sargeant didn't seem to want to be seen at all. He tucked his head deeper into his coat and, if it were possible, grew smaller.

"Okay, fine," I said and hurried to keep up. The gray sky threatened, though I wasn't sure whether it would deliver rain or snow. We weren't the only pedestrians braving this miserable day, but the sound of tires slicking against pavement, the echoes of car horns in the distance, and the wind whistling between buildings were lonely sounds just the same. A gust of cold air shot past as we crossed a dark corridor — wider than a gangway but narrower than an alley — between two restaurants. About halfway down the dark space, three men stood outside a side door to Tous le Monde, taking a smoke break. All three wore kitchen whites and surly expressions. One also wore a shabby trench coat. He looked up as we hurried past.

The icy wind lifted my hair, creating goose

bumps that danced across the back of my neck. I shivered. I was glad Lexington Place was our final destination for the day. As much as I didn't want to credit Sargeant, taking a cab back to the White House might not be a bad idea.

We were a few steps past the alleyway when I heard a shout and the unmistakable sound of someone running. Too many unwelcome surprises in the past few years had made me wary of anything even slightly unusual and I spun defensively, turning just as the intruder emerged.

The man in the shabby coat looked harmless enough. Short, with a full head of dark hair streaked with gray, he stopped long enough to focus before scurrying over. He, too, held his collar tight against his neck. His unbelted open coat flapped as he ran. Nothing about him would have been the least bit remarkable except for the fact that his full attention was focused on us. On Sargeant, to be specific.

"Petey!" he shouted.

Sargeant had continued walking without me. At the man's shout, his shoulders dropped and he turned. His face went through a series of contortions I'd characterize as pained.

"Petey?" I asked.

16

I swore he snarled at me. In the two seconds it took for the man to reach us, Sargeant jammed his fists into his sides. "Milton —"

The guy was breathless. "You told me you might stop by. But you just rushed right past without even looking in."

" 'Might,' " Sargeant said through clenched teeth, "I said 'might' stop by. Something came up." Pointing at me, he added, "I'm with a colleague. I'm busy."

Sargeant referring to me as a colleague? Would wonders never cease?

"I knew you'd try to blow me off," the man said. "Good thing I was keeping an eye out."

Fresh cigarette smoke wafted off his body, surrounding our little group. I took a step back. Milton, whoever he was, didn't seem to notice. Beneath the ratty coat, his kitchen whites were badly stained. I hoped to heaven he wasn't a cook. His fingers were tobacco brown and the whites of his large, droopy eyes a sickly yellow. Red veins spidered across his cheeks and nose, leading me to believe he and Jack Daniels were close personal friends.

Sargeant was clearly not happy to see him. "We'll talk later," he said, backing away from the man.

With an uneasy smile, Milton moved in closer toward Sargeant, clapping the other man's upper arms, looking ready to pull him into a bear hug.

Visibly repulsed, Sargeant flinched. "Kindly remove your hands."

Milton's cheeks darkened slightly, but he shrugged and backed off. "It's been too long, Petey."

Prissy as ever, Sargeant brushed down the sides of both his arms as though to flick away germs. Silently I watched their interplay, slowly realizing that Sargeant and Milton shared more than just short stature. Though less pinched and certainly more friendly, there was something in Milton's face that reminded me of Sargeant's. Agewise, they were close. "Are you two brothers?" I asked.

Milton brightened, but Sargeant bristled. "No."

"Pete's my uncle," Milton said.

I couldn't hide my reaction. "Uncle?" I repeated. "But —"

Sargeant practically chewed the words before spitting them out. "My sister was much older."

"Pete was a bonus baby," Milton offered with a grin. "We're only six months apart, but I'm his nephew. We went to school together, even. Kind of like growing up as brothers. Well, except for fifth grade, when he made me call him Uncle Pete." Milton laughed at the memory.

Sargeant was not amused. He looked at his watch. "We have to go. We're late."

We weren't, but I wasn't about to correct him.

Milton rubbed his fingers, as though itching for a cigarette. He had a hopeful look on his florid face. "Did you get a chance to talk to the chief usher for me? I sent my resume weeks ago, but I haven't heard from him. A good word from you would —"

"I haven't had time, Milton. I'm very busy, you know."

"Please, Pete. Just this one time. A word from you and I'm set. I'll make you proud of me again. I swear."

This was more family drama than I should be privy to. I took that moment to step back. Pointing in the general direction of Lexington Place, I said, "How about I meet you there?"

A man hurried toward us, head down. Not seeing him, Sargeant took a step closer and answered my question with a vehement thrust of his arm. "No!"

Just as he did, the man rushed by, crashing into Sargeant's outstretched appendage

19

and knocking our sensitivity director off balance. Milton grabbed his uncle to keep him from falling. "Hey!" Milton shouted. The man didn't stop, didn't turn, didn't apologize. "You just bumped a White House official. You know, you could be arrested for that."

The guy stopped in his tracks and turned fully around. He was too far away for me to notice much beyond his dark jacket, blue jeans, athletic shoes, and thick head of hair. I expected him to deliver some hand gesture in response to Milton's shouts. Instead, he hunched his shoulders and turned away again, disappearing around the next corner.

"I really wish you hadn't said that," I said. "We don't like to be outed in public. It's not good for the image. Not good for security, either."

"Some people have no respect," Milton said. "They ought to be taught a lesson."

Sargeant shrugged off his nephew's protective hold. "You're hardly in a position to do the teaching. For once Ms. Paras is right. There have been far too many skirmishes in the past involving staff members" — he glared at me — "to take our personal security for granted." He tapped his watch. "Don't you need to get back to work? Tous le Monde isn't a dive, you know. These people won't stand for your shenanigans." His gaze roved up and down, assessing his nephew's appearance. "It also wouldn't hurt if you tried a little harder to at least look professional."

Sargeant started away without a backward glance. I turned to Milton and raised my hands helplessly as though to apologize for his uncle's behavior. Like an abandoned puppy, Milton tilted his head and gave a sad smile. He'd known Sargeant a lot longer than I had. No doubt he was used to the man's cutting remarks by now.

"Call me," Milton shouted.

Sargeant raised a hand but didn't turn. I double-stepped to catch up with him. "What was that all about?"

He waved me off.

"He wants a job at the White House, I take it," I said, as though we were conversing normally and Sargeant wasn't doing his level best to ignore me. I didn't ask why Sargeant refused to put in a good word with our chief usher, Paul Vasquez, because I already knew the answer. Although one should never judge a book by its cover, in the two minutes I'd gotten to know Milton, I knew he wouldn't be a good fit in the president's home.

"I just have one question," I said.

Sargeant glanced sideways. "He's had a tough life. Is that what you want to know? Most of it is entirely his own fault. He made his bed, let him lie in it."

"That wasn't what I was going to ask. I wanted to know why you told him you were going to be in the area today. It's pretty clear you had no intention of stopping by."

Sargeant ran a hand up his forehead, frustration tightening his features. This had to be one of the first times he'd exhibited an unguarded, human reaction — at least in front of me. "Milton changes jobs like most people change channels. When he called, I thought he was still working on the other side of town. He wanted to meet for lunch, but I told him I'd be out here on official business. Little did I know he would be, too."

"He seems tenacious."

Sargeant glanced at me, his eyes flashing with anger. "It's unfortunate he never used his tenacity to make a better life for himself. We both started out in the same place, yet look at where I am as compared to —" When Sargeant cut himself off, I didn't push it. His family issues were none of my concern.

We slowed as we approached Lexington Place. Built in the late 1800s, the Romanesque building was set back from the street behind a wide driveway. Even I could tell this was perfect for limos to drop off occupants behind a screen of Secret Service lookouts. We climbed the half-dozen marble steps up to the giant glass entry doors that had been retrofitted into the façade.

The green glass whispered open, allowing us entry. It was pretty quiet today. When not being used for black-tie dinners or other such illustrious affairs, Lexington Place served as a temporary gallery for fledgling artists. Free and open to the public during showings, Lexington Place had arranged for portable white walls to be set up cubicle style in its high-ceilinged, pillared lobby. Local artists — some classically trained, some self-taught — vied for spots inside. From what I understood, it was quite a coup to be featured here.

Today's bad weather and the early hour apparently combined to prevent art lovers from venturing outdoors and into this space. Too bad. Even a cursory glance told me I'd enjoy spending time here. We looked around, but it appeared completely vacant. "Hello?" I said.

No answer.

Other than the hollow, clicking noises our footsteps made as we ventured into the lobby, the place was quiet as a tomb.

A female security guard came around one of the back cubicles. Wearing a wary look and a blue blazer two sizes too small, she ambled over. "We're here to meet Patty Woodruff," I said. "Is she here yet?"

The guard sized us up. "You the two from the White House?"

"We most certainly are," Sargeant said, fussiness back in place. "Ms. Woodruff is expecting us."

The guard glanced at her watch. "Yeah, that's what she said." Waving absently to the east, she continued. "She's been here all morning up on the second floor. Elevator's over there." She pointed to the south. "Or you can take the stairs. Whatever suits you."

"Is the kitchen on the second floor?" Patty wanted me to scope out the food preparation facilities. I intended to do that first. On my own, if possible. It was always much easier to focus and concentrate without one of the First Lady's assistants or Peter Everett Sargeant breathing down my neck.

"She said she'd be waiting for you in the kitchen," the guard replied. "West side of the second floor. Through the wooden door that reads PRIVATE, then take a right."

There went the idea of exploring on my

own. "Thanks," I said and headed for the stairs.

Sargeant glowered.

"Take the elevator if you want." I set off toward the wide marble steps at the very back of the lobby, resisting the urge to add, "I'll beat you," because Sargeant was not a playful man. To my surprise, he fell into step beside me.

"Are we the only ones here today?" he asked as we made our way up. With a noise of disgust, he added, "They call themselves green. How much heat do they waste keeping the building open all day? Not to mention electricity. Thousands of dollars wasted on the chance that some sightseers might drop in. It's a shame."

Sargeant's mood was always foul when I was around, but after our encounter with Milton, it'd gotten worse. I decided to ignore his complaint. I didn't know enough about green technology to offer up an argument, but I imagined the building's certification had more to do with the methods it employed than solely on how many hours it remained open to the public each day.

The hallway at the top of the stairs was completely dark. I hesitated, unsure of proceeding, but the moment we cleared the last step, overhead lights went on to illuminate our path. "There you go," I said, "conservation." More lights automatically popped on as we headed down the hall.

"Hmph," he said.

I pushed through the door marked PRIVATE, less reluctant now to venture into the dark. As they had before, sensors tracked our movement and provided illumination. "I guess Patty hasn't been out in the hall in the past few minutes," I said. "I wonder how long the lights stay on before they shut themselves off."

"I don't like it," Sargeant said.

Truth was, I didn't like it, either. Dark rooms were never inviting and I got a sudden tingling along the back of my neck. "The guard did say Patty was in the kitchen, right?"

He didn't answer. As instructed, we took a right at the first corridor. Though long and dark, two circles of light — windows in far doors — kept us moving forward. I wiggled my shoulders, trying to shake off the eerie sense of two big bright eyes watching us approach. I felt like a character in one of those "Don't go through the door!" movies. When hallway lights popped on above, exposing a bright white set of swinging doors with porthole windows, I heard Sargeant breathe a sigh of relief.

"Patty?" I called, pushing through the right-hand door. "You here?"

The kitchen was empty. Dead-silent empty. "What's going on?" I asked.

Sargeant looked around the room, confused as I was. "Ms. Woodruff must have just been here. The lights are still on."

I'd been thinking the same thing as I moved toward the wall switch. "Nope," I said, pointing. "This room is set to stay on until manually shut off. It's an override just in case the person working here doesn't move around enough to keep the sensors happy. I've seen things like this before."

"Well then, where is she?"

Like I would know. I wandered around, hoping she'd peer around a corner but I couldn't shake the sense that this floor was utterly devoid of life. "Until she shows up, we might as well get to work," I said. "We're here to assess, right?"

This kitchen was at least twice as big as ours. Stainless steel countertops, sinks, and work areas weren't so spread out as to limit efficiency, but were nicely spaced. I made a circuit of the room, checking out their ovens, equipment, and preparation area, growing more impressed by the minute. At the room's far end, I pushed open another set of doors. Lights in that short corridor snapped on and I poked around. When I came back, I said, "That leads to the banquet room."

Sargeant clicked his tongue. "So where is she?"

"We are a little early."

He checked his watch. "Not by much."

Shrugging, I continued my perusal. "She's got to be here somewhere, or else she would have called. I'm going to check out the rest of the kitchen. Might as well make good use of the time we have." I wandered through, brimming with envy. This place had everything. Not only that, but everything was brand-new. The White House had to make do with what we already had. While we were never denied a necessary piece of equipment when we requested one, we were expected to nurse all current utensils until they fell to shreds on the floor. Even then, if there was any chance of refurbishing rather than replacing, we did so.

I made my way down a tiny hall in the room's eastern corner. One side was an office, the other a long wall of stainless steel. I recognized the walk-in refrigeration and freezing units immediately. When I pulled at the heavy handle, unlocking the massive door to peek in, the lights went on. I looked around. "You could feed an army with what they've got stored here."

As was my habit, I checked the door handle to ensure it could be opened from the inside. Equipment this new was probably safe, but it never hurt to check. I pushed it twice, watching the latch move with each attempt. Just fine. I was about to walk deeper into the unit to take a closer look at the inventory when Sargeant called.

"Olivia?"

I couldn't remember him ever calling me anything but "Ms. Paras," and the tone of his voice was strained.

"What is it?" I hurried back into the main part of the room.

"What do you think this is?" he asked.

I was about to lapse into smart-aleck mode and answer that it was a sink, but then I noticed where he was pointing. A thin line of red ran along the outer seam.

"At first glance I missed it. Anyone would have. But look." He pointed to a single drop of red on the white industrial floor.

"Not yours, I take it?"

"Maybe Ms. Woodruff cut herself," he said, "and went for help?"

I crouched to look more closely at the red line snaking its way down the stainless steel side, then stood to view it from above. I brought my head even with the edge of the sink and tilted to get the light's angle just right. "I think someone wiped this clean," I said. "See that dull spot? It looks like a smear."

"Should we call someone?"

I was about to answer when I noticed the two tilt-skillets just a few feet to my left. Giant rectangular boxes that sit about three feet off the floor, tilt-skillets are wonderful for creating crowd-sized portions of soups, stews, or other concoctions that require a heck of a bigger container than a standard Dutch oven. I loved our tilt-skillet at the White House and used it on a regular basis. Whenever it wasn't being used, we almost always kept it open.

These two were closed.

I started for the one closest to me.

"Don't!" Sargeant shouted.

I jumped. "I'm sure there's nothing in there."

"I think we should call the police."

"And report what?" Swallowing past a suddenly dry throat, I started to reach for the handle. On second thought, I pulled the edge of my long sleeve top out from beneath my coat sleeve, covering my fingers with fabric.

"What are you doing?"

"Being silly. Letting my imagination run

away with me."

He backed up. "Just the same . . ."

"There's nothing to be afraid of."

With that, I flung the tilt-skillet lid open.

I gasped, staggering backward. Patty's cramped, twisted body had been jammed into the small space.

Sargeant yanked his handkerchief from his pocket and held it up to his eyes. "I think we found her."

CHAPTER 2

I stood paralyzed for several seconds, momentarily forgetting to breathe. "Call the police," I finally said. Although there was no way Patty could be alive, not so perfectly still, not with that bloody gash across the back of her head, I had to check. I took a step closer.

"What are you doing?" Sargeant practically shrieked.

"We should feel for a pulse."

"Oh my. Oh my." Wringing his hands and looking ready to faint, Sargeant started for the door.

"Use your cell phone," I said. "Don't leave the room."

"But the security guard . . ."

"Just use your cell," I said, focusing on Patty. I reached in to press two fingers to her neck. She was still warm. "What if whoever did this is still here?"

Sargeant took a step closer to me, dragging a cell phone from his pocket. When the dispatcher answered, the sensitivity director had regained his composure. "We need the police," he said, and provided the address. "There's been a . . ." Faltering, he stared at me. ". . . an accident?"

I pressed my fingers against several places in Patty's neck, searching for any trace of a pulse. When Sargeant looked at me, I shook my head. "Have them send an ambulance anyway. You never know."

He repeated the request into his handset. "We're on the second floor in the kitchen. And," he added, "we're with the White House. Make it fast."

I stepped away from Patty's body, trying to force myself to think. By touching the tilt-skillet's handle, even with my sleeve, I might have smudged a fingerprint. I hoped to God I hadn't.

Sargeant's little eyes were as wide as I'd ever seen them. "Shouldn't we alert the guard?"

I was torn. What if the guilty party was still nearby? What if leaving this scene unattended was the wrong thing to do? What if staying was the wrong thing? I couldn't focus. One thing I did know: Of all the choices spinning through my head right now, splitting up seemed the worst idea of all. I turned to look at the swinging doors with the porthole windows. Sargeant followed my gaze. The corridor beyond was dark again. "At least that means there hasn't been any movement out there," I said.

"Not yet."

It dawned on me that the security guard might have the capability of sealing off the building. "On second thought, let's go. We'll do this together."

With Sargeant behind me, I summoned the nerve to push through the porthole doors again. We had no idea what we were walking into, but this had to be done. I tamped down the raging fear that pounded in my heart like a jack-hammer. Praying I wasn't stepping into a trap, I took a long stride forward, readying myself for the lights to come on and brighten our path.

Nothing.

"Why aren't they working?" Sargeant asked. Close enough for me to feel his hot breath on my neck, he was a whole lot deeper into my personal space than I'd ever expect Sargeant to be. Or me to allow.

I reached behind to grab a handful of his trench coat sleeve. "Let's move," I said, "fast, okay?"

There was enough ambient light from the portholes to see our way clear to where we needed to take a left, but from there on the darkness was pitch. "Don't they believe in windows around here?" he whispered.

"Not for the working areas," I said, keeping my voice just as low. "Keep it utilitarian. No frills, no distractions."

"Shameful," he said, "worker conditions like this."

Behind me, I could feel him trembling, and though my legs felt rubbery and weak, we plowed ahead, our inane conversation helping — in a bizarre way — to keep us from freaking out at the thought of Patty's motionless form in the kitchen behind us.

The wooden door marked PRIVATE on the other side was just ahead. One second before I grabbed the handle and pulled, I prayed it wouldn't be locked. With a sigh of relief, I dragged it open and Sargeant and I ran for the main staircase, no longer clinging to each other. I wished I'd noticed the security guard's name. I shouted, "Guard!"

"Guard!" Sargeant's voice was louder, more shrill.

We spotted her trudging up, looking ready to chastise us for making too much nose. "The police are on their way," I said breathlessly. "Patty has been . . ." My mouth moved but no words came out. ". . . hurt. They're sending an ambulance and police.

Can you lock down the building?"

"Whoa, hold on. Slow down a minute. What are you saying?"

Though short, I pulled myself up to my full height and injected authority into my voice. "Shut the building down," I said, "now. Only open the door for the cops. Get it?"

She squinted at me and began to argue.

"Just do it, you fool woman," Sargeant shrieked in a pitch so high I'd only ever heard it before from dolphins. "There's been a murder upstairs."

The police and ambulance took only moments to arrive. Whether their nearly instant response had anything to do with Sargeant mentioning our White House connection or if they were always just that prompt, I didn't know. Cops tumbled in by the dozens, some in uniform, others clad in black, like a SWAT team. Belatedly, I realized they'd expected to encounter a presidential emergency. Expecting big trouble, each one wore a helmet and body armor and carried an enormous automatic weapon in his or her hands. The uniformed officers were ordered to secure the first floor while the SWAT-type guys corralled Sargeant, the guard — whose name was Jorjanna — and me.

"Who called us?"

Within moments, Sargeant and I gave them the basic information they needed to proceed. Jorjanna told them she'd done her best to secure every exit.

Grudgingly, she remained down by the front door as Sargeant and I took the police and paramedics upstairs. The lights were still not working and the officers pulled out flashlights to illuminate the creepy corridors. Two officers led our group, two brought up the rear. Sargeant was too close, yet again. At the porthole doors, I said, "In there."

The two lead cops peered in before turning around to silently gesture that we and the paramedics should wait. The two cops at the rear jostled forward, holding up when the leader held up three fingers, then two, counting down. Just as he reached "one," the cops burst through the swinging doors to swarm the kitchen. I watched through the window as they looked up, down, around every corner, into every nook. One by one, they shouted to let us know areas were clear. The young man who had been the leader removed his helmet and wiped sweat from his brow. He stared.

For half a second I panicked that the body was gone, that it had disappeared while we ran for help, like bodies so often do in movies and on TV. But then he shouted, "Bring the paramedics in here."

They rushed past us, banging through the swinging doors into the room. Sargeant and I followed, tentatively. When the lead cop pointed at Patty's body, I surreptitiously checked out his name badge. Kooch. "You knew her?" he asked.

Knew. Already using the past tense. Even from here, even before the paramedics turned to us and shook their heads, everyone could tell she was dead.

Sargeant crawled close. I could smell the fear radiating from him. "Her name is Patty Woodruff," I answered. "We were supposed to meet her here. She's an assistant to the First Lady at the White House."

Kooch rubbed his face. "Was."

I glanced over. What a terrible place to die. "Yeah."

"Sir," one of the other team members raised his voice, "over here."

Kooch gripped his gun and shifted to where the other cop pointed. The second tilt-skillet. After finding Patty, I hadn't thought to check the other one. Maybe because I hadn't wanted to. Muffled noises came from inside the stainless steel box. A voice. Female. We hadn't heard any noises before. We certainly would have noticed. I exchanged a look with Sargeant, who was as pale and still as a frozen turkey. Though we couldn't make out the words, the voice moved with an odd cadence, as though we were listening to a television program through the skillet's metal lid. Three officers surrounded the piece of equipment and gestured for us to back off. We didn't need to be told twice.

"Police," Kooch shouted. "Come out if you're able to. Or knock to let us know you're trapped."

The blathering continued for a moment, then music, then nothing.

"Come out," he repeated, "or knock."

Complete silence except for Sargeant's shallow panting next to me. I took another look at his terrified face. "Maybe you should step outside for some air," I whispered to him.

He shook his head.

"At least breathe slower, then," I said. "You'll hyperventilate."

"I'm fine."

Kooch gestured toward the door with his chin, the message in his eyes unmistakable. "Get out of here."

I couldn't move. My legs were lead weights, immobile. At least until I knew what — or who — was in that other tilt-skillet, I wasn't going anywhere. I inched backward a few feet to appease him, nearly toppling over Sargeant as I did so.

With their guns trained on the giant skillet, the police locked eyes and nodded another countdown. At "one" Kooch stepped forward and threw open the lid.

"Oh my God," Sargeant said, gripping both my arms from behind. A second later he let go as he slid to the floor. "Oh God."

Jammed inside the second tilt-skillet was Mark Cawley, the White House chief of staff. And from the looks of his blue-tinged skin, he'd been here a lot longer than Patty had.

CHAPTER 3

We stared down at Chief of Staff Cawley for a breathless, silent moment. A diminutive man, shorter even than Sargeant, he was dressed in a dark suit and wore his trademark cherry red tie. Unlike Patty, he didn't have a huge gash on the back of his head. In fact, except for being tightly crammed into the coffin-like skillet space and his deathly skin color, he looked relaxed, as though he were simply sleeping.

Just as Kooch leaned in to get a better look at the official, the radio voice leapt back to life, this time not so muffled. Everyone in the room jumped. Sargeant yelped. Kooch held up two hands as though to assure us everything was under control, then reached in and pulled up a cell phone. He studied the display, his face unreadable as his finger sought the silencing button. Unable to quiet the device fast enough, we were treated to two repetitions of Cawley's ringtone. Set to play a recording of a local female DJ talking about the next selection, it was unusual to say the least. You could hear the smile in her velvet voice: "For all you lovers out there celebrating tonight, this one is for you . . ."

Opening notes from one of Barry Manilow's hits followed, the song cutting off just before the lyrics began. The ringtone then looped back and repeated the DJ's sultry announcement and the song's first few measures. I recognized the classic "Mandy." An odd choice for a ringtone. We'd recently hosted the White House chief of staff and his wife at the White House. Her name was Susan.

"Who was calling him?" I asked.

Kooch glared. Without even knowing me, he was irritated by my question. "This will go into evidence." Another officer approached with an open plastic bag. Kooch placed the phone inside. "Cell phones offer lots of clues."

"Patty!" I said, startling everyone, including myself. "Where's her cell phone?"

Kooch looked at me as though I'd gone crazy. "If it's here, we'll find it. Why don't you step outside until we're finished?"

"You don't understand," I said, "Patty has a special White House cell. All staff mem-

42

bers have them. If someone gets their hands on it . . ." I let the thought hang.

Kooch nodded and, to his credit, didn't try to kick us out again. One of his team had already called for backup. While we awaited their arrival, Kooch made a methodical examination of Patty's resting place. Her purse had been wedged in behind her bent knees.

"I don't want to disturb the crime scene," Kooch said, "but in the interest of national security, I will take a look through her purse."

He poked through her turquoise bag using a black plastic wand, moving sideways to allow me a better view. "You see it in here?"

I didn't. Taking a critical look at Patty this time, trying to block out the sadness as I did so, I realized she had no pockets in her skirt and wore no outer jacket over her silk blouse. Unless the phone was tucked beneath her body, it was not here. "She must have a coat nearby," I said. "It's too cold to have gone out without one."

Kooch dispatched two of his men to look for it. "The other victim isn't wearing one, either."

Good thing. At least from the killer's perspective. Tilt-skillets are not huge, and fitting a full-grown adult into one couldn't have been easy. Mark Cawley, though not a large man, was still considerably bulkier than Patty. He barely fit in the tilt-skillet.

"Looks like he was shot," Kooch said as he examined Cawley. "Back of the head, execution style." He held both arms out. "Everyone back up. We've contaminated this scene enough." Waving to the EMTs, he said, "Wait for us on the main floor. Secret Service is on the way. I'm certain they'll want to talk with you."

Within minutes, more Metro police, a wave of Secret Service, and every authority I could imagine flocked to Lexington Place. Mostly men, they crammed into every available space outside the perimeter Kooch had established. Amid murmured discussions and shouted directives, I understood they were waiting for the scene to be processed. I grasped Sargeant's arm again, pulling him into a small area as far from the active crime scene as possible.

We shared a corner of the huge kitchen, a nook just big enough for us both to sit in as long as we kept our knees up. Sargeant leaned against a portable refrigeration unit facing me, looking like a well-dressed little boy forced to sit in the corner until he behaved. I leaned against the tile wall facing

44

him. Except for the many law enforcement legs running back and forth between us and the tilt-skillets, we had a direct view of everything.

"Why won't they let us go?" he asked, "Doesn't it make more sense to get us out of here?"

"They'll want to talk to both of us while everything is still fresh in our minds."

"Fresh in our minds!" His voice grew loud enough to catch the attention of the officers nearest us. Sargeant pretended not to see them, continuing in a whisper, "Do they really believe I'd be able to forget a moment of this tragedy? I'm not like you. I don't stumble across things like this on a daily basis. I will be as accurate a witness tomorrow as I am right now. In fact, I would prefer to go home for the day. I've had quite enough."

He began to rise, but I stopped him with a look. "Peter, they're going to want you to walk them, step by step, through every move we made in here. They need to figure out where we left fingerprints, hair, DNA. They need to see everything through your eyes. Just be patient. They'll come for us soon."

"Easy for you to say. You're the expert on criminals and their behavior."

"Gee, thanks, Peter." Little did he know

that for all my calm talk I was shaking in my shoes. Sure, I'd been involved with violence and crime before, but I'd never gotten used to it. I certainly never expected to come across dead bodies stuffed into kitchen equipment.

"You think they were murdered?" he asked, stealing a glance to his right.

"They didn't climb in there by themselves."

He shuddered.

I texted my second-in-command, Bucky, with a cryptic message that said I'd been delayed and didn't know when I'd be back. I suggested he handle the rest of the day himself.

Less than a minute after sending, my little phone registered an incoming text from Bucky. *Uh-oh. What happened now?*

After many hours of fielding questions, repeating answers, and clarifying those answers with more people than I usually talk to in a week, Sargeant and I were finally released. I hesitated at the front doors. "Hang on a minute," I said, backing up. "Look out there."

Beyond the yellow crime scene tape that quivered in the breeze, dozens of reporters waited outside, eyes bright, microphones ready, itching to snap up juicy details.

"I don't want to go out there," I said.

Sargeant sniffed. "I thought you liked being the center of attention."

I shot him a withering look.

Jorjanna sidled up. "I can't leave. They need me to stick around until the building's representatives get here." She looked at her watch with disgust. "Where are they, anyway? New Zealand?" Pointing toward a side door, she said, "Nobody is camped out on that side. I'll call you two a cab."

Total relief. "Thanks, Jorjanna," I said. "I owe ya."

Ten minutes later, Sargeant and I were safely ensconced in the back seat of a taxi.

"Where we headed?" the driver asked.

Sargeant started to say, "The White —"

I interrupted. "The W Hotel. Fifteenth street side."

Sargeant looked at me like I'd grown a second nose. I ignored him. The W was practically next door to the White House. With all the activity out front here at the Lexington, and once the full story broke, our taxi driver might try to make some quick cash by reporting our White House drop-off. Let him think we were tourists. Weak, but better than the alternative.

"You don't owe her anything, you know,"

Sargeant said the moment the driver took off.

"Huh?"

"You told that security guard that you owed her. For calling us a cab? I think she owed us that much at least. Now that you said it, she'll try to cash in. Mark my words."

I waved away his concerns and stared out the window. I had too much to think about right now to deal with Sargeant's paranoia. I was sure it was just his nervousness talking, but the man had been downright mean to me since the day he started. I didn't feel like cutting him any slack.

Instead, I focused on everything that had just happened. I tried to force myself to relax on the short cab ride, but it didn't work. Did one person kill both Mark Cawley and Patty? I was no expert, but it looked to me as though some time had elapsed between the two deaths. Patty had been killed shortly before we arrived. I suppressed a shudder, thinking about her lifeless form. How long had Cawley been there? Hours? Days? He hadn't been reported missing that I knew of.

Sargeant was talking again. Muttering, actually. I'd missed it. "What did you say?"

"I should never have agreed to work with you. You're bad luck." He turned to face the window as the driver pulled up to the hotel. "Look what you've gotten me into."

The moment we alighted, Sargeant — such a gentleman — headed straight away at a brisk pace, leaving me to settle up with the driver. "Thanks," I said, and asked for a receipt. By the time I made it across 15th Street, Sargeant was at least fifty feet ahead of me. I didn't bother trying to catch up.

Bucky had everything under control, just like I knew he would. Over the past few months since Virgil Ballantine had joined the White House as the First Family's personal chef, we in the kitchen had found it necessary to adapt. Technically speaking, Bucky, Cyan, and I were no longer responsible for preparing daily breakfasts, lunches, and dinners for the president and his family. Virgil had made that point quite clear when he started here. I'd originally chafed at the change, but with the amount of entertaining the Hydens did, I slowly came to appreciate Virgil's contribution, such as it was.

Kitchens as busy as ours can't exist with such rigid divisions and I'd recently noticed a shift in the personal chef's attitude. Though Virgil remained protective of his responsibilities, he would occasionally ask

49

for help. In turn, we invited him to join us when preparing for a major event.

That didn't mean we always got along. When Virgil was stressed, he was intolerable. I'd tried, repeatedly, to talk him down when I sensed he was about to explode. Rarely was I successful. We'd discussed this issue several times but hadn't found a compromise. Yet.

Virgil looked at the wall clock when I walked through the door. "I can't believe how long you were gone. Everything is done here except to serve and plate dinner. I thought the four places you were visiting today were within walking distance. Where were they? Maryland?" He gave a light laugh as though making a joke, but nobody thought it was funny.

Ignoring Virgil, I sent a meaningful look to Bucky and Cyan as I made my way to the computer at the far end of the kitchen.

"I knew it," Bucky said. "I knew it as soon as I got your text. What happened this time?"

Cyan said, "Oh, Ollie."

Virgil's face was a total blank. "What are you talking about?"

I didn't say a word. I merely clicked onto one of the sites we relied on for breaking news and turned up the sound. At the time of the recording, reporters were beginning to gather outside Lexington Place's front doors. Scrolling headlines reported the "deaths of certain high-ranking officials" but didn't disclose the victims' names until their families could be notified.

"Geez," Bucky said.

"You were there?" Virgil asked.

I didn't answer him.

He tried again. "Did you see who was killed? Who were the high-ranking officials? Someone we know?"

Cyan's eyes, bright green today, were sad. "Oh, Ollie," she said again, placing a hand on my shoulder. "Why is it always you?"

"Why indeed?" I asked.

Virgil's face contorted, probably with confusion and pain at being left out of the conversation. "Will someone please tell me what's going on?"

Bucky sent Virgil a baleful look. "In case you missed it, Ollie has a knack for getting into the middle of things," quickly adding, "not her fault. Well, not always." He leaned back, tapping a finger against his lips as though sizing me up. "If I were to venture a guess, she definitely knows who was killed and how it was done. If I were a betting man, I'd even wager she was first on the scene."

"Nice summary," I said, "but I can't confirm or deny."

Bucky shrugged. "No need. We get it."

"But why are you all feeling sorry for Olivia?" Virgil asked. "Seems to me you should be feeling sorry for the victims here. Whoever they are."

"He's right," I said. "Sargeant and I had a rough afternoon, but nothing compared to what . . ." I couldn't finish, so I shifted gears into more comfortable territory. "I know I'm late, but now that I'm here —"

"Sargeant?" Bucky asked. "He was there, too?"

"Yeah, remember? The two of us were planning to meet . . ." I faltered again.

Cyan's face went white. "Nooo . . ." she said, "not Patty."

I pressed my lips together, angry at myself for not being more careful and sorry for the bad news I'd inadvertently imparted. "I'm so sorry, Cyan. I never meant to let that slip. I shouldn't have come back here to-night. I should have waited until you all saw the news. But" — I shrugged — "you guys are my friends and I trust you. Please keep this to yourself until it breaks, okay?"

"Oh my God," Cyan said, "she was so young."

"Cyan . . ." Words failed me.

The phone rang. Virgil didn't move, so Bucky answered. After a moment, he handed it to me. "It's for you," he said, "it's Paul."

I felt my shoulders drop. Of course our chief usher would have been apprised by now. Of course he would want to see me. "Ollie," he said when I answered, "how are you holding up?"

We'd had similar conversations so often, the question was almost laughable. But then I thought about Patty and Mark Cawley squeezed into their tilt-skillet coffins and my throat caught. "I've been better."

"If you're up to it, please stop by my office. I need to talk with you and Peter. He's here now."

"On my way."

I hung up and looked at my team. "Gotta go. I'm sure Paul wants to warn me about talking to the media. Listen," I said, thinking ahead, "without getting too specific, I need to let you all know that tonight may turn out to be an all-nighter for the president and First Lady." I thought about it. "And their staffs. Let's prepare for that. The butlers will be here 'round the clock, but they'll need plenty of food to keep everyone's energy up."

"What happened, Ollie?" Virgil asked.

"There's more to it than you're telling us."

"I'll tell you what I can, when I can. Until then, let's keep ourselves in a position to help."

Cyan's focus was back on me. "Good thing Tom isn't here, huh?"

"Yeah," I said as I headed to see Paul, "good thing."

Cyan patted me on the shoulder, a sad look on her face. Tom MacKenzie and I had had a romantic relationship until my involvement in extracurricular activities, like this one, drove a wedge between us. As head of the Presidential Protective Division here at the White House, his job was to oversee the protection of the First Family. Mine was to feed them. Problems arose when I inadvertently encroached on his turf.

From the scuttlebutt, I knew Tom had moved on. In fact, he was back home this week, visiting with his high school sweetheart. They'd recently reconnected and from the little I'd heard, she was perfect for him. A tall, pageant-winning blond. As opposite as you could get from a short, dark-haired, carb-watching kind of girl who happened across dead bodies on a regular basis. I was happy for him.

I was happy for myself, too. I'd begun to move on as well, though no one knew it yet.

I hadn't shared anything about this new relationship with anyone. Not even Cyan. I'd vowed to keep my personal life personal this time.

Despite the fact that Tom's presence, or lack thereof, wasn't affecting me emotionally, I was still glad he was out of town. Whenever I got drawn into one of these complicated situations, he was quick to blame me for interfering. But this time it had truly just been bad timing and worse luck. I resolved to stay as far away from the investigation as I could.

CHAPTER 4

Paul stood up when I walked into his office. "Thanks for coming, Ollie." His salt-and-pepper hair seemed to be growing whiter and thinner by the day. "Close the door," he said, then gestured for me to take the open seat next to Sargeant, who watched me with disdain.

Paul began. "I've spoken with the First Lady —"

But Sargeant interrupted to fill me in. "Paul says we can't have Secretary of State Quinones's birthday party at Lexington Place for obvious reasons. In fact, we're not even supposed to breathe a word about Lexington Place ever being considered or anything about our visit there today. The White House is stepping away from all this until everything can be sorted out."

Eyes tight, Paul folded his hands atop the papers on his desk. He was a more patient person than I. Thank goodness. When

Sargeant sat back, pleased with himself, I exchanged a look with our chief usher. He had been through a lot over the past few years, but today he looked worn out and older than he should. "That about sums it up," he said. "Ollie, have you mentioned this to anyone?"

I cringed, remembering my gaffe in the kitchen. "My staff knew I was meeting Patty at Lexington Place. Cyan asked me if Patty was one of the two victims mentioned on the news . . ." I hesitated. "She — they — put two and two together."

Sargeant made a *tsk*ing noise. "Loose lips sink ships."

Ignoring the interjection, Paul jotted a note. "I'll talk with them to make sure no one breathes a word to the press. At this point, it looks like you two made it back without the media sniffing you out."

"There was the security guard at Lexington we interacted with," I added, "Jorjanna. And the taxi driver, but we got out at the W Hotel, so maybe he won't give us a second thought."

"Good thinking." Paul scribbled more notes as he chewed his lip. "The guard could be a problem. I'll look into that. For now, both of you need to lie low. Did you mention going to Lexington Place to anyone else? At any of the other locations you visited?"

"We didn't want anyone to know who they were up against," I said. "Wait!" Snapping my fingers, I turned to Sargeant. "You told Milton."

If looks could kill, I'd be crammed into a tilt-skillet with the lid slammed shut.

"Milton?" Paul asked. His gaze shot toward a pile of papers on his right. He reached to grab them and began to riffle through. "The same person you and I planned to discuss, Peter? He sent me another resume with a letter begging me to give him a try."

"As I told you before, he's no one of consequence."

"He isn't a relative, then?"

"One chooses one's friends," Sargeant sniffed. "Unfortunately the same cannot be said for one's relatives."

Hand poised to jot another reminder, Paul pressed the issue. "That's fine with regard to the job question; I wouldn't have considered him without your recommendation. The more important issue, however, is what was said to him today. I need to know everyone at risk to leak this to the press."

"I'll speak with him immediately and ensure his cooperation."

Paul looked skeptical.

Sargeant was quick to change the subject. "What about Secretary of State Quinones's birthday party? Is that still on the agenda? If so, and we're no longer having it at Lexington Place — a decision I highly support, I might add — then where?"

"Unsure at this point," Paul said. "In fact, as you already surmised, the entire event may be postponed indefinitely. Once word gets out about the two murders, the White House will be required to display proper respect." Paul seemed to catch himself. "Which, of course, is exactly correct, given the circumstances."

Paul was off his game today. Not nearly as smooth and strong as usual. In addition to wondering what was on his mind, I was beginning to question what purpose I served here. The little bit of conversation that had applied to me could have been handled over the phone. Paul must have sensed my impatience because he lowered his voice and leaned forward. "There's one more thing," he said. "I wanted you both to hear this from me."

The crow's-feet on either side of Paul's eyes suddenly looked less like smile lines and more like the ravages of age.

"I'm . . ." He took a deep breath. ". . .

leaving the White House."

Total silence. I stared at him in disbelief. "Why?"

He fiddled with his pen. "My wife is having health problems and I need to be with her. It's serious and sudden, but maybe with the right care . . ." Trying to muster a smile, he said, "The First Family is aware, and I have their full support. Time is of the essence, and I had planned to announce my resignation to the staff tomorrow and to the media the day after. This new situation makes that timing awkward."

"Paul, I'm so sorry," I said. "Is there anything I can do?"

"There is. You both know Doug Lambert. He's been an assistant here for several years. Until a permanent successor is named, Doug will serve as interim chief usher. I want you both to work with him as you would me." He lifted his phone's receiver and pressed an intercom button. "Whenever you're ready," he said into the mouthpiece before hanging up. "In a terrible way, today's events are working in my favor. I'm leaving immediately — this evening — so that I can be with my wife. News of my resignation will have to wait for a few weeks. No one else on staff is to know I'm gone permanently — not until it's decided the time is right for the announcement."

"We have to keep this secret?" Sargeant asked.

"To the rest of the world, I'm just away for a while," Paul said. "Doug will handle the fallout from today's tragedy. I would have preferred a smoother transition because he isn't quite ready. Doug's going to need your full cooperation. Although he's been briefed on most of what transpired today, I want to bring him in on your involvement."

As though on cue, Doug Lambert knocked and entered. I'd worked with him a little in the past but hadn't gotten to know him very well. About my age, he was dark-haired and tall, with a narrow, peninsula-shaped bald spot that ran from his forehead to the back of his head. Carrying about thirty extra pounds and with his persistently pink cheeks, he would have looked about twelve years old — if it weren't for the lack of hair.

"You all know each other," Paul said, standing up.

Doug pulled a chair from the corner and sat down to join us. "I'm sorry to have to take over under these circumstances," he said, "but I understand we have a situation that needs to be handled discreetly. Let's get started."

■ ■ ■ ■

After about an hour of discussion, our little meeting broke up. I came away feeling the same about Doug as I always had: He was eager and earnest, but lacked the polish and confidence needed for the job of chief usher. I sure hoped he was a fast learner.

Paul had excused himself to talk with the Secret Service about Jorjanna, the security guard at Lexington Place. When he returned and after Doug had been completely apprised of the situation and our involvement, we were finally cut loose for the night. Sargeant murmured sympathetic sentiments to Paul and left, promising to get in touch with Milton immediately.

Paul grabbed his coat as Doug took the chair behind the desk. "I'm sorry to see you go," he said.

Paul's eyes grew bright. "I'm sorry to be going." He shook hands with Doug, then crossed back to accompany me out. "Keep in touch. I'm always available by phone."

Paul closed the door behind us. "Walk with me."

We stepped into the darkened entrance hall and made our way toward the stairs, neither of us saying a word. At the room's very center, just in front of the north doors, Paul took a long look around. "It's quiet right now."

I didn't say anything.

"In a few hours this place will be a madhouse. Again."

I thought about the press getting wind of the double murder. "Madhouse" was an understatement. "I know."

He flashed a glance back the way we'd come. "I hope Doug is up to it."

"I do too."

Paul seemed to want to say more, but instead he gave the area an extended, loving look. I knew he was saying good-bye. In a moment he started again for the stairs. When we reached the bottom, where he would go east to exit and I west to the kitchen, I took his hand in both of mine. "I hope your wife makes a full recovery," I said. "Let us know from time to time, will you?"

He promised he would. "Ollie," he said, "of everyone on staff, you've proved to be the most . . ." He scanned the air for the right word. ". . . challenging. But the White House is better for having you here. Don't ever forget that."

Paul was taking the time to bolster *me?* I would sorely miss this man. "Thank you."

"Ollie." This time his voice held an edge. "I'm not going to tell you not to get involved this time because you already are. Just please, watch your back, okay? Doug doesn't know you the way I do. Keep him updated. Regularly. Don't do any end-runs around him. He's a good guy and I'm confident he'll do right if you do right by him."

"I will," I said, "but I don't plan to get further involved this time."

A small smile curled Paul's lips. "You never do."

"No, really . . ."

"Ollie, one more thing," he said in a low voice, stopping me mid-protest, "about Sargeant. This is between you and me and . . ." He gestured toward the nearby protective case. ". . . the Remington sculpture. The Hydens aren't too taken with our sensitivity director."

"No?" This was news.

"Steer clear of him as much as you can. He's been making . . . mistakes lately. Several of them. I think he senses the First Lady's displeasure, and you know Sargeant. He'll do anything to push blame on someone else. And he's always kept a target on your back. Just be careful."

I nodded.

"And be patient," he added quickly. "They

won't cut him loose anytime soon. One more misstep on his part, however . . ."

"I get it," I said. As much as I didn't wish bad luck on anyone, I knew life would be much happier with a Sargeant-free White House. After all the bad news today, this was a little bit of a day-brightener. "Thanks for letting me know."

"You take care of yourself," Paul said, giving my hand a squeeze. "And don't be a stranger."

"What's wrong, Ollie?" Cyan asked when I made it back to the kitchen. "What did Paul say?"

"Same old, same old," I lied. "Keep everything under wraps. Don't talk to the media. Yadda, yadda, yadda. Where's Virgil?"

"Went home right after you went up. Bucky's gone for the day, too. I stuck around to make sure you were okay. And before you ask, we have everything under control. There are literally hundreds of items that can be put together for snacks or even full meals. We're good."

"I knew we would be," I said, "but I may just stay around to keep an eye on things."

"After the day you had? No way. Jackson's covering the night shift. And you know how good he is."

I did. "Maybe it is better I head home. After today, I could use a hot shower and a good night's sleep."

She eyed me critically. "You need more than that."

I didn't want to go down this road right now. "Are we in good shape for the morning?"

"Don't change the subject. You need someone to come home to. You haven't had a date since Tom."

"Trying to forget that one you arranged for me?"

Cyan's face colored. "I didn't actually arrange it. That just sort of materialized while I was around. Anyway, I mean besides that one." She pressed on, "You need to get out a little."

"Thanks, but I'm very happy right now," I said, "very happy."

Again the critical look, but this time there was a sparkle in her eyes. "Is there something you're not telling me?"

I opened my mouth to discourage further discussion, but she interrupted.

"What's his name?"

No way. Not yet. Indicating the computer, I asked, "Any further updates on the big news? Have they identified the victims yet or shared any details?"

"I haven't checked. To be honest, I don't want to hear it. I could tell by your face that Patty was one of them." She put her finger to her lips. "I know not to say anything to anyone until I hear it on the news, but the idea that someone so young and so full of energy could have her life snuffed out . . ." Cyan's eyes teared up. "What's wrong with people?"

I didn't have an answer for her. "Tomorrow's going to be crazy around here. When the news finally does hit, it's going to be big."

"Not just because of Patty?"

As much as I wanted to, I couldn't tell her who the second victim was. "Believe me, it's going to be a very bad day tomorrow. I plan to get in extra early."

"Got it, Ollie. See you then."

I resisted the urge to check updates online before I left. If the news about White House Chief of Staff Cawley and Patty Woodruff hadn't hit already, it would soon. Coverage would undoubtedly go on all night.

Poor Doug Lambert, taking over for Paul in the midst of this chaos. I wished him the best and vowed to do whatever I could to make his job easier. Part of me seriously considered staying here through the night. And part of me was utterly relieved to be going home.

All of a sudden I craved quiet, though not solitude. Even though no one waited for me back at my apartment, I hoped to be able to talk about all the events tonight with the one person I knew I could trust and who — conveniently — possessed the clearance to hear it all. There were times I wished I possessed the clearance to hear everything *he* knew, but you can't have everything.

I glanced at my watch and frowned at the little timepiece. At least another hour before he'd call. That is, *if* he called. Today's events could drag him into meetings that lasted far into the night.

Thank goodness the days are getting longer, I thought, as I ducked my head against the freezing wind to make my way across Pennsylvania Avenue. Despite the unpleasant weather and dusk settling in, there were still several dozen tourists outside the White House fence, staring between the iron bars and posing for pictures.

There were also tourists taking pictures of the tent directly across the street from the White House. Connie was a fixture on Pennsylvania Avenue in Lafayette Park, where she maintained her steady vigil against nuclear arms. Our neighbor of sorts, Connie had occupied the same spot since the early 1980s. From what I understood, her campaign was one of the longest-running continuous political protests in history, if not the longest.

She had to be over sixty by now, but living outdoors had aged her beyond her years. I worried for her, particularly on days like this. Every so often I stopped by and dropped off a few dollars. It was the least I could do.

I hoped she was keeping warm inside her tent tonight. I also hoped that the last tourist, a hat-and-scarf-wearing man still reading her posters, would pull his hands out of his pockets long enough to drop a donation before he left. Whether he supported her protest or not, the poor woman had to eat.

McPherson Square station was a few blocks from the White House. Most days I found the walk enjoyable. Not so much this evening. The other pedestrians hurried along as fast as I did, fighting the chill that nabbed us in its icy grip.

As I made my way north on 15th Street, I became aware of a person walking quickly behind me. I turned to see the same man who had been outside Connie's tent, hurrying as though to catch up. He lifted a hand in greeting. "Excuse me," he said, raising his voice to be heard over the noise of the street, "can you help me?"

I glanced around, slowing my pace. I was ever suspicious of strangers, but there were plenty of other people around and he looked harmless enough. "What do you need?" I asked.

Wearing a brown fedora, dark jacket, and red plaid scarf across his mouth and nose, he puffed out a dramatic breath. "Thank you. I may be lost." Nothing about him set off any alarms, but when he took a step closer, I stepped back.

"I'm supposed to meet someone at a restaurant around here." He stretched his left arm out and tapped the watch on his wrist. I'd expected a Rolex, but it looked more like a department-store Swatch. "I'm late and I can't remember the name of the place. Which stinks, because I'm starving."

He didn't scan the street for potential meeting places, he stared at me — studying me in a way that made me feel uncomfortable. I didn't like that I couldn't see his whole face. "There are a lot of restaurants around here," I said as I inched away, "why don't you call your friend and ask?"

He stepped closer. "Left my cell back at work. Hey," he said as though the thought

70

had just occurred to him. "Can I borrow yours? Just for a minute?"

There seemed to be far fewer pedestrians than there had been just moments ago. I was definitely getting the creeps from this guy now. As he took another half-step closer, I said, "It won't do you any good if his number is in *your* phone's memory."

He blinked. "Right." Switching gears, he continued, "You seem a little frazzled. Rough day at the office?"

This conversation was very wrong, and I needed to get away without making any sudden moves. I worked up a smile of my own and took a step back, making sure to memorize all I could about this weirdo, just in case. Twenty-five to thirty-five years old, by my limited best guess. Dark eyes. No moles, no birthmarks in the part of his face I could see. "I hope you find your friend," I said, giving a little wave. I started away at a brisk clip.

Within seconds, he was at my side again. "Maybe if I describe the restaurant to you. It's supposed to be famous for its gourmet menu. Do you know anything about food?"

I didn't slow my pace, didn't look at him. "Not much."

"You're a terrible liar."

Instinctively, I glanced over. I couldn't tell

whether he knew who I was or whether he was just socially inept. He shrugged, said, "Women always know the best restaurants," then studied the streets, as though looking for an opportunity. "Where do you work?"

Picking up my pace, I pointed east. "There's a great steakhouse about a block from here." I gave him the name. "On the next street. If that isn't right, I'm sure they'll be able to help you find the right one." I tapped my wrist. "Gotta run."

"Wait —"

I didn't. I flat-out ran the rest of the way to McPherson and reached the entrance to the station panting. My hungry friend didn't follow, thank goodness, but when I peered back around the corner, I swore I saw him pull out his left-at-work cell phone and make a call.

What had just happened?

CHAPTER 5

My own cell phone had run so low on power that I didn't risk making a call unless it was an emergency. I kept the little device tight in my sweaty hand as I waited for the next Metro train. There were two men on the platform with me. One was a large fellow wearing a hat, a cell phone tight to his ear.

The other man was elderly, white-haired, with bushy eyebrows. He leaned on a four-foot aluminum cane and stared down the tunnel as though awaiting the train's arrival. Except he was staring in the wrong direction.

Not that it mattered. The train came soon enough and I readied myself to get on, wondering if the elderly man needed assistance. Just as the doors opened, however, the man in the hat was behind us, nudging the old fellow in. I couldn't tell for certain whether the two knew each other or whether the younger man was just impatient. Either way, you didn't push people with canes. It just wasn't right.

Once inside the car, I made sure to study each and every commuter. Two young women chattered about an upcoming wedding. Neither gave me a passing glance. They were safe.

The hat-wearing younger man sat behind the two girls, while the older man took a seat by the door. Apparently they didn't know each other after all. Across the aisle from him, a younger man sat with his legs wide apart, bouncing on the balls of his feet as though ready to leap into action. When I walked past him, he gave me a curious look, but maybe that was because he'd felt the weight of my stare.

Paranoia and I made our way to the middle of the car, choosing one of the many empty aisle seats. My senses were so heightened by my recent encounter that I sat ramrod straight, trying to quiet the thrumming of my heart. Again I wondered what had just happened outside. "Come on," I whispered, urging the train to depart. I needed to get home. Today's gruesome discovery was weighing heavily on my mind and was undoubtedly the source of my intense suspicion. *Deep breath,* I told myself, *it's safe now. It's okay to relax.*

The man with the hat got up just as the Metro doors closed. I watched as he lumbered over. He wore a business suit under an open, camel-colored trench coat, and his hat was pulled low over his eyes. All I could see of his face was the deep cleft of his chin, until he pushed back the brim of his hat, made eye contact, and took the aisle seat across from me. "Cold draft over there," he said.

There were plenty of other choices in the nearly empty car. Why pick one so close to mine?

Annoyed, I gripped my phone tighter, snugged my purse under my arm, and pretended to brush debris off the seat next to me. With a shake of my head and a disappointed huff, I stood up and walked farther back in the car, proud of my dramatic talents. Three rows behind the guy with the hat, I had a wide, unobstructed view of all occupants. I liked it much better this way.

To my relief, the guy stayed in his seat. He pulled a Metro map from his pocket and spread it open across his lap, studying it for a few minutes before jamming a finger near the bottom to hold his place while he looked around. Apparently pleased by whatever he saw, he folded the map up again and slid it back into his pocket. Probably an out-of-towner on a business trip.

The two women and the antsy young man got off at Foggy Bottom, leaving me with the elderly gent with the cane and Map Man for company. The older fellow's head drooped lower and lower and I thought I heard him snore. The man with the map kept his hands folded as he read the ads on either side of the car. Neither of those two seemed particularly interested in me, so I tucked my phone back into my purse and stared out the window, able to relax a little, finally.

Two stops later, we hadn't picked up any passengers, but by then the old guy's snores had taken on a life of their own. During an extended open-mouthed gurgle, Map Man turned to me and spoke in a stage whisper. "Should I wake him up? What if he misses his stop?"

I shrugged. "If he's not awake by Crystal City, maybe we should wake him then."

"Is that where you get off?"

I looked away and pretended I hadn't heard him.

He pulled his map out again, but instead of reading it, he tapped it against his leg and kept looking at the elderly gentleman whose head bobbed and wagged with each bump and joggle of the train. We sailed through the next two stops without the old guy waking up. Map Man kept up a staccato rhythm against his leg, its tempo getting faster by the second as the old guy's snores reverberated around us.

"Maybe I'd better ask him." Map Man got up and shook the sleeping fellow's shoulder. "Hey, Gramps. You okay there?"

Startled, the older guy blinked and leaned away from the intruder, clearly terrified. "What? What?" Frantically looking around, he asked, "Where are we? Is this my stop?"

Our train began to slow as we approached Crystal City. I stood up.

Map Man rolled his eyes. "Don't know. Where do you get off?"

He coughed. "Clarendon."

Oh no. I was about to offer to help when Map Man's words froze me in my tracks. "Gramps, you got a problem. You didn't just miss your stop. You're on the wrong train. This is Blue. You should have switched at Rosslyn." He pointed to the floor. "This is the wrong train, mister."

I stifled my surprise. Unless he possessed a photographic memory, an out-of-towner wouldn't know that information off the top of his head. I fought the queasiness that took hold of my stomach. This could be nothing. A misunderstanding on my part. But I wasn't about to take chances. Without making eye contact with Map Man, I approached the older gentleman.

"Let's get off here," I said, taking his elbow and helping him to his feet as the train came to a stop. "I'll get you onto the right train."

Map Man seemed surprised. "Is this your stop?" he asked.

The doors opened.

Map Man followed us out. "Let me help you."

"I'll handle this, thanks." I turned to my elderly charge. "What's your name?"

He dragged the back of his hand across his mouth. "Bettencourt," he said, pulling his arm from my grip, "Benjamin Bettencourt."

Map Man gave me a skeptical look over the back of Mr. Bettencourt's head. "You sure you want to handle this on your own?"

"I'll be fine."

"Suit yourself."

Visibly vexed, Mr. Bettencourt stamped his cane on the ground. "For the love of Pete," he said, "would you two stop acting as though I'm an idiot who's lost all my marbles?"

"I'm sorry," I said, "I just thought . . ."

"I know what you thought," he said, voice rising. "Just because I'm old doesn't mean I'm feeble. Wait until you're my age, girlie, and some do-gooder tries to manhandle you."

"My apologies," I said, backing away. "I'm sure you'll be fine from here."

"Darned right I am. This is my stop."

"I thought you said Clarendon," I said.

Bettencourt worked his mouth. "Yes, well. It's none of your business where I get off. I just got confused for a minute. I was having a good dream before I got shaken awake."

Map Man pushed his hat farther back on his head and shot me an amused look. I didn't return it. All I wanted was to get away. "Are you sure you don't need help?" I asked Bettencourt.

His face contorted as though highly annoyed. "My daughter will be waiting for me outside. She's very important, you know."

Not totally convinced he really knew where he was, I was reluctant to leave him to his own wiles. And, selfishly, I figured that if I took charge of him, Map Man would back off. With any luck he'd get on the next train and disappear. "Tell you what," I said, "I'll go with you and wait until your daughter shows up. It's getting late."

"You do-gooders are all alike," he said,

but at least he didn't argue. As we set off for the escalators, he gripped my arm and spoke under his breath. "I may need to call her."

"Of course." I turned to Map Man. "Another train should be here in a minute. Thanks for your help."

"This is my stop, too."

Oh great.

With that familiar "something is not right" feeling tingling up my back, I pulled out my cell phone and dialed. With any luck I'd have enough juice for this important call and another to Bettencourt's daughter.

"Who are you calling?" Map Man asked.

I ignored him.

Mr. Bettencourt cleared his throat several times as the number went to voicemail. "Hey," I said into the receiver, "it's me. I'm just getting off at Crystal City. Can you . . . can you meet me?" I didn't know what else to say, so I hung up.

We reached the top and made it through the turnstiles. "So, what's your name?" Map Man asked.

Again I ignored him. "Come on, Mr. Bettencourt, we're almost there."

Map Man was nothing if not persistent. "My name's Brad."

He looked like a Brad.

"No need to give me the cold shoulder," he said, trailing us through the exit and outside into the windy chill. "I'm just trying to be friendly."

When the frigid night wind hit me, I questioned myself. Maybe he *was* just trying to be friendly. To help out an older person. Why else would he hang out here in the cold if he didn't have to? Maybe he knew the Metro system well and had brought home a map for a friend. Maybe he didn't have an evil agenda and my fears were completely unfounded. I often picked up on conspiracies before others did. Trouble arose when I thought I detected one where none existed.

"I'm sorry," I said, "long day."

I looked up and down the street for Mr. Bettencourt's daughter. "Is this the exit where you'll meet her?" I asked. "Will she walk or drive?"

Bettencourt wrinkled his nose as he stared upward, clearly looking for landmarks. He didn't seem very sure of himself when he nodded. "Yeah. This is it."

"I hear you about the long day," Brad said. "Mine was a bear." He studied the landmarks, too. "You live around here?"

I was spared answering because Mr. Bettencourt thought the question had been directed to him. "Not far. She'll be here in a minute."

Brad shifted his weight and looked ready to launch into a new round of questions.

"You can go ahead," I said. "I'm sure we'll be fine."

"I don't want to leave you out here by yourselves —"

"Trust me, we'll be fine. I have a friend meeting me."

"No, you don't. You only left a voicemail," he said. "No telling when *your friend* will get the message."

Brad was smiling in a way that scared me. But I couldn't take off, not without making sure Mr. Bettencourt was all right. I had slipped my cell phone into my pocket and now I reached in to grip it again, ready to dial James at the front desk of my building. He'd be quick to send help if I so much as squeaked.

"Mr. Bettencourt, do you have your daughter's phone number?"

The question seemed only to confuse him further.

"How about I call a cab?" I asked.

Still looking around, Bettencourt seemed to grow less certain by the moment. "I don't know."

"Hey!" Brad snapped his fingers and

pointed at me. "I know you."

"Mr. Bettencourt?" I said, turning my back to Brad. "I'm going to call a cab. If your daughter comes in the meantime, I'll just take it myself."

My apartment was within easy walking distance, but I didn't want Brad offering to accompany me. I also didn't want to hear how he thought he knew me. I pulled up my phone again to see if I had a local taxi company on speed dial. Low on battery juice, the handset gave a warning beep. "I know," I said under my breath, "just one more call."

Brad came around to face me. He tipped his hat very far back to look me straight in the eye. I got a much better look at him. Dark blond hair. Thinning. Tiny ears, small eyes spaced far apart, and a pudginess around his features that let me know his excess bulkiness couldn't all be blamed on the coat. "I knew you looked familiar. You're the chef."

My stomach lurched. "Don't know what you're talking about."

"The one who was on TV today."

"What?" My attention no longer on the phone display, I stared up at Brad's wide-set eyes.

"Got your interest now, huh?" he said.

"You're the one who found the White House chief of staff dead. Murdered, right? It's all over the news."

I felt all the blood drain from my face.

"Who's dead?" Bettencourt asked.

"Not you, Gramps. Not yet, at least." A corner of Brad's mouth curled up. "What was that like — finding the body? Two of them, right? That girl got murdered, too." He went on before I could say a word, "Did you see who killed them?"

Who was this guy? Every single hair on my body stood on end. My voice croaked, "No idea what you're talking about." Still scrolling even with trembling fingers, I finally found the taxi number. "You must have me confused with someone else."

I hit the call button just as headlights swung past, making me blink in their brightness. At first I thought it was Bettencourt's daughter, but the car was moving too fast. As it approached, I took a closer look and nearly jumped straight up. Waving my hands, I called, "Hey, over here."

The squad car slowed, coming to a stop across the street. The cop rolled down his window. "Is there a problem?"

From my handset, I heard the taxi dispatcher answer. I hung up.

"No," Brad said, waving the officer away.

"We're cool."

"Yes," I said.

With a resigned look, the officer pulled his car to the curb and got out, flashlight beaming right at us. Fifty-something, he was of average height, a bit wide around the waist, and had deep-set eyes. The weariness in his demeanor made me believe we'd interrupted a long-overdue break. "What seems to be the problem?"

Brad lowered the brim of his hat against the flashlight's brightness. I tried to speak, but he talked over me. "Nothing at all, Officer. I was just giving this young lady directions. I think she's lost."

The cop scratched the back of his neck. "Where are you looking to go, miss?"

"I am not lost." I was about to add that I lived nearby, but didn't want to share that information in front of Brad. I took hold of Mr. Bettencourt's arm. "But this gentleman may be."

"Who are you?" he asked me.

"I'm just trying to help out here."

To Brad: "What about you?"

"Just walking by and giving directions, Officer."

"That's a lie," I said. "He followed us off the Metro. He says he knows me."

Brad laughed. "Delusions of grandeur, lady."

"All right, there seems to be more going on here than either of you care to admit. Show me some ID."

Brad nodded. "No problem, Officer."

I started to dig in my purse.

Brad made a show of searching through his wallet. "I've got ID in here somewhere," he said. "Maybe I need more light." Pointing to the nearby streetlamp, he said, "Hang on a minute," and walked a few feet away.

The cop grunted, then flashed his light directly into Bettencourt's face. "You, too." A couple of seconds later, his head jerked back in surprise. "Hey! Aren't you —" His hand reached back, hovering over his holster. All politeness disappeared in a flash. "Put your hands up," he growled at me.

"What?"

When the cop turned to face Brad, I turned, too. "Hands up. Both of y—"

Brad was gone.

CHAPTER 6

When I finished going through mug shots at one of the detective's desks, Officer Ellis handed me a cup of coffee. "You're telling me you didn't know Mr. Bettencourt was missing and presumed kidnapped?"

"No."

"You don't even know who he is, do you?"

"Who is he?"

"Where have you been? It's been on the news all day." He lowered himself into a rolling chair. It squeaked, the sound bouncing off the walls in this airless room. High-gloss walls, metal desks, tile floor. Cold, gray, uninviting.

"I've been busy. No time for TV." I held the cup of steaming coffee in both hands and stared down at the dark liquid. No cream. I hoped there was no sugar. He hadn't asked, but right now I didn't much care. I took a sip. Scalding and soothing at the same time. "By the way, where is he?"

The moment we'd arrived at the station, two detectives had rushed up to take charge of the elderly man. I hadn't seen him since.

"On his way home."

"Good. He said his daughter would be at the station to pick him up."

Ellis gave a snort. "You really don't know, do you? Don't they have televisions in the White House kitchen?"

I didn't answer.

"Shame what's going on over there today."

"What have you heard?"

He blinked at me. "Oh come on. You had to have heard about the murders."

"Fill me in."

Ellis knew about the double murder at Lexington Place. Knew the victims were Chief of Staff Cawley and Patty Woodruff. The news had covered most of it. "No leads yet." He took a deep slurp of his coffee.

I nodded. Clearly the news hadn't mentioned how the victims were found, nor the fact that they'd died in separate attacks. Most important, the news could not have mentioned my involvement. If they had, Ellis here would have made the connection.

Brad's comment about me being on the news made my stomach twist with fear. Had he been waiting for me at the Metro platform? Did I just get lucky to stumble upon lost Mr. Bettencourt, who'd helped me escape with my life?

Ellis was still talking and I didn't interrupt. These musings needed to be shared, but not with local cops. I needed to talk with the Secret Service. Now.

"Maybe it was a murder-suicide."

"Yeah." I didn't feel much like talking, or even listening. Ever since my identification had been verified, I'd been a-okay in these cops' eyes. Right now I waited while the Secret Service sent an agent to escort me home. Ellis here had evidently drawn the short straw, and was stuck babysitting until then. I glanced at my watch. Could this day get any longer?

"So you're saying you never saw that guy who called himself Brad before tonight?"

We'd been over this already. "Not until he got on the Metro. He tried to sit by me."

Ellis scribbled a note. "You think he recognized you as somebody from the White House?"

My head hurt. "He said he did."

The cop took another slurp of his coffee and smacked his lips. "What made you notice him in the first place? Most people just go about their business. Did you think maybe you'd seen him before?"

How could I explain that by now I was

suspicious of everyone? I certainly couldn't tell him that I was as skittish as a rabbit after the morning's adventure with Sargeant. I hedged. "Before I got on the train, there was this other man —"

Ellis sat forward. "Boyfriend?"

"No," I said a bit too sharply. "Listen, I kind of have a history of running into bad guys."

He sat back. "Not boyfriends?"

I ignored that. "On my way to the Metro, this man in a scarf started acting suspicious."

"Suspicious how?"

Right now the lost fellow looking for a restaurant seemed perfectly harmless. "Hard to explain, but I got that all-is-not-right feeling from him."

Ellis finally seemed to understand. "Go on."

"I was in a hurry to get away. I ran, actually." Wrinkling my nose, I stared at the gray walls. "The encounter made me jumpy. I started paying close attention to anyone who so much as made eye contact."

He'd put his cup down and begun scribbling again.

"Since I missed all the news," I said, "would you tell me who the elderly man was? He told me his name, but it didn't mean anything to me."

"Benjamin Bettencourt is the secretary of state's father-in-law," he said as though that explained everything.

I waited.

"He went missing this afternoon. Gone from his home. Family was frantic with worry and they were afraid he'd been abducted."

"But he just wandered off?"

"I don't know," Ellis said. "Something doesn't smell right. With the murders today and now this, the administration is under siege, if you ask me. 'Course, nobody's asking me. I got a sense about these things." He tapped his temple. "Lot of years on the job tells me there are too many incidents happening at once. That guy — Brad — who took off knew more than he wanted to tell, that's for sure. Wish I could have had a chance to talk to him."

A young kid, probably a cadet, appeared in the doorway. "Officer Ellis?"

He turned around.

"Her ride is here."

"Got it."

I stood and held up my half-finished coffee. "Where do I put this?"

"Just leave it," he said with a wave. "I'll get it. You go home and get some rest."

My ability to get rest would depend greatly on which agent they'd sent to escort me home. I'd had run-ins with several, and didn't feel like being used as a stepping stone for one of the newer agents to make a name for himself at my expense. There were a couple I endeavored to avoid.

"This way," the cadet said. He led me down a long hall to a metal door. He swung it open with a smile. "Have a good night."

As I stepped into the waiting room, I started to say, "Thanks —" The rest of what I would have said died on my lips when I saw who was waiting for me. "I thought you were out of town."

Tom MacKenzie, my ex-boyfriend and head of the PPD, looked just about as happy to see me as I was to see him. "Flew in about a half hour ago," he said. "This was on my way."

"Great."

We fell into step and made our way outside where I took a breath of the fresh, cold air. "I didn't realize how stale it was in there. Smelly." A bright star twinkled above. Closing my eyes, I made a wish. But when I opened my eyes again, Tom was still there.

"What happened?" he asked.

At least he didn't start with "Why is it always you?" the way he usually did.

"I think I'm being followed."

He pointed his key ring at a shiny, dark Mustang in the lot's far corner, beeping it open.

"New car, huh?" I said as I got in. "It's nice."

He settled himself behind the wheel and started it up with a roar, not looking at me. "Kim picked it out."

"Yeah? How's that going?"

"Good." He pulled out of the lot. I think the fact that he didn't have to ask directions to my apartment was not lost on either of us. "Very good, I mean. Great."

"I'm glad."

"What happened today?"

I didn't feel like rehashing every little detail. "How much do you know?"

"Everything. Except how you got mixed up with Bettencourt. That's too much. Even for you."

"Even for me? Nice."

"You know what I mean."

"The guy who followed me on the Metro knew about my involvement at Lexington Place today," I said.

"What?" Tom yanked the steering wheel so hard the tires squealed against pavement. He pulled to the curb and banged the car into park. "Talk to me."

"He said it's been all over the news."

Fury made Tom's words come out clipped. "It hasn't. We kept you and Sargeant out of it."

"I figured. Otherwise the cop who hauled me in would have known. He clearly didn't."

"You didn't say anything to the local guys, did you?"

"Give me a little credit, would you?"

Tom rubbed his forehead. "Just what we need," he said as he started driving again. "You've done it again, haven't you?"

Tom had never trusted me, despite the fact that I'd proved myself again and again. That was just one of the issues between us. I stared out at the moonlit trees and dark buildings as we flew down the deserted streets. By the time we made it to my apartment building, I'd finally managed to work my anger down to a manageable level. Enough to say good night without biting his head off, at least.

He made the left turn that took us up the driveway to the front doors. "I'll officially debrief you tomorrow. After all that's happened today, it's been decided to send an agent here in the morning to pick you up. What time do you want him here?"

I didn't even ask if that was necessary. Grabbing my purse, I readied myself to get out. "I'll need to be in early. Have him here by four. Any idea who it will be?"

"Probably —"

I followed Tom's gaze to find what had stopped him from finishing. A tall fellow leaned against the side of my building, in the shadows. He pushed himself from the wall and ambled over. All the anger I'd bottled up disappeared like magic. Like happy fizz bubbling up from a champagne bottle.

Gav opened my door. "Hey," he said, taking my hand to help me out, "you've had a rough day."

Now *that* was how to treat a woman who'd discovered a double murder.

Tom leaned over. I couldn't read his expression, but his tone was just this side of sneering. "I guess Agent Scorroco doesn't need to show up here in the morning, does he?"

Gav bent down to face him. "Orders haven't changed. Please see to it that Ms. Paras is escorted to and from the White House tomorrow. And for as long as necessary."

Even in the scant light of the Mustang's overhead dome, I could see Tom's face color. "I just assumed . . ."

"You have your orders. Good night, Agent

MacKenzie." As soon as Tom pulled away, Gav turned to me. "He thinks there's something going on between us."

"Isn't there?"

"You know what I mean. We're taking things slower than most people do these days."

With my long hours, Gav's unpredictable schedule, and a few issues we'd yet to work out, slow was the only choice we had. Special Agent in Charge Leonard Gavin's responsibilities kept him on call 24/7 and out of town much of that time. I glanced back at the road. "I just hope he doesn't share his assumptions with anyone."

"He won't. He's a good man, Ollie."

"He is," I agreed, "but I have my sights set on someone even better."

That got a smile out of him.

"Got time to come up?" I asked. "Hungry?"

"Can't. As you can imagine, there's too much hitting the fan tonight to take any personal time."

"But . . . you're here."

"By the time I got your message you'd already been taken to the police station and we'd all been apprised of the situation. I volunteered to pick you up, but they said MacKenzie was already on his way."

"You came anyway?"

"I wanted to see you."

My stomach somersaulted like a smitten teenager's. I tilted my chin up. "I'm glad."

I waited a breathless moment, silently willing him to kiss me. Really kiss me. We'd been here before. So close. Maybe this time . . .

But there was that look in his eyes again. The one that had become so familiar these past weeks. Another reason we were taking things slowly.

"Ollie," he said in a voice so gentle it sent shivers up my back, "if we're going to have a relationship, we're going to do it right. So it lasts."

"I know."

"Be patient with me."

"Always."

With a smile he said, "That's my girl," and kissed me on the cheek.

CHAPTER 7

As expected, the White House was crazy the next morning. Media trucks got as close as they could, a press briefing was scheduled for ten, and those reporters not lucky enough to be invited to attend were left to stand in the cold, waiting for word from their colleagues inside as they spoke somberly into television cameras, the White House their backdrop.

Bucky came in fifteen minutes after me. "Can you believe the crowds out there?" he said as he peeled off his coat. "I could barely get past them. One of the uniforms had to physically restrain this one girl who tried to tackle me. For an update!"

"What happened to her?"

"No idea. Don't these people have any sense of decorum?"

I sighed. "It gets worse." I told him about the prior night's adventure on the Metro.

"When was the last time you took a vacation?" he asked.

"Time off is a luxury I can't afford right now."

Bucky pulled out a bag of potatoes, emptying the spuds onto the countertop with a soft *thud-thud-thud.* Their earthy smell filled the quiet kitchen, and if I closed my eyes I could pretend it was just a normal day. Just me and Bucky, making breakfast for the president. But I knew better. Virgil was upstairs doing that. I looked at my watch. Or maybe not. Chances were, the president had already finished and was on his way to the West Wing.

"I don't know." Bucky hefted a potato and began to peel. "I think you can't afford not to. Look at how tightly wound you are."

"If it weren't for Virgil trying to take over —"

"Don't give him power he doesn't deserve."

I glanced over at my second-in-command. "I don't."

"Sure you do. He's good, and he's got the First Lady's ear, but you're making a name for yourself with this family, too."

"Thanks, Bucky."

"Just telling the truth. He's good. You're better." With a cock of his head, he added, "*I'm* better."

I started to smile, but it died on my face as Doug Lambert came in. He looked as though he hadn't slept all night.

"How did it go?" I asked him.

His voice was hoarse. "You know about the press briefing, but there's a change," he said. "Before talking about the tragedy at Lexington Place, the president will allow Secretary of State Quinones a few moments at the microphone. He will be accompanied by his wife and father-in-law. Quinones wants to thank the public for helping bring his wife's father home safely. After that announcement, the president will discuss the double murder, announce what arrangements are being made to help the victims' families find justice, and finally take questions. It's going to be a rough one. Nothing like this has ever happened before."

I thought about what Ellis had said last night. "It's almost as though the White House is under siege."

Doug seemed to slump. I was sorry I'd opened my mouth.

"At least the kids and First Lady are away for this. When will they be back?"

"We're in discussions about that right now. Until we know more, the president is suggesting that his wife and kids stay out of Washington. They're with family in Florida

100

but are due back tomorrow."

"Oh no."

"Mrs. Hyden is scheduled for a goodwill trip to Africa. As far as we know, she will return for the funerals, take the kids to Camp David for a few days, then continue with her African plans."

"Will the kids go with her?"

"We're thinking of having the kids' Grandma Marty accompany them to Camp David, where they will stay until all this is cleared up."

"What about their schooling?"

Doug looked like a beaten man. "We're working on it."

I was sorry to keep bothering him. "No one is aware of my involvement, right? In either of these situations?"

"Officially," Doug said with a meaningful glance, "Mr. Bettencourt was found by police in Crystal City. Unofficially, the Quinones family is very grateful to you."

"They didn't need to know it was me."

Doug swallowed loudly, then massaged his throat. "They insisted. Mr. Quinones wants to thank you personally."

Anything but that. I started to protest, but Doug's pitiful expression stopped me. Belatedly I realized that arguing did little more than make his job harder. "I would have preferred otherwise, but since they know, I'll cooperate. Whatever works for you."

Doug gave a lopsided smile. "Thank you."

"Go gargle with saltwater or something," I said.

He waved and was off.

Cyan arrived a few minutes later. "Do you have any idea how bad it is out there?"

"Crowds or weather?" Bucky asked.

"Both. How can that many people stand to wait outside in this mess? I could barely make it through. I thought I'd be crushed."

"They'll probably be there all day," Bucky said, "ready to greet us when we leave for the night."

Cyan shuddered. "They were all asking me for a statement. Like what could I know?"

Bucky smirked. "Maybe they know you have an in with" — he gestured with his chin — "the person who found the bodies."

"Let's hope no one makes that connection," I said.

Bucky said, "This morning I got so angry at all the people with microphones, I told them to . . . well, let's just say I told them off."

Cyan giggled. "I'll bet you did. Me? I just pretended I didn't speak English."

At that I laughed out loud. "Red hair . . ."

I peered to see what color contacts she was wearing today, "blue eyes, and they believed you?"

"I held up my hands and kept repeating *Nein, nein.* I didn't know how to say anything in Gaelic, so I pretended I was German."

Bucky snorted. "I'm sure that fooled them."

"I'm here, aren't I?"

"Breakfast was wonderful," Virgil said as he bustled into the room carrying two huge bowls and what looked like a set of fuzzy red, white, and blue slippers. Except there were three of them.

"What in the world are you carrying?" Cyan asked.

He set the bowls down. "These take up too much room in the family's kitchen. There are plenty of other suitable choices up there. I figured we could use these oversized versions down here."

"Not those," Cyan pointed to the fuzzy things, *"those."*

He looked at her as though she were a simpleton. "Golf club covers."

Bucky waved a potato in the air. "And we need them because . . . ?"

Virgil expelled a sigh of annoyance, but the look in his eyes was gleeful. "They are a gift. The president received them from a well-wisher, but he already has a set he prefers. He thought I might like these."

Before any of us could respond, he made sure to add, "You know the president and I golf together occasionally."

"Yes, we remember," I said. "They're very nice. You may want to put them away before they get splattered."

"Whatever you say." He tamped down his smile with obvious effort, picked up his fuzzy gift, and started out.

"Uh-oh," Bucky said.

I looked up. Sargeant blocked Virgil's path and for several seconds the two of them did that dance-in-the-doorway thing until Virgil eventually stepped aside. "Fine!" he said.

Sargeant didn't seem to notice the assistant chef's irritation. Instead, he made a beeline for me. "Why were you escorted in today? Do I need an escort, too?"

I told him everything that had happened on the Metro the evening before. With only Bucky and Cyan in the kitchen, and because Sargeant and I had discovered the double murder together, I thought it appropriate to warn him about my encounter with Brad. I even told him about the man looking for a restaurant.

When I was finished he almost smiled. "I

guess I should be grateful that my face isn't on the front page of the newspaper as often as yours is. At least no one would recognize me."

"My face hasn't been in the paper recently," I reminded him, "yet Brad knew I was involved. How could he if he wasn't involved himself?"

Sargeant bit the insides of his cheeks.

"It wouldn't hurt to be careful," I said.

Sargeant sniffed. "You and I still need to submit our reports about the other three venues," he said. "When do you want to discuss our findings?"

"Discuss? With you?" My question took him aback and I softened my response immediately. "Sorry, Peter, I didn't mean to snap. I just assumed you and I would submit our recommendations independently. I should have mine ready soon, though I don't imagine party plans are very high on Doug's agenda today."

"Do you have a copy of the guest list?" he asked.

"No," I said. "The kitchen doesn't get the list until it's finalized and until the invitations are written out. That way we don't prepare special menus for guests who don't make the final cut."

"Oh," he said with a smug lilt. "That's

where your responsibilities and mine differ. I get all the guest lists. Every one. In fact, if I so choose, I can recommend names to be cut."

Only when it's known that certain guests don't interact well with others, I thought. That's what a sensitivity director *should* do, but I didn't want to deny him his happy little moment of one-upmanship. "Good for you. Now, if there's nothing else, we need to get back to work."

Sargeant left, but our blessed respite turned out to be only temporary. He returned a short while later, waving a manila folder. "These are my venue impressions and the notes I made on our visits. You can check to see if there was anything you missed."

"No, really?" Bucky clapped his hands in front of his chest. "You would do that for Ollie?" To me: "Wasn't that thoughtful of Mr. Sargeant to come all the way down here just to help you out?"

"Knock it off, Bucky," I said under my breath. Sargeant was about the last person I wanted to work with, but we'd been assigned a job and I intended to get it done to the best of my ability. There was a chance, however slight, that he might have picked up on a problem with a venue that

I'd missed. "Sure," I said to the sensitivity director, "I have time now."

We'd just gotten started when Doug came in. "There you are," he said. We all turned. His tie was off center, the left side of his hair was disheveled, and his cheeks were even pinker than normal.

"Who are you looking for?" I asked.

"You," he said. "The press briefing is in less than an hour."

Sargeant's eyes went wide. "*You* have been invited to the briefing?"

"Nothing of the sort. There's just . . ." I didn't want to explain about Secretary of State Quinones's insistence on thanking me personally. "I have to talk to someone who will be there, is all."

Doug continued, "I came to give you a heads up. Keeping everything moving today has been" — he started walking away — "challenging."

I wondered why he hadn't simply picked up the phone or sent an e-mail. As though I'd voiced the question, he said, "There are too many people in my office. Explaining why I need to bring you to Secretary Quinones would just open up a can of worms. It's going to be tough enough to get you to talk with him one on one without anyone noticing." He started for the door again. "I'll be back in a bit to escort you upstairs, Ollie. I'll figure something out in the meantime." I thought I heard him mumble, "I don't know how Paul stayed so calm all the time."

Sargeant started after him. "Just a moment, Doug."

He turned.

Sargeant pointed toward me. "We're working on our venue recommendations for Secretary Quinones's birthday party. How soon would you like them on your desk?"

I thought Doug might reach over and smack Sargeant upside the head. The look on the chief usher's face was one of total disbelief. "No rush on that, Peter," he said. "I've got a lot more pressing issues to juggle today."

Sargeant nodded. "Yes, of course. How silly of me to even ask."

Doug was out the door without another word.

Bucky sidled up to me to whisper, "Very *sensitive* of Sargeant, wouldn't you say? He's just so perfect for this job."

I jabbed Bucky in the ribs but had to admit it was funny.

"Get him out of here," Bucky said. "He's in the way."

"Why don't we work on this later?" I said to Sargeant. "I need to make sure I'm presentable enough to be seen upstairs."

Sargeant would not be dissuaded. "I can keep working here for a while. When you get back, you can read my notes and see what I've included."

Bucky's level of exasperation was at an all-time high. "Don't you have something else to do? New protocols to memorize or something?"

Sargeant pulled himself up to his full height. "I have more to do than you could ever hope to appreciate."

Bucky pulled out a tray of shrimp to be cleaned. "I have no doubt."

Sargeant's nose twitched. "I will speak with you later, Ms. Paras. Until then."

The moment he was gone, Bucky wiped his hands on his apron. "That's the most civil he's ever been to you. He was almost pleasant. What's going on?"

"I think he's scared," I said. "He and I happened across a horrific scene and I bet he can't get the images out of his mind. I know I can't." I thrummed my fingers on the countertop. "He and I are in the exact same boat. I think he believes that if we stick together, we'll stay safer that way." I thought about it. "Or should I say, he hopes *he* will stay safer that way."

Cyan laughed. "Just what you need, Ollie,

Peter Everett Sargeant as your best bud."

"Just lucky, I guess."

When Virgil returned, Bucky's mood still hadn't improved. "Where did you go to put those club covers? Maryland?" he asked, mimicking Virgil's comment to me the day before.

Virgil smiled, showing teeth. "You're hilarious. You should be on television."

I knew what was coming.

Virgil went in for the jab. "Because then I could shut you off."

"Boys," I said, "let's not get out of hand. We'll probably be feeding a lot of people again tonight. There's no time to waste."

"Speaking of time," Virgil said. He waited for us to bite.

No one did.

"*Time* magazine will be interviewing me."

Okay, that caught our attention.

"Don't tell me," Bucky said, "Man of the Year?"

"Ha-ha. Not exactly. The piece isn't for *Time* magazine itself," he amended. "It will appear in one of its sister publications."

"Congratulations, Virgil," I said.

"I'm not sure when the interview is to take place, but they definitely want pictures of me at work on the First Family's meals."

"You know you'll have to clear that with

Doug," I said. "Plus, it would be nice if we had a heads-up so we can make this place presentable."

"Not down here," he said. "They want pictures of me working in the family kitchen. Upstairs."

"Good," I said, "then it doesn't really affect us."

"Except you'll have to handle the First Family's meals while I'm tied up."

"I thought that's what they were here to document."

"I'm not making myself clear. They're coming here to do a story on me and on what I do day to day to feed the First Family. I won't actually be preparing their meals that day. I'll be demonstrating my kitchen prowess."

"Oh," I said, "my mistake." With so much on my mind, the last thing I needed was to worry about Virgil's not-ready-for-*Time* interview. "Just let us know when you'll be gone. Fair enough?"

Doug appeared in the doorway. "Ollie, we're ready for you."

"So soon?" I asked. I hadn't had time to change my smock, but it looked presentable enough. I untied my apron and threw on a sweater to make me look less kitcheny. "Okay, let's go," I said and followed him out the door.

We made our way to the press briefing room via a different route than I expected. I'd been worried about how we would get past the press in their cubbyholes if we took the direct route through the Palm Room. But Doug veered outside along the West Colonnade, taking us back into the West Wing near the Cabinet Room before doubling back to the briefing room from the other side.

As we stood just outside the doorway that led to the Brady Press Briefing Room, I shivered from being outside, even for that short walk. This was the doorway where all the big shots always stood before facing the cameras. What in the world was I doing here? I felt small yet ridiculously conspicuous.

I couldn't see around the doorway to watch the goings-on, but I was okay with that. If I couldn't see the press, they couldn't see me. Here in this bustling back room they had plenty of monitors; I staked a spot near one of them to watch as the president and Quinones family took the podium. President Hyden, looking very somber, talked about the goodness of strangers and how Secretary Quinones's father-in-law, Mr. Bettencourt, had been returned to safety because people in this world care enough to look out for one another. At that point, he turned the lectern over to the secretary of state.

Quinones was a large man — tall and muscular but not fat. His features were well-defined and his hair still full and dark. I guessed him to be about fifty-five years old. While he'd once been President Hyden's political rival, the two now worked together on foreign policy with the fervor of lifelong friends. One of the reasons Mrs. Hyden was organizing this big birthday bash was to cement their new friendship. According to all pundits, President Hyden had chosen well for this position. Quinones was a powerful ally, universally loved by his constituents.

He didn't speak for very long. He simply offered sincere thanks for the safe return of his father-in-law. The camera angle widened to encompass the secretary, his wife, and her father. If there had been any intention of having Mrs. Quinones take the microphone, those plans were quickly scrapped. Holding on to her father's arm, she tried without success to fight back sobs.

Quinones finished, then stepped aside for President Hyden to take the lectern. "We are all very pleased that Mr. Bettencourt has been returned home," the president said, "but now I must turn the discussion to a very grave matter . . ."

At that point, the White House press secretary came through the doorway, escorting Mrs. Quinones and her father. Secretary Quinones brought up the rear.

Mrs. Quinones's face was even more red and puffy than it had appeared on television. Although her hair and makeup were perfect, her face was crumpled and she hiccupped with nearly every breath. Her father patted her hand and asked if everything was all right.

"I'm just so relieved," she said between breaths, "relieved you're safe."

Bettencourt smiled and continued to pat her hand.

The press secretary led the two away as Doug presented me to Secretary of State Quinones. He towered over me. Gav was tall, but Quinones beat him by several inches at least. The man smiled down at me. "So you are the angel who saved the day for our family," he said, grasping my hand with both of his. "Thank you so much, Ms. Paras. You have done a rare and wonderful thing."

"No," I started to say, "anyone would have —"

"Don't be modest," Quinones said, with a

glance in the direction his wife had gone. "I only wish Cecelia could have thanked you personally as well. But she's very emotional right now. I know she will feel terrible later that she didn't take the time to speak with you."

"It's fine, really," I said. "I understand."

"If there's anything I can ever do for you," Quinones added as he let go of my hand, "just say the word. We owe you."

I just wanted to get back to the kitchen. "Thank you."

Sargeant was in the kitchen when I got there. "How did it go? Did they mention us at all?"

I was about to answer when I noticed Virgil removing his apron. "What's going on?" I asked.

"His big interview has been rescheduled," Bucky said. "They just called."

"What?"

"He's taking off for the day."

"Virgil," I said, "this is not acceptable."

"The First Lady wants us to be accessible to the public," he said. "Do you want me to tell her I'm not allowed to leave the kitchen?"

"Today? Of all days? Don't you think that your interviewers are just trying to get a scoop on the murder story? Don't you find the timing a little convenient?"

"They're here to talk to me. That's it. We will be upstairs in the residence for the entirety of the interview. This has nothing to do with your murders."

"They aren't *my* murders," I said, feeling heat swirl up my chest. "Did you clear this with Doug?"

"He knows about it."

"Does he know you plan to do this *today?*"

Virgil looked at his watch. "They'll be here in less than an hour. I have a lot to do upstairs. Don't worry, I'll talk with Doug."

I raised both hands in a gesture of surrender. If the interviewer and camera crew hadn't been cleared for today, there was no way they were getting in. *Good luck with that, buddy.*

Sargeant, as always, injected himself into a conversation where he didn't belong. "You go right ahead, Virgil. This group managed without you before. I'm sure they can do so again."

With a smug look on his face, Virgil left.

I turned to Sargeant. "Exactly when did you take over the kitchen, Peter?"

"You know as well as I do that you'd lost that argument. Whatever the First Lady wants, she gets."

"That doesn't mean you can just prance

in here and take over."

Sargeant waved me off. "Did anyone at the press briefing mention us?"

"I didn't stay. But I doubt it. They're working hard to keep our names out of it."

"That's a relief."

"My guess is that plans for the secretary of state's birthday party will be abandoned. Especially in the wake of this tragedy."

He didn't seem to want to leave.

"Is there something else, Peter?"

He looked around the room as though searching for an answer. "What are you preparing today?"

Our pastry chef, Marcel, had recently shared some of his renowned puff pastry with us. I was eager to put it to good use. "We're working on a few new appetizer and entrée ideas. Why, did you want to help?"

He frowned but still didn't leave.

One of the pages knocked on the wall of the kitchen. "Chef Paras?" she said. "There's someone at the gate requesting to talk to you."

"I'm not expecting anyone. Who is it?"

She consulted her cell phone. "A Mr. Milton Folgate."

"Milton?" I turned to Peter. "Isn't that your nephew?"

Bucky said, "What?" and Cyan looked

confused.

Sputtering, Sargeant stepped closer. "Tell Milton we refuse to see him."

The page glanced to me for approval. Smart girl. "Whoa, a minute there, Peter," I said. "He asked for me." I turned back to the page. "Any idea what he wants?"

"I didn't talk with him directly." She consulted her phone, reading the message. "But the guard at the gate says that Mr. Folgate wants to tell you that it was really nice meeting you on the street the other day. And he says he might be able to help you find the person you're looking for." She looked up. "Do you have any idea what that means?"

I sure did.

Sargeant started to shoo the page out. "I told him to leave me alone. Not to bother me here. You tell him —"

"Just a second," I said. "I'll go."

Sargeant was apoplectic. "What?"

"Let me just get my coat," I said to the page. "Which gate?"

"He's waiting at the Northwest Appointment Gate. Do you want me to show him in?"

"No, keep him there. But let him know I'm on my way."

Sargeant was practically hopping with

fury. "Fine. Have it your way. But I'm going with you."

Cyan and Bucky looked ready to attack with questions, but they'd both been through enough situations with me to know I'd fill them in later if I could. Milton's visit was unexpected, but the message he was delivering was clear.

The minute we were outside, Sargeant lit into me. "Don't you understand? If you show Milton any compassion, if you give him even a glimmer of hope about getting a job here, he will be relentless forever. We won't ever be able to get rid of him."

Although we were another day closer to spring, the wind still buffeted us on the short walk, taking my breath away. "That's exactly why we have to see him."

"I don't understand."

"Didn't you hear what the page said?"

"Of course I did. Milton wants to talk to us about getting a job —"

"He specifically mentioned meeting us on the street."

"So what?"

"And he said he could help us find the person we're looking for."

"I'm not looking for anyone." He gave me an up and down look. "Are you?"

"Peter," I said sharply, hoping to get him

to focus, "did you talk to Milton like Paul asked you to?"

"I didn't have time."

I'd been afraid of that. "Well you should have made the time. Don't you understand? He knows we were at Lexington Place that day. He also knows about the double murder. Your nephew may not be the sharpest knife in the drawer, but he's trying to tell us he put two and two together and that if we don't at least talk with him, he may spill the beans to the press about our involvement."

Sargeant huffed. He shivered, pulling his suit coat closer.

"You should have gotten your overcoat," I said. "I would have waited."

"You don't really believe Milton is threatening us, do you?"

"I don't know him as well as you do. What do you think?"

Sargeant didn't answer.

Milton stood just outside the guardhouse, hopping from foot to foot, blowing air into his red, chapped hands. "Hi Milton," I said as we approached, intent on keeping things light.

The uniformed guard came out to confirm clearance. He offered to let us come inside, where it was warmer. Milton looked ready to jump at the offer, but I declined.

"Suit yourself," the guard said and went back inside.

Sargeant grabbed his nephew's arm and pulled him far away from the guardhouse. With the wind outside and the building tightly closed, there was no chance of being overheard, but Sargeant seemed frantic to make sure of it. "What were you thinking? Why did you come here?"

I tried to interrupt. "Peter . . ."

He continued to berate his nephew, who took it all with disaffected resignation, making it obvious that similar scenarios had played out their whole lives. For a minute I worried that the spit shooting out of Sargeant's mouth would freeze into icy missiles and ping against Milton's pudgy face. "You can't just show up unannounced and demand to see me."

"I came to see her."

Sargeant looked about to launch into another unhelpful rant when I asked, "What do you want from us, Milton?"

"You know what he wants," Sargeant said. To Milton, "It isn't going to happen. You have no business here. Go on, before I tell the guard you threatened us."

Unfazed, Milton directed his attention to me. "Listen, Chef Paras, I know what went down the other day at Lexington Place. I also know what the papers aren't telling anybody. You and Petey were there." He pointed at me. "I've read about how you get involved in all sorts of crazy things at the White House, so I figured it was you who found the two dead people. Am I right?"

I didn't answer. "What do you want from me, Milton?"

"Nothing more than what's fair," he said. Looking sheepish, he worked his mouth. "All I want is an interview. Let the job be mine to win or lose, not Petey's to decide. I can work in the kitchen. I'm a real good cook. I can work as a server, too. I'm good at getting orders just right. I could be a butler, even."

Sargeant made a noise of disgust. "I'd sooner put a gorilla in a tuxedo to serve the president."

Milton dug into his pocket and pulled up his cell phone. "A gorilla wouldn't have the local news station on speed dial."

"We can have you arrested for threatening us," I said.

"I don't think so," he said almost apologetically. "I mean, all I'm saying is that the news media folks have a right to know you two were in the vicinity." He pointed the phone at me. "And with your reputation —"

Sargeant jumped on that one. "This is all your fault," he said to me. "You get involved in the White House business far more deeply than you ought. I never should have agreed to accompany you the other day. You're trouble with a capital *T*."

"Gee, thanks, Peter. Now tell me how you really feel."

Milton shifted foot to foot. He was losing us. "How long were the two people dead?" he asked me.

I took a step back. "Listen, I think we all need to —"

"Because I think the guy who bumped us is the guy who killed them."

"What are you talking about?" I asked.

"Remember the guy who almost knocked Petey over?" He hesitated a moment. "You got upset with me for shouting at him."

"You think that's the killer?" I asked. Even as I heard the skepticism in my voice, my brain zinged into high gear. Hadn't the stranger stopped and looked back at us when Milton shouted?

"I do," Milton said with some pride.

Sargeant threw his hands in the air. "Bah," he said. He began to walk away.

"Even better," Milton continued, "I think I saw him again."

"Where?"

Sargeant had made it about fifteen feet. "Are you coming?"

I ignored him to focus on what Milton was saying. "I saw him walk by the restaurant where I work. Couple of times. I'm sure it's him. I'm gonna follow him next time."

"You should go to the police," I said.

"And tell 'em what? Wouldn't that be a fast track to getting your names in the paper?"

Sargeant had doubled back. "I don't want my face in the paper."

"It's more important to follow any leads. The chances of that being our guy . . ." I let the thought hang.

"It *is* the guy," Milton said, "I can feel it. And from the look on your face, you can, too."

"Then go to the police."

He shook his head. "Ain't happening."

"Then I will," I said.

"In the meantime," Milton said, "don't forget who gave you this information. Maybe you can put in a good word for me with the chief usher."

I knew the answer, but I asked anyway. "You sent a resume?"

Milton brightened. "I did. He should have it by now. With a good word from you —"

Sargeant looked ready to pop. I headed

off any further outbursts, explaining, "Paul Vasquez is out for a while." I couldn't very well let on that Doug Lambert had taken over when most of the White House staff hadn't yet been informed. Time to sell the party line. "He's on vacation for a few weeks. He won't be able to look at it until he gets back. And I'm not exactly sure when that will be."

Milton's face fell. "Do you promise to talk to him about it when he gets back?"

Sargeant pivoted. "I'm going in. With or without you."

"I will talk with the chief usher about you at some point," I said. "I can't promise more than that right now."

"Will you recommend me for the job?"

"Can't promise. All I can do is make sure he sees your resume."

"What if I bring you more information about the guy who bumped us?"

"Milton," I said, repeating words that had been directed to me more times than I could count, "stay out of it."

I signaled to the guard to show Mr. Folgate out. "I'll be in touch," Milton said.

The tenseness of the conversation had made me forget the cold. Now, as I returned to the White House, I felt it whip my hair around and race down my neck, making me shiver.

The trees offered little protection from the slicing wind and I ducked my head, hurrying back. Just as I passed a giant tree, someone jumped out at me.

My hands went up and I screamed. A half-second later, I was furious. "Peter, you scared me."

He seemed surprised by my reaction. "I was waiting for you." Hands shoved into his pockets, his nose was bright red.

"My lucky day."

"Are you really going to tell the police what Milton told us?"

"It would be foolish to ignore a clue." I mulled it over. The police didn't know me and they might not understand the significance of Milton's report. "I'll tell the Secret Service. They'll know what to do with it."

That shut Sargeant up for a minute. Unfortunately, not long enough. "You're just going to get in deeper, you know. I think we should both just forget Milton's visit here."

"Why are you so against him? He's your family."

Sargeant didn't answer.

"Look," I continued, "I don't see him as White House material, either, but it wouldn't kill you to be nicer to him."

"He will never work in the White House."

"What did he ever do to you?"

The look in Sargeant's eyes was one I'd never seen before. Angry, yes, but also oddly vulnerable. "Nothing I care to discuss with you."

CHAPTER 8

Friday morning, Virgil was humming when he returned from preparing breakfast upstairs.

"How did it go yesterday?" I asked.

"Very well."

"No trouble getting the camera crew in?"

"None whatsoever."

I was surprised to hear it. Yesterday had been a zoo, which meant that our Secret Service agents were ten times more likely than usual to push back. Getting interviewers and camera crews in on such short notice was unheard of.

"Peter Sargeant made sure they got whatever clearances they needed," he said.

That couldn't be right. "How? He didn't leave the kitchen." That had been the standing joke yesterday, that Sargeant simply would not leave. That is, until he and I had gone outside to talk with Milton right about the same time Virgil was being interviewed.

"He must have made a call, or sent an e-mail, or . . . I don't know. Whatever he did, he got me what I needed. That's what counts, right?"

None of my business. I shrugged. "I suppose."

The phone rang and Bucky answered. "For you," he said when he hung up. "Doug would like you upstairs right away."

Being summoned to the usher's office "right away" sounded ominous.

"What's up with Paul, anyway?" Bucky asked. "It's not like him to stay away during a White House crisis. I expected him to rush back from wherever he was as soon as the news broke."

I held up my hands in a helpless gesture. "Maybe he can't get away?"

"Paul not putting the White House first on his list of priorities? Nah, I think something is up." He looked at me shrewdly. "Is there?"

Avoiding answering, I held my hands up in a helpless gesture, untied my apron, and washed my hands. "I'll be back as soon as I can."

Doug looked up from his paperwork as I entered his office. I wondered if I'd ever get used to seeing him sitting behind Paul's

129

desk. "Good morning," he said. "Have a seat."

I did. "Is this about me talking to the Secret Service yesterday?" I asked. "Because I stopped by here a couple of times to let you know about it, but you weren't in."

I could tell I'd confused him. "Secret Service? What are you talking about?"

"Yesterday," I said, "I alerted the Secret Service to a possible clue in the double-murder case."

Doug perked up. "What are you talking about?" he said again.

I took a deep breath. "It's a long shot, and maybe not even very reliable, but I promised Paul I would keep you informed. Yesterday, Peter and I . . ."

"What about me?"

Doug smiled as Sargeant entered. "Thanks for joining us. I have some important news to discuss with both of you. But first, Ollie, please continue."

Sargeant's expression darkened as I told Doug about Milton's visit the day before. By the time I'd finished explaining the encounter, Sargeant wore a deep scowl. "I don't believe my nephew's involvement needed to be discussed at this level."

"I disagree," Doug said. "Thank you for letting me know, Ollie. Did the Secret

Service tell you how they intended to proceed?"

I gave a short laugh. "Do they ever?"

"Good point." Doug scratched at the back of his head. What little hair he had was standing on end as though he'd been grabbing it with both hands and trying to yank it out. His eyes were bloodshot and small. "Okay, before I get to why I called you up here, is there anything else we need to cover about the incident at Lexington the other day?"

Incident? Doug made it sound more like an unfortunate wine spill rather than a case of double murder. "No," I said.

"Have you heard if the police have any leads?"

"The media is continuing to pursue the rumor that Chief of Staff Cawley and Ms. Woodruff were having an affair, but I think we all know that's ludicrous."

"Was the medical examiner able to determine how much earlier than Patty Mr. Cawley was killed?"

"Why on earth would you care?" Sargeant asked.

"I like when things make sense. You and I both know that Cawley and Patty were killed at different times. There has to be a reason. If the police are able to figure out why, they may have a clue to who killed them."

He made a noise that sounded like *har-rumph.*

"No idea, Ollie," Doug said. "They keep me updated on a lot, but there are details I'm not privy to. All I know is that the police aren't squelching the affair rumor because it keeps the media on the wrong track."

If Doug didn't have any idea about the two victims' times of death, he surely wouldn't know why Cawley's phone was set to play the opening bars of "Mandy," so I just said, "What's on your mind, Doug?"

"As we discussed before, the First Lady has decided not to hold the secretary of state's birthday party at Lexington Place."

"But she's still planning to host it?" Sargeant asked.

Doug nodded slowly. "It's a tough call, but there's more at stake than just a simple party. This event promises to bring two groups together. Groups that don't ordinarily mix, let alone work together. The president and First Lady are working hard — and very shrewdly, I might add — to build consensus. Throwing a lavish event such as this one is a brilliant move. If it goes well, this could be the start of significant harmony in our government."

"And if it doesn't go well?" Sargeant asked. Always the optimist.

Doug wore a grim expression. "We need to make certain it does, and that not one single thing goes wrong." His hands curled into fists so tight I could see the whites of his knuckles. "Not one."

"Okay," I said, "what do you need us to do?"

"First of all, thank you for the reports you sent me. I know I told you I wouldn't need them immediately, but it turns out I did and I appreciate it. We're moving ahead with these plans, despite the recent tragedy, because we all know how much lead time is necessary to get a project of this scope under way. There's no time to waste."

Doug was talking in circles, but maybe that made it easier for him to keep control of the many balls he was juggling.

"Based on Patty's preliminary reports, which she recorded before her death, and the opinions you two submitted, Secretary of State Quinones's birthday party will now be held at Jean-Luc's. I believe both of you pegged that as your second choice. You probably also realize that Patty's colleagues are having a difficult time dealing with this." He waited for us to nod.

"Chief of Staff Cawley's funeral is scheduled for Monday. I'm not quite sure about Patty's arrangements yet. I haven't heard from her family. Regardless of when her services will be held, her loss is being felt all over the East Wing. The people she worked with are some of her closest friends. You may not be aware that she worked with Mrs. Hyden and several of the other assistants in the past. They're very close and this loss has devastated them.

"With that in mind," Doug went on, "we ought to give them a hand. They're all professionals, yes, and we will eventually be able to depend on them to make the secretary's birthday party a success, but right now they need our help."

"Absolutely. What do you need us to do?" I asked.

Sargeant looked ready to backhand me out of my chair.

"I'm glad you asked, Ollie," Doug said, "because I would like for you and Peter to take over Patty's responsibilities until another assistant is appointed to take her place."

"Exactly what do you mean by 'take over'?" I asked. "Neither of us is qualified to organize a White House affair — I mean, beyond our regular responsibilities."

"The two of you have been part of the

decision making on this project from the very beginning. All I'm asking is that you both step it up a notch. Work together to get all the preliminary legwork done."

Sargeant fairly leaped out of his seat. "You can't be serious."

I tried to look at the bigger picture. Maybe Doug wasn't asking us to do the impossible, but the sinking feeling in my gut told me differently. "I thought all the preliminary legwork *was* complete," I said. "What still needs to be done? You do realize that we know nothing about organizing an event of this magnitude."

"You're both resourceful and smart. Additionally, I have notebooks explaining every step. Complete with checklists." He smiled, but it was clearly for our benefit. Wasn't working. "You'll coordinate with the social secretary regarding the list of invitees. Obviously that information needs to be disseminated to various departments, not the least of which is Secret Service. Peter, you will assess any sensitive conflicts between guests and investigate ethnic and religious observances. Ollie, you'll plan an appropriate menu, with options for those who require them. Simple."

Notebooks? Checklists? "There's a lot more to it than you're telling us," I said.

He shrugged as though it was nothing. "Sure, there's more. For instance, you'll have to coordinate floral arrangements with Kendra. Make sure the final guest list gets to the calligrapher's office. Arrange for social aides to be there that night. As long as you keep very detailed notes and keep everyone informed, this should be a breeze."

"You're serious," I said.

Sargeant, shell-shocked, sputtered, "But, but, but . . ."

Doug's expression hardened. "I'm not talking about setting up the entertainment or choosing an evening theme. Others will handle that. I'm not asking you to write out the invitations by hand or personally arrange flowers. Your job will simply be to act as liaison. To facilitate."

"What you're saying is —"

"That you two will coordinate efforts between Jean-Luc's and the White House. Pretty simple if you think about it. Patty was new to the job and no one doubted she could handle it. You two have far more experience than she had. There's really nothing to it. Keep in mind that we'll be getting one of the assistants to take over as soon as we can. You're just interim organizers. Just like I'm the interim chief usher." Doug looked at us with tired eyes. "I'm doing the best I can. All I'm asking is that you both do the same."

He was in over his head on this one, drowning in a sea of chaos and dragging us under with him. "This is so far out of our purview," I began, "we won't have any idea —"

Sargeant joined me. "This is ridiculous. I'm the sensitivity director, for goodness' sake. You can't make me into a social director just because you don't care to oversee this project yourself."

Doug threw his pen down. "This isn't a request." Rather than quietly trying to settle us the way Paul would have, he worsened the situation by raising his voice. "Both of you *will* take this over." His hands curled into fists of frustration. "No one else is prepared to do so right now. Once the other assistants come back on board, you'll be able to resume your regular responsibilities, and serve simply as consultants. What we need now, however, is a consistent hand at the helm. That's where you two come in."

Sargeant waved a finger at him. "You said 'consistent hand.' That would be singular."

"I hate to admit it, but I agree," I said. "A single hand. His or mine, I don't care." Truth was, I did care. But one battle at a time. "This is not a good idea."

Sargeant went on, "And you're missing the most glaring obstacle of all. Ms. Paras and I do not work well together."

Doug's voice trembled as it rose again. "This is not a matter for discussion. You two are in charge. Get used to it."

The words were strong, the delivery — not so much. Doug was out of his league, and I could read hesitation in his eyes. Right or wrong, he'd made his decision. Unfortunately, we were stuck with it.

Sargeant looked at me and I at him. I could feel waves of contempt radiating at me.

"Jean-Luc's, huh?" I said just to lessen the room's tension.

Doug cleared his throat and consulted his notes again. "We have time constraints. I understand you're both busy, and I don't want to put you in an impossible situation."

Too late.

Keeping his eyes on his scribbles, Doug kept talking. "With that in mind, I'm assigning you an assistant. One of our social aides is currently on medical leave from his full-time military position." Quick look up at us. "Broken wrist." Back down at the notes. "His infirmity shouldn't hamper him from assisting you two. I don't anticipate any heavy lifting. His job will be to help you get to know the players."

Social aides were an interesting breed. For the most part they comported themselves well. Tall, impressive-looking, wearing their dress uniforms and gold braid aiguettes across their chests, their job was to mingle at White House and other official events, chat up the guests, and dance with lonely wallflowers. Social aides were brought in to ensure that a good time was had by all.

I pulled out my notebook. "Who is it?"

Doug seemed relieved to be able to dictate without getting an argument. "Wyatt Becker. He's meeting you there today."

"I don't know him," I said.

"I do." Sargeant got an unpleasant look on his face. "He's arrogant, talkative, and ineffectual. I don't care for him."

"Great, I'll probably adore the guy." I stood up, ignoring the look of surprise on Doug's face. Everyone in the White House knew there was no love lost between me and Sargeant. No sense in pretending differently now.

Then I remembered Paul's prediction. This may very well have been a set up to grease Sargeant's dismissal. "I'm sorry," I said to both of them. "That was uncalled for. I'm just feeling the stress of everything. I'm happy to help wherever I can."

Doug nodded. "Thank you, Olivia." Peter, of course, remained silent.

"How often do you want updates on the event's progress?" I asked.

"Oh . . ." Doug shuffled papers around, "um . . ."

So he hadn't thought it through that far. That gave me a real feeling of comfort. "How about we check in as necessary?" I said in an attempt to put him at ease and maintain a little control. "We've got this one."

Sargeant stared at me, open-mouthed.

"Come on, Peter," I said, "we've got work to do."

"Wait, so you're not only in charge of the food for Secretary of State Quinones's birthday party, you're also in charge of overseeing its entire organization?" Cyan's incredulous expression was reminiscent of Sargeant's in Doug's office.

"It gets better. I have a partner to help me."

"Who?"

"Sargeant."

The kitchen exploded with surprise. Bucky slammed a towel onto the stainless steel counter. "This is ridiculous."

"You're telling me."

Virgil wasn't bothered. "I catered a birthday party for the Hydens once and I handled everything just fine. Maybe the new usher should assign me instead. At least then he'll have a win for his first big project in the new job."

Cyan rolled her eyes. "Doug is just standing in for Paul while he's on vacation."

Virgil looked amused. "Is that what you believe?"

"Virgil," I said, my voice a warning, "didn't Paul tell you? He's on vacation. Doug is just stepping in as interim chief usher."

"He's interim, all right. But that's only until all this murder business dies down. Then they'll figure out who's in charge permanently. The First Lady confided in me. She told me that Paul is out. Gone. Hasta la vista, baby."

For the second time in as many minutes, the room exploded. "Ollie, did you know about this?" Cyan asked.

Rather than answer her, I advanced on Virgil. "That was supposed to be kept quiet, until we were told it was all right to share the information. What business do you have spilling it to us? What other White House confidences have you broken?"

Virgil backed up. "The First Lady told me

because she trusts me."

"Look how you repaid her: by breaking that trust."

"Are you kidding? The three of you won't tell anyone." He pointed at me. "I wasn't even sure you knew yet. But if we're all supposed to work together here, shouldn't we be able to share what we know? I mean . . . don't you trust us?"

Cyan turned to me. As did Bucky. Virgil's words had struck a nerve with them. He had a point. Even if I didn't like the way he'd made it, I had to acknowledge the truth of his statement.

"Maybe I should have trusted you with that information," I began, "but in my defense, I was told not to. Not only that, but I think you, Cyan, and you, Bucky, know that I have never broken a confidence you've shared with me. I felt the need to protect Paul's privacy because he asked me to. He's a friend, and I choose to protect him the same way I protect both of you." I glanced over. "I would do the same for you, Virgil."

No one said anything, but I thought I saw understanding in Bucky's and Cyan's eyes. That's all I asked for.

Sargeant arrived in the kitchen, wearing his winter coat. "Are you ready?"

I wasn't ready to leave, not now. But duty called. "Yeah," I said, "just give me a minute." As I grabbed my own coat, I went over the day's list with Bucky. We had several hastily planned dinners coming up over the next few days. Bucky and Cyan could handle these with no problem, but all final decisions rested with me.

"Believe me, I'd much rather be here," I said as I pulled my coat on.

"And we'd want you here," Cyan answered.

Virgil walked away. Bucky smirked and leaned in, lowering his voice, "How much you want to bet he'll try to take over while you're gone?"

"My money's on you," I whispered back.

"I'll call if we run into any problems," he said.

I didn't expect any. "See you soon, I hope." I took a long look around the kitchen. They might not run into any problems, but I had a feeling I would.

CHAPTER 9

Jean-Luc's was within easy walking distance of the White House, but the Secret Service insisted on escorting us there. With all that had transpired recently, I didn't particularly mind. As the car slowed in front of the four-story, ultra-modern structure, Sargeant leaned toward me. "Doesn't this building seem more likely than Lexington Place to win a green award?"

"You know what they say about appearances being deceiving," I said, but I agreed with him. Everything about Jean-Luc's was sleek, shiny, clean, bright. It didn't just stand out between its elderly neighbors, it sparkled. Jean-Luc's was not only the new kid on the block, it was the one with all the toys. When we'd visited last time, I felt like I was walking into the future. But I, and everyone else, had preferred the classic lines and the old-world elegance of Lexington Place.

Remembering our visit to the kitchen there, I hoped there were no surprises waiting for us here today. I suppressed a shudder. But not well enough.

Sargeant peered at me. "I wish we weren't here, either," he said.

As we alighted, a doorman greeted us with a big smile and a tip of his hat. "We are delighted to welcome you. Let me show you in." He held out an arm toward the steps, which led up to the towering glass doors.

Our Secret Service escort instructed us to call when we needed to be picked up. As he drove off, something caught my eye.

"Hang on," I said.

Sargeant was already halfway to the stairs. He turned, glancing warily up and down the street. "What now?"

"Someone was watching as we pulled up. Whoever it was ducked out of sight." I pointed toward the space between Jean-Luc's and its next-door neighbor building. "Give me a minute," I said over my shoulder.

I sensed Sargeant's presence behind me as I reached the edge of Jean-Luc's. My heart raced even as my nose wrinkled. The narrow space was just wide enough for a single vehicle. Rotting garbage in overstuffed and split bags poured all over the uneven ground. Sourness swirled around me. If this had been the middle of summer, the stench would have been overpowering. This access alley provided for deliveries, with plenty of dark doors out of the public eye. Unfortunately, it seemed to be a convenient staging area for garbage as well.

With surrounding multi-storied walls on either side, the alleyway was rife with shadows. It wasn't dark enough, however, to obscure the person who had been watching us. She cowered when I turned the corner. Squatting next to a giant plastic bin, she stared up at me with apprehension while wrapping one arm around three ratty shopping bags. "Go away," she shouted, waving the other hand over her head.

A homeless woman caught being nosy.

"Sorry," I said.

She blew raspberries at me and tightened her grip around her belongings. With a huff, she stood and wobbled away with an uneven gait. She kept glancing behind as though to make sure I wasn't following her.

Sargeant had come to stand next to me. "Do you always rush into danger like that?" he asked. "No wonder you get into trouble."

"She's harmless."

"You didn't know that until you got this far," he said. "What if it was the guy who followed you the other night, hmm? What then?"

"I knew it wasn't . . . the body shape and the movement were different. Besides, I don't like people watching me from shadowy corners. I just had to see for myself who it was . . ." I let the thought hang as I took a look at the surrounding area. I stepped deeper into the alley. "Do you see this?"

"I've seen plenty of detritus in my life. Let's go. The doorman is waiting for us."

"No, look," I said. "This alleyway is bad enough, but do you think Doug realizes how decrepit the building next door to Jean-Luc's is? I didn't even notice it on our first trip here." Graffiti covered the irregular walls and broken equipment sat just outside its doors.

"Of course not. Our job isn't to inspect the neighborhood, it's to determine the viability of a location for our purposes. Why would we notice this?"

"No reason. It's just . . ." I put my hand up against the brick wall. Mortar crumbled out. "This is pretty bad." Skirting scraps of bent and twisted metal, I gingerly walked a few feet farther to face a set of scratched and graffiti-covered black metal doors. One was ajar. "This place looks like it hasn't seen civilization in twenty years."

"Its neighbors have. They're using it as a dump."

"It's a terrible background for photo ops. Not to mention a security risk."

He glanced at his watch. "I'm beginning to see why you generate so much controversy. If it makes you feel better, you can talk to your friends in the Secret Service about your concerns. But right now we have a job to do and I, for one, would like to get this over with as soon as possible."

"Fine," I said, following him back to the sidewalk.

When we finally made it up the steps, the doorman wore a look of apprehension. "Is there a problem?"

I pointed. "What is that place?"

"Originally it was a bank. Like, way before your time. Before my time even. Over the years it's had a bunch of different owners, all trying to make a go of it. The location is great, but it just seems the place is cursed with bad luck."

"Did something bad happen there?"

"Picked up on that, did you?" He grinned. "All hearsay, of course. Back when it was first opened, decades ago, maybe even nineteenth century — I don't recall — couple of robbers stormed in and demanded money. The teller refused. Robbers shot everybody in the place. Just like that."

"That's terrible. Were they caught?"

He squinted. "Yeah. Cops caught up with them. Had a shoot-out, and both thieves were killed. The money was returned, but still so many dead. Such a waste. To this day, they say that the teller who refused to give up the money haunts the place because he feels guilty."

"That's a sad story."

He held a hand toward the abandoned building. "Could be why no tenants stay longer than a year. I've worked in the surrounding area all my life and I've watched businesses come and go. That place has been almost everything — a restaurant, a business office, a health club. Nobody can make it work."

I thanked him and started inside with Sargeant.

"Why do you care about the building next door?" he asked the moment we were out of earshot.

"I was just curious. Nothing wrong with that."

"Of course not. But now we know there are ghosts next door. You think that's helpful?"

"You don't believe in ghosts, do you, Peter?"

"Certainly not." He waited a moment, then said, "But I can't help but think there might be two haunting Lexington Place now."

Inside, our young host, Barb, took us through the spacious lobby to the main reception area, eventually leading us into the banquet hall. With so many shiny, flat surfaces and no one there besides us, our shoes clicked loudly wherever we went. Inside the banquet area, Barb was quick to point out the balcony, where security could oversee the entire affair, and the space's many amenities. Jean-Luc's could easily handle the seating we required. "Great," I said. "Can we get another tour of the kitchen and work areas?"

"Of course."

"You know the Secret Service will come out and do their own reconnaissance," I said. "They'll be in touch as soon as we get them this preliminary information."

She giggled. "I can't imagine how crazy things will be here once the Secret Service steps in."

Sargeant wore a sour expression. "No, I don't believe you *could* imagine it."

Geez. Couldn't he tone it down just once?

I sent Barb an apologetic grin as she led us into the kitchen. The prep space was more than adequate. Although it was not quite as spacious as Lexington Place's, it nonetheless benefited from being dead-body free.

I was in the middle of examining the refrigeration area when Barb's cell phone rang. She answered it, spoke a few words, and hung up. "Your colleague just arrived," she said.

"Who?" Sargeant asked.

"That social aide," I said, "remember? Wyatt Becker?"

Sargeant pinched the bridge of his nose. "Oh, yes."

Barb smiled. "You two take a look around. I'll go get him and bring him here."

As soon as she left the room, Sargeant said, "It's bad enough we've been assigned these liaison duties. What are we supposed to do with him?"

"Tap into his expertise. He's been to a lot more of these events than we have."

"Then why not let him handle the whole thing? Why drag us into this?"

"You and I are senior staff members in the White House and have been through enough of these events to do them in our sleep." That was an exaggeration, but by bolstering Sargeant, I helped convince myself. "We should be able to handle it. I'm just glad we don't have to worry about preparing the guest list or deciding the entertainment. That would be a nightmare."

"It already is." He ran a finger along the edge of the stainless steel sink and examined it. "Not bad."

"I think this Wyatt fellow will do us some good. According to Doug, he's here to help us. We're supposed to be able to rely on him for anything we need. Let's use our resources wisely."

Sargeant started grumbling again. "You don't know Wyatt . . ."

"Yes?" Wyatt Becker strode into the room, followed by Barb. "I heard my name. Was there something you needed, Mr. Sargeant?"

Sargeant looked ready to spit. "No," he said. "Olivia, what's next?"

Ignoring Sargeant, Wyatt stepped over to me, extending his hand. "It's very nice to meet you, Ms. Paras. I've heard a great deal about you."

Though not bad looking, Wyatt wasn't particularly handsome, either. His features were soft — rounded nose, wide cheeks, and high eyebrows that made him look as though he were in a constant state of surprise. Still, he was trim and tall, as social aides are required to be. Best of all, he had bright eyes and an expression that suggested he was eager to help.

He carried a clipboard, which he shifted as we shook hands. I guessed him to be in his early thirties. I realized I'd seen him around the White House. In fact, he'd been one of the busy people present the other day after the president's news briefing. I just never knew who he was. "It's very nice to meet you, too, Wyatt. I'm surprised we haven't met before this."

"I'm usually on the main floor," he said, his smile never wavering, the eyebrows never relaxing. "The other social aides retreat to the ground floor more often than I do to eat and relax. I prefer to remain where I can be of the most use."

"That's . . . commendable," I said for lack of anything else. "I understand you're here to help us get things organized for the secretary of state's birthday."

"Exactly." Turning to Barb, he said, "I think we'll be fine here. We'll call if we need you."

Sargeant and I exchanged a look.

"I thought you had a broken wrist," I said with a glance at Wyatt's arm.

He waved it. "Cast just came off, but the doc wants me to take it easy for a couple more weeks."

"I don't anticipate any manual labor, so I'm sure you'll be fine."

"Yes," he said without inflection. "From what I understand, this party is not a surprise to the secretary of state, am I right?"

"That's our understanding as well. Secretary Quinones is fully apprised of our plans."

"Good. Makes things so much easier that way." He consulted his clipboard. "With all the official dinners and events I've taken part in, I thought it would be helpful to share my insights with both of you. After all, you both perform your duties in the background, but as one who has actually participated as a guest, of sorts, I believe my help will be invaluable. I've taken the liberty of compiling a list of what needs to be done over the next several days." If it were possible, he smiled even more brightly.

Sargeant snorted.

"Excuse me, Mr. Sargeant, do you disagree?" Wyatt asked.

"You act as though we're the assistants and you're in charge. It's the other way around, young man. You're here to help us."

Wyatt's smile never dimmed. "I never meant to imply otherwise. I just want to do my best to offer my help in the most efficient way possible. My duty is to the White House, same as yours." He tapped his clipboard. "Shall we begin?"

After an hour, I was seeing the myriad benefits of having a social aide on our team, but I found myself wishing it was anyone but Wyatt. I hated to admit that Sargeant had been absolutely correct in his assessment of the guy.

"Lastly," Wyatt continued, pointing toward the stage, "when dinner is complete and you both are released, the entertainment will begin. It's too bad you won't be here to enjoy it. We social aides have so much fun when the entertainer is a big name. Who do you have performing this time?"

"Doug didn't tell us yet," I said. "I'm not even sure it's been settled. Usually one of the First Lady's assistants handles it, but obviously . . ."

"Oh," Wyatt said, "no idea? That's a shame. Do you know if any of the former First Ladies are attending?"

Sargeant fielded that one. "As a matter of fact —"

"Because they always ask me to escort the most important female guests. I'm the first choice for that duty and I take great pride in it."

Sargeant mumbled under his breath again.

I was about to start doing so myself. We'd been treated to Wyatt's stories about how he had been in charge of keeping Barbara Bush company for several hours during one major event. She'd recently suffered a minor spill and wasn't up to dancing, so Wyatt had been assigned to keep her company in the Red Room for the entire night. Poor woman. "Mrs. Bush was an absolute delight," he said, not for the first time. "She wanted to know all about my service record, my family life, and how I got to be the top social aide. She got me talking about myself for *hours*. She couldn't get enough of me."

Next to me, Sargeant murmured, "I've certainly had enough of you."

I decided to steer the conversation away from either of them. "How about we finish up here so we can all get back to the White House? Let's review our to-do list, shall we?"

"Of course," Wyatt said. "By the way, did you know that Mrs. Campbell almost named her cat Denise? One of her kids wanted Patches instead. Good thing, huh? Wouldn't that have been terrible to have the new First Lady share a name with the prior First Lady's pet?"

"Good thing," I said. "About the list . . ."

"Another interesting tidbit you may not

156

know is that the current secretary of agriculture's great-uncle used to be a butler at the White House. Back in the day."

Wyatt was an endless font of useless information. I expected Sargeant to pop a cork, but he remained surprisingly quiet. Wyatt not only went over the list we'd created — which was understandable to make certain we were all on the same page — but he also interspersed each to-do with a light reminder of his importance in the event's success.

"When the food is prepared," he said, "do the butlers take care to ensure that no guest is served an item he or she is allergic to?"

"Yes, of course. We have a lot of experience in ensuring food safety." I thought back to one guest who hadn't been so lucky. Fortunately for me and for my kitchen staff, that tragic incident hadn't been our fault.

Wyatt jotted a note. "It would be helpful to know who we had for entertainment," he said. "The First Lady has been vocal about how much of an Elton John fan she is. Do you think he might be our guest for the evening?"

"It's not a good idea to speculate," I said.

"One time —" Wyatt began.

Sargeant stepped to the far side of the room. "I need to check something over here before I forget."

Yeah, right.

Oblivious, Wyatt went on. "We had Tina Turner come to perform in the East Room. That was with the Campbells, of course."

"Of course," I parroted, not really listening.

"Anyway, do you know Governor Pakled?"

"I know of him."

"Turns out he had a friend who was this huge Tina Turner fan."

"Okay . . ."

"Pakled was one of the few invited to meet with Ms. Turner right after the concert. You know all the big shots get perks like that. Pakled ran into this fan-friend at the dinner — a guy he went to school with who got invited because of his service to the community."

"Where is this going?" I asked.

"Huge dustup right before the concert," Wyatt said with no small amount of pride and no indication that he planned to get to the point soon.

Sargeant had disappeared. I wished I could disappear.

"Pakled wanted his friend to meet Tina. But his name wasn't on the list."

"What happened?" I asked in spite of myself.

"They started causing a bit of a scene and I stepped in to handle it. Pakled wanted his friend's name added to the list, but I couldn't do that."

"What did you do?"

Sargeant reappeared. From behind Wyatt, he tapped his watch and made a "Let's get moving" face at me.

"I handled it, of course," Wyatt said. "I told him to meet me in the Entrance Hall right after the concert."

"I don't understand."

"Ms. Turner was meeting everyone in the Blue Room. There was no way the guy could get in there without me. And I knew he'd wait until I got there."

"Go on, I can't stand the suspense."

"I left him there."

"Waiting?"

"Yes."

"Where did you go?"

"I went downstairs to hang out in the coat room until the post-concert reception was over."

I exchanged a look with Sargeant, who rolled his eyes.

"So how did that solve the problem?"

Wyatt seemed puzzled by my question. "He didn't get to meet Tina Turner."

"That's not solving a problem," I said,

"that's avoiding it."

For the first time all day, the social aide's expression turned sour. "I got the job done," he said. "I know how to put people in their place." He looked side to side, as though searching for Sargeant. He wasn't aware that the sensitivity director was right behind him. "For instance, there are some people you and I both know —"

I couldn't stand another one of his stories. "We'd better get moving," I said. "Lots more to do. Thanks for your help, Wyatt, but I think Peter and I can take it from here."

"You sure?"

"Absolutely," I said, my brain screaming: *Just go away.*

When he saw Sargeant standing there, Wyatt blanched. I wondered what he'd been about to say that he hadn't wanted our sensitivity director to hear. His discomposure was fleeting, however, and with a tip of his head, the smile was back. "I'll see you both tomorrow, then."

I could see Sargeant about to ask, "Tomorrow?" but I stopped him with a look. Any argument would just prolong Wyatt's stay. He wasn't a bad person, just incredibly self-absorbed. Not to mention dull.

As soon as he was gone, I turned to

Sargeant, who stared at me with a smug expression on his face.

"Where did they pick him up?" I asked. "And how did we get so lucky?"

"He's their top aide."

I cringed. "He's the best of the best?"

"I said he was the top, not the best. He's moved up the seniority ladder. His father's some big military hero. Lots of honors, lots of connections. Wyatt served in combat but never measured up."

I looked out the way he'd gone. "He sure knows a lot of tedious detail."

"I think it's a job requirement. They have to memorize books of stuff."

"They certainly chose well, then. That guy is a walking, talking White House encyclopedia."

We returned to the White House prepared to head back to our respective departments, but as soon as we hit the guard entrance, we were told to report to Doug's office. "What now?" I asked rhetorically.

"Maybe he wants to put us in charge of the budget deficit."

Dutifully we headed straight to the usher's office. Doug stood behind his desk with his back to us, talking on the phone as he stared out the window. "Yes, I understand," he said. "It will be taken care of. Yes. Yes. With discretion. Yes."

When he turned and hung up, he saw us standing there. He seemed to have aged ten years in less than a week.

"Tough day?" I asked.

"Have a seat, both of you."

That didn't bode well.

"Ollie," he began without preamble, "that was Ethan Nagy on the telephone."

"He's Secretary of State Quinones's right-hand man, isn't he?" I asked. Whatever Doug had promised, he had promised to do so with discretion. My nerves tingled. I waited.

"It's actually the fourth time he's called today. He wanted me to talk to you."

"Me?" My voice fairly squeaked.

"As you know, Secretary Quinones is coming to a dinner meeting tomorrow night."

"Has something changed?"

"Ethan Nagy will accompany him."

That seemed unusual. "Why is that?"

"Is it your job to question why anyone is invited to the White House?"

Stung, I tried again. "I don't know if we have any information on Mr. Nagy's dietary restrictions."

"We'll get that to you today. But that's

not why I called you in here. Secretary Quinones's wife, Cecelia, wants to give you a small gift to thank you for rescuing her father."

"Oh, no," I said, "that's not necessary. I would feel terrible accepting anything."

"That's beside the point. She wants to do it, and Secretary Quinones intends to present it to you personally. You don't say no to the secretary of state."

"I suppose not."

"No, you don't," he said unnecessarily.

Doug needed to learn that once he won his point with a subordinate, he didn't need to put an exclamation point on it. Doing so only added tension, disconnecting us from wanting to help him in the future. Paul had had a gentle yet powerful demeanor. I'd heard his technique described as having a velvet fist. In contrast, Doug wielded a hammer. Worse, he didn't have particularly great aim.

Sargeant cleared his throat. "And this concerns me how?"

Doug placed both hands atop his desk, fingers spread. "I'm getting to that next." His eyebrows came together and his lips pursed, as though he were weighing his next words. "Peter, why did you cut Mr. and

Mrs. Baumgartner from the party guest list?"

Sargeant sat up. "What are you talking about?"

"This could have been a mistake of great proportion. Mr. and Mrs. Baumgartner are Hyden-family friends and are among the key people the First Lady expects to attend the secretary of state's affair."

"I didn't . . ."

Doug picked up a piece of paper from his desk. "I have it right here. You removed the Baumgartners from the guest list. I need to know why."

Sargeant was without words. He turned to me. "Do you have any idea what he's talking about?"

I shook my head.

"Peter," Doug said slowly, "we all know how much you dislike our executive chef. Things will go much better for you if you own up to your actions. If this was a simple error on your part, just say so."

"I don't understand," Sargeant said. "I have provided no input on the invitation list yet. Why do you think I touched it?"

"You weren't supposed to, true. But you went in and took the Baumgartners off. There's no disputing that. The document was sent from your computer. No one has access to it other than you, am I right?"

"My office?" he said. "Couldn't someone have gone in when I stepped away?"

"To what end? Who on staff would care whether the Baumgartners attend or not?" Doug took a deep breath. "I'm sorry, but this incident will have to go into your file. If you had admitted the mistake, we could have possibly —"

"I didn't do it," he said, then pointed at me. "She probably did it. She can't stand me."

I put both hands up. "No, no, no. Don't get me involved here."

Doug looked confused.

Truth was, I almost felt sorry for Sargeant. I believed he had nothing to do with removing the Baumgartners from the guest list, but how had the change been made from his computer? Either there was a glitch in Doug's information, or someone on staff had it in for Sargeant — which didn't exactly narrow the field.

Sargeant pulled himself up to his full sitting height. "I don't have an answer for you, but I will endeavor to find one. This was not my doing, but as it happened on my computer, I do take responsibility." He leaned forward to jam an index finger onto Doug's notes. "Put that in my file, will you?" With that, he stood. "If there is nothing else, I will attend to this matter immediately."

When he left, we both looked after him.

"We're just lucky a sharp-eyed staffer noticed this," Doug said.

"Who was it?"

He named one of the assistant calligraphers who worked in the East Wing. I knew her slightly. Thin and mousy, she usually kept her scraggy blond hair pulled back into a ponytail. She was timid enough for Sargeant to easily manipulate if he wanted to, but I just couldn't see it. I couldn't imagine him interacting with her, nor her trying to get him into trouble.

"We're missing something here," I said.

"Yeah, maybe," Doug said, but I could tell he'd already moved on to something else.

CHAPTER 10

"Another successful day in the kitchen." Bucky swiped the countertop with a flourish. "Everybody fed. Nobody dead."

"That isn't funny," Virgil said.

Bucky shrugged. "Maybe not, but it's accurate. You've only been here a few months. You don't know the trouble we get into."

Virgil was leaning over one of the side counters, poring over notes. "What have we heard about tomorrow?" he asked. "How many for lunch?"

"It's on the computer," I said, "updated regularly."

"I prefer working with paper and pen."

"Suit yourself. But the rest of this kitchen works on the computer, and if there are any updates we need to be aware of, they're there."

"Speaking of which," he said as he made his way over to the monitor, "any more updates on the wakes and funerals of the chief of staff and that girl?"

"That 'girl' has a name," Cyan said. "Patty Woodruff. Just because she wasn't a big hot-shot here doesn't make her death any less significant."

Virgil wisely chose not to argue the point. "Patty, then. Have we heard any more about the arrangements? Will you go?"

"We're not required to," I said, "but I feel as though I should."

"Finding them murdered doesn't make you responsible," Virgil said. If I thought our newest chef was suddenly expressing compassion, I was slapped back into reality when he added, "I should be the kitchen representative for Chief of Staff Cawley's wake. He and I golfed together many times. I found him to be a delight. Such a waste."

I thought Cyan's glare would burn a hole through the back of Virgil's head.

"That's your decision," I said. "I'm sure his family would appreciate it."

"I'm sure they would."

A little ping went off in my brain. "You were friends with Mark Cawley, then?" I asked.

Virgil was sitting in front of the computer. "Of course. You golf with a man, you know him."

I wanted to delicately ask him about that

ringtone we'd heard when the bodies were discovered. I knew that detail had not been leaked to the press, so I didn't want to break any confidences. This might take a couple of clever dance maneuvers.

"Was he a big Barry Manilow fan?"

Virgil barked a laugh. "Barry Manilow? Mark wasn't that old. He was younger than me, in fact. What would make you ask that?"

"Something I heard." That wasn't a lie. "I guess I was mistaken."

Virgil went back to studying the monitor, but I could see his focus shift. He stared over the top of the monitor for a moment. "Now that you mention it, there was a Barry Manilow song he liked. We were in the car once and it came on. He turned it up."

"Which song was it?"

"Why do you care, Ollie?" Cyan asked. "Does this have to do with the investigation?"

I needed to be vague, so I stretched the truth a little. "When we were talking about entertainment for the Quinones birthday party, Wyatt asked me who the entertainment would be. Barry Manilow is a possibility."

"For Quinones's age group, yes," Cyan said, "but you're asking about Cawley. He's much younger."

169

"I just thought how sad it was that he would be missing this event," I said. "Especially if he was a fan."

Cyan screwed her face up into a look of utter disbelief. She leaned in close to whisper, "Lame."

Maybe, but Virgil seemed oblivious. He was staring at the wall, hand over his mouth, deep in thought. "I remember it clearly because I made fun of him. Of course in his car, he picks the music. For the life of me, I can't remember which song it was."

" 'Copacabana'?" Cyan asked.

Bucky piped up. " 'I Write the Songs'?"

Come on, I urged silently. Somebody suggest "Mandy."

Cyan again, " 'Looks Like We Made It'?"

" 'Can't Smile without You'?"

Virgil snapped his fingers. "I got it! 'Mandy.' "

" 'Mandy'?" I said. "That is an old one."

"Yeah." He laughed. "But Mark said it made him smile because it reminded him of someone he cared about."

"His wife's name isn't Mandy, or even Amanda," Cyan said.

Thank you! I waited for Virgil to pick up on that. He didn't disappoint. "No, his wife's name is Susan."

"Weird," I said, striving for noncommittal.

170

"Could he have been having an affair?" Cyan asked. "With somebody named Mandy?"

"Maybe that was the name of his dog," Bucky said. "Wasn't that the rumor about that one, anyway?"

"I think that was 'Shannon,' " I said, "not a Manilow tune."

Virgil had been pondering Cyan's question. "I don't think Mark was having an affair, but then again . . ."

"Did the Secret Service or the police talk with you about that?" I asked.

"They asked me if I thought he was having an affair with Patty, but I told them absolutely not. She's much too young. Cawley was a decent guy. Patty was just a kid."

A decent guy? Stepping out on his wife? I took a breath. No sense getting ahead of myself. But I couldn't help thinking that if we knew who'd inspired Cawley to include that intro to "Mandy" as his ringtone, we might have a clue to his killer.

"What, Ollie?" Cyan asked. "You just went white."

"What if whoever killed Cawley and Patty *believed* they were having an affair?" I asked. "What if Cawley's wife did it?"

"She lives in Vermont," Virgil said. "Plus, I heard they investigated her. It was in the

171

paper. Airtight alibi."

"Oh, yeah," I said, "I seem to remember that now. Forgot." I hadn't forgotten at all, but I thought it better to make that suggestion than to share what was really on my mind. That whoever this Mandy was had done the dirty deed herself.

"And they give you kudos for solving crimes." Virgil laughed. "You're days behind everyone else."

"Yeah," I said.

Bucky and Cyan were watching me, but Virgil didn't pay them any attention. Bucky had a warning look on his face. "Ollie would stay out of things if she knew what was good for her."

Cyan's expression matched Bucky's. "Especially this time. She's too involved already."

With his back to us, Virgil was missing all the subtext. "Maybe next time you should check with me when you're looking for answers. I know a lot more than you give me credit for."

I winked at the other two. "I'm sure you do."

Agent Scorroco drove me home again at the end of the day. No one had made any further attempts to accost me, but to be fair, no one had had the chance. My new best buddy made sure to deliver me safe and sound to my building every evening and was there every morning bright and early to pick me up. He also insisted I sit in the backseat. I hated that.

For the past trips home, he'd asked if there was anything I needed on the way. There hadn't been. And even though I didn't need anything today, either, I wondered why he hadn't asked. Agent Scorroco came across like a man of routine and I was curious what was up.

I leaned forward. "Not going to ask me about stopping along the way today, Agent Scorroco?"

His hands were set precisely at the ten and two position and his attention never wavered from the road. "Not today, ma'am," he answered in his soft Kentucky drawl. "Orders are to take you straight home."

"Oh, do you have somewhere else you need to be?"

No answer. I'd learned that trying to engage Agent Scorroco in conversation was a futile endeavor, so on the ride to Crystal City I sat back, pulled out my cell phone, and dialed Gav.

"Hey," he answered.

"Wow, first ring, I'm impressed." It was

rare when we didn't play telephone tag for several hours before finally connecting. "You busy tonight? It's been a heck of a day."

He didn't answer.

I sneaked a look at my driver, who appeared to be utterly uninterested in what I was saying. "I could use company."

"You *had* company."

"I don't understand."

"You will."

"What are you talking about?"

"See you in a few."

He hung up. I tapped the back of Agent Scorroco's seat. "Is something going on?" I asked him.

"I'm not at liberty to disclose any information."

"But it's about me." It wasn't a question and he didn't answer.

I sat back hard, folded my arms, and stared out the window.

I usually waited for Agent Scorroco to give me the all-clear before getting out of the car, but the moment he threw it into park, I was up and out the door, looking for Gav.

Agent Scorroco jumped out and called from the driver's side, "Ms. Paras."

The outside of my apartment building was

quiet as ever. No one loitering in the shadows, no one waiting near the door. The way Gav had said "See you in a few" led me to believe he was here already, or at least on his way. But then again, would he want Agent Scorroco to see him? Probably not.

Coming around the front of the car now, Agent Scorroco tried a more chastising tone. "Ms. Paras," he said, "you can't run out like that until I make sure —"

I waved him silent. "I'm fine. I'm going straight in. You can take off."

He looked unconvinced. "But my orders —"

"Your orders were to get me here safe and sound. I'm here. I'm safe. I know that ensuring I'm sound isn't always possible . . ." He didn't laugh. Fine. I pointed to the glass entryway. "If it makes you feel better, you can watch until I get in."

At that moment four men came running up, two from the street end of my apartment building and two from the far side. I jumped, then relaxed. All four wore suits, held grim expressions, and had wires running up to their ears. Not only that, but they all had the pin-of-the-day on their respective lapels. I'd recognize Secret Service agents anywhere.

In the seconds it took for me to wonder

175

why they were swarming my apartment building, Agent Scorroco had rushed up and grabbed my arm. "Back in the car, Ms. Paras."

I didn't fight him.

One of the agents came over to talk to Agent Scorroco, but with the door closed, I couldn't hear what was going on. I tried rolling the window down, but they were electric and Agent Scorroco had taken the key. All I could make out were muffled voices — very muffled, because they both talked so low. The three other agents were talking among themselves near the front door. From their body language, I could tell they'd all been looking for something. Or someone.

My phone rang. Gav.

"What is going on?" I asked.

"Stay put. I'll be right there."

Again he hung up.

The four agents and Agent Scorroco surrounded the car, standing in a rough circle with their backs to me. I was surprised not to see James peeking out the front doors to see what was going on. A quick stab of panic. I hoped nothing had happened to him.

A few minutes later, just as I thought I might go stir-crazy, I spied Gav coming out.

He spoke briefly to the agents, then waved them back.

He opened my door. "Ms. Paras," he said, without changing the expression on his face. "You can come out now."

"Thanks." I stepped out onto the sidewalk and stared at the agents flanking the front door. "What in the world is going on?"

Gav gestured me forward. "I'll explain inside." As we passed the five, only Agent Scorroco made eye contact with Gav, who released him for the day. "You can go back. The rest of you gentlemen remain here until I brief Ms. Paras. I'll give you further orders momentarily."

James at the front desk looked like a five-year-old who'd just been given a pony for his birthday. He practically danced from foot to foot as we approached. "Ollie," he said, "they wouldn't tell me what was going on, just that there might be someone after you. Is that true?" He pointed to Gav. "I've seen this fellow before, but those other guys are all new." Still pointing, he said, "I let him into your apartment. That was okay, wasn't it?"

"You did the right thing, James."

The worry lines faded as he smiled. "Thought so. You always have some excitement going, don't you, Ollie?"

"Seems so," I said, trying to keep my tone upbeat, but there was nothing light about this situation. Gav's expression was unreadable.

"There was a ruckus here earlier," James said in an effort to help.

I knew how much I was about to disappoint my elderly doorman, but I resisted the urge to ask him any questions. "Several of Special Agent Gavin's agents are waiting outside," I said. "He needs to debrief me upstairs before he can release them." James's face fell. "I'll tell you all about it later. I promise."

Gav and I were silent as we walked to the elevators, but once we were out of earshot, he turned to me. "What are you going to tell him?"

"Maybe I'll have an idea after I find out what's going on."

"It could be nothing," he said, "but we like to be careful. After Wednesday night's encounter on the Metro, we don't want to take any chances."

"But nothing actually happened?"

"Not that I could tell."

"But you were in my apartment."

He nodded.

As we waited for the elevators, I felt another stab of panic. But this one had nothing to do with anyone's well-being. I suddenly remembered what I'd left on the kitchen table.

This morning as I'd made up a to-do list for the next several days, I'd also doodled. It was a habit I had when my mind wandered. My artwork — if you could call it that — stunk. This morning, however, I'd gone beyond mere doodles. With Gav on my mind, I'd amused myself with a game girls used to play in grammar school when we liked a boy. Boy's name on one line, girl's on the next. Through a complicated series of steps where we crossed out letters and added up numbers, you could determine if the boy you liked was your one true love. I hadn't goofed around like that in years, and I wasn't even sure I remembered the rules right. But accuracy wasn't what worried me right now.

I'd left those scribbles right in the middle of my table.

Whatever might have happened in my apartment that brought Gav in couldn't be as bad as him seeing my schoolgirl-crush handiwork. I'd doodled hearts all over that paper, too. With arrows. And our initials.

I couldn't look at him. I was afraid my face would give me away. "Did you find anything . . . strange or wrong?"

He waited for me to meet his gaze, but I couldn't read his expression. "There was nothing in your apartment that shouldn't be there."

Well wasn't he Mr. Enigmatic? "Was there some reason you thought there would be?"

"Yeah." Gav stared up at the numbers as we reached my floor and the car came to a smooth stop. "I need to make a detour," he said when the doors opened.

There weren't too many options at this point, so I wasn't terribly surprised when he knocked at Mrs. Wentworth's door. She opened it immediately and I could read relief on her face when she saw me standing there. "Well?" she said to Gav, stomping her cane on the ground. "What of it? Did you catch him?"

"I'm sorry to report that we did not, Mrs. Wentworth," he said, "but I do thank you for your diligence in reporting what you saw."

Her eyes flicked over to me, back to Gav, and back to me. "He hasn't told you what went on, has he? Not much more than an hour ago, I'd say." She held up her watch and squinted at it. "Not that you ever keep regular hours, Ollie, but I expect it was someone who hoped to find you at home." Her face crinkled up and her eyes narrowed.

"Shady character. I don't think he intended for you to ever leave here, either."

Speechless, I turned to Gav. He didn't look at me. Instead, he kept up a conversation with Mrs. Wentworth, all the while holding on to my elbow in a way that was neither comforting nor helpful. "You did the right thing," he said. "Any time you hear or see anything out of the ordinary, you be sure to call." Gav let go of me long enough to dig out a business card. He handed it to her. "My cell phone is on there. I'll be the first to admit that I'm not always reachable at that number, but do you see the one under it?"

She held it low, at arm's length. "Yes."

"You can call that one anytime day or night. They'll find me. Better yet, they'll send help immediately."

Looking very pleased with herself, Mrs. Wentworth tucked the card into the pocket of her pink sweatshirt. "I'm happy to help any way I can. But can I make a suggestion?"

"Absolutely."

"Maybe if you stayed the night once in a while, I could sleep easier knowing Ollie's protected."

Gav coughed. His face went bright red. "Yes. Well. I'll take that under advisement.

Good night."

But Mrs. Wentworth wasn't finished with him. "You're going to stay tonight, aren't you?"

Gav looked to me for help, but he was totally on his own here. "I'm afraid I'm needed elsewhere."

She made a face that told us exactly what she was thinking. With a very unladylike snort, she shook her head. "Seems to me you're needed here." She shut her door.

We both stared at it for a moment before she shouted, "Good night."

"She's a pistol," I said.

"And a good neighbor."

I pulled out my keys and let us both in. "Start at the beginning."

"I don't have long."

"I gathered that, from the contingent of agents downstairs."

My apartment looked exactly the way it had when I left this morning. Messy, with newspapers strewn on the kitchen countertop, mail piled up on the side table near the door, and an unmade bed. I wondered if Gav had gone in there.

"Have a seat," I said, leading him to the living room. I wanted to get a peek at the doodles I'd left on the kitchen table. They were just scribbles on scratch paper, but I had to know if Gav had seen them.

"I don't have time," he said. "Where are you going?"

"To get a glass of water. Want some?"

As I passed the kitchen table, I saw the corner of the scratch pad peeking out from under newspapers. I must have tossed them on top before I left the house. Whew. My secret was safe.

"Ollie," he said with some impatience, "we need to talk. Right now."

"No problem," I said, returning to the living room. "What happened?"

"About an hour and a half ago, a man Mrs. Wentworth described as having dark hair and wearing a dark coat managed to get past James and up to this floor. He was at your door when Mrs. Wentworth shouted at him to get away. He took off, apparently without leaving anything, and she called for help."

"She could have been hurt," I said, newly terrified. "What if he'd turned on her?"

"She's a tough one," Gav said with a dose of admiration. "When one of my agents told her she'd been foolish to confront the intruder, she waved him off, claiming it had been her excitement for the day."

I rubbed my eyes. "She watches too many cop TV shows." But something nagged at me. "Why are you here? I mean, didn't she call the police?"

"She called the White House and demanded to talk to the Secret Service. I don't know how she got through, but she did." Gav chuckled. "It isn't funny, but she mentioned your name. Your reputation is legendary."

"Great."

"Mrs. Wentworth apparently noticed that you were being picked up every morning and dropped off every night by one of our own. She's feisty all right, but she's sharp, too. She thought about how your bodyguard detail started immediately after the two victims were found at Lexington Place. She put two and two together and figured you were somehow involved."

I sat. "Of course she did," I said with resignation. "I have to be careful if I want to keep secrets around her."

"I don't think you can. The two of you are too similar."

"Hey," I said, suddenly remembering, "speaking of Lexington Place, did we ever find out who it was calling the chief of staff's cell phone? You heard that it played the song 'Mandy,' right?"

"We're following up, but we're hitting brick walls. The caller used a prepaid cell phone bought at a Walmart. Paid cash. Almost impossible to track down. But that's not our priority right now. The authorities are working on the theory that whoever called most likely did not know Cawley was dead. That means they're not a suspect."

"But the ringtone?"

"Yeah, I know. Unanswered questions. We even questioned the DJ whose voice is part of the recording. She checks out. No connection to the case. Apparently Cawley had saved the prepaid phone's number to memory and assigned that ringtone, but there's no way to determine who 'Mandy' is."

"He saved it to memory? What name did he assign?"

"Three guesses. And your first one is right."

"Mandy. No last name."

He nodded.

I took all that in. "Even though she, or he, isn't a suspect, I bet knowing who Mandy is would help."

"It could. But this one really is out of your league."

I was afraid he'd start lecturing me the way Tom used to, but he surprised me by adding, "Knowing you, though, you'll probably stumble across a clue the rest of us miss. Keep your eyes and ears open. But most important, stay safe."

"I plan on it."

"We're not taking any chances. An agent will be posted outside your apartment around the clock."

"I appreciate your concern, but —"

He started pacing my small living room. "Not just my concern. People out there know you're involved with the double murder. And they know you helped rescue Mr. Bettencourt. When they find you, they aren't going to play around. Or go away. Not until they get their jobs done. There's a very real threat against the administration, and you're right in the thick of it."

"Again."

"Yes, again." He stopped at the balcony doors and stared out the glass. "You should keep these covered," he said and pulled the drapes closed. The room was suddenly dark. I could see him across the room, but his features were in shadow when he turned. "I'd be lying if I said I wasn't concerned for you personally, but first and foremost I'm doing what's best for the country. I thank God I'm able to protect you this much." He ran both hands through his hair. "I used to get aggravated with you because I thought you were a smart aleck who didn't know what was good for her."

"And now?"

"You're still a smart aleck who doesn't know what's good for her, but now I'm not aggravated — I'm terrified. You could get hurt, Ollie. Seriously hurt."

I made a move as though to get up, but stopped when I saw him wince. "You don't want me near you?" I asked.

"That's the problem. I do."

"Because you're afraid."

He didn't answer. He didn't have to.

"Having a guard outside my door twenty-four/seven means you won't come visit, doesn't it?"

"It means you'll be safe."

"But . . ."

He came over to where I was sitting and crouched next to me. He took my hands in his. "Let's just get through this, Ollie. Maybe when this is over . . ."

"Then what?" I asked. "Will you want to continue as friends, or will we take a chance and move forward?"

"Understand this: When it comes to keeping you safe, I never take chances."

That wasn't what I meant and he knew it. "But . . ."

He put his finger over my lips. "I know,"

he said. "I'm not ready. Not yet."

As he left, I wondered: Would he ever be?

CHAPTER 11

In the morning I showered, grabbed a quick bite, then remembered I had a Secret Service babysitter waiting outside my door. I poked my head out to see a female agent pacing the hallway. "Good morning," I said. "Have you been here all night?"

She glanced at her watch. "You're an early riser. But no, I just got here at three." She came over to shake my hand. "I'm Agent Rosenow."

"Olivia Paras."

She gave me an amused look, as if to say, "I know."

I opened my door wider. "Please, call me Ollie. Would you like coffee or something? Are you hungry?"

Agent Rosenow had a nice smile. Older than me by just a couple of years, she was tall and muscular, with super-short cropped blond hair that looked about a week overdue for a touch-up. She thanked me but declined. "You're not scheduled to go in to the White House today. Why are you up so early? Big plans we need to know about?"

"There's an important dinner tonight I need to handle, so I am going in." With Virgil covering the president's breakfast and lunch, my single focus today would be tonight's event — a working dinner for the president and some of his most trusted advisors. I'd slept far past my normal four o'clock wake-up because I knew the evening could go late. "It's already six-thirty."

"I wasn't informed," she said, "but we will adjust. How soon will you be ready to leave?"

"Ten minutes. Five."

"I'll call for a car."

She opened her cell phone and began to dial. I ducked back into my apartment to make sure I had everything for the day. Tonight's working dinner would be a relatively easy event. We had originally planned for ten guests plus the president, which made eleven, but now with Nagy's addition, it would be an even dozen. Even though we'd planned for several new dishes with intricate preparations, we'd taken care to ensure every single dietary requirement would be met. I was eager to get in and get started. Days off could wait.

Agent Rosenow knocked a moment later.

"A driver will be here shortly," she said. I must have looked confused, because she quickly added, "I'm here alone on site all day. I can't leave. Our information said it was your day off and we didn't expect you to be up and out so early. I can't leave the building until ordered to do so."

"I feel so . . ." I wanted to say "hemmed in" or "restricted" or "claustrophobic," but that would have sounded rude.

"Protected?" she suggested.

"Exactly."

"The car won't be here for at least ten minutes. Possibly longer."

I smiled and nodded. *Just great,* I thought as I shut my apartment door behind me. A ten-or fifteen-minute delay wouldn't kill me, but it certainly wasn't optimal. Grabbing my coat, cell phone, and a handful of notes I'd scribbled as I'd gotten ready this morning, I emerged from my apartment less than five minutes after I'd gone back in.

"The car's not here yet," Agent Rosenow said. The look on her face told me she wondered how I could possibly have not understood.

"I just want some fresh air," I said. "I'll wait downstairs."

Agent Rosenow wasn't pleased, but she

didn't refuse. "Let's go."

"Honestly," I said as we rode the elevator down, "I doubt if anyone will try anything at this early hour of the morning. I'm sure I'd be fine on the Metro."

She gave me a look that told me exactly what she thought of that idea. I hadn't really expected my suggestion to fly, but even after one night I was getting itchy knowing that my every movement was being watched.

As much as James wanted to man the desk all day every day, he, like most humans, required sleep from time to time. I waved hello to his replacement. As we passed, the elderly gentleman brightened and said, "Good morning, Olivia!" and I felt guilty for not remembering his name.

Though temperatures were slowly beginning to climb, it was still unseasonably cold. The brightening sky promised a clear day. Fragrant damp dirt hinted at new growth. I took a deep, appreciative breath the moment I cleared the doors. Agent Rosenow followed. "Where's your coat?" I asked. "Don't you have one?"

"I didn't think you meant to wait outdoors," she said, pointing toward the parking lot. "It's in my car."

"Why don't you go get it?"

She shook her head. "I'll be fine."

"It'll take you less than a minute, and I'm not going anywhere."

"I'll be fine," she said again.

"At least button your jacket," I said.

"Can't."

Oh that's right. Secret Service agents never buttoned their jackets. "I feel guilty," I said. "Let's wait in the lobby, then."

Agent Rosenow was about to reach for the door when her cell phone rang. As she stepped to the side to answer it, I noticed movement in the shrubbery to my far left. Not like a squirrel or a gopher; we were talking significant movement. Sneaking around in the shrubs.

I took a few steps back when I heard branches snap and leaves rustle. The shadow moved behind a cluster of tall evergreens planted there to create a berm between our apartment building's property and our neighbor's. To make it look pretty. Not to shield peeping Toms.

"Hey," I started to say.

Still on the phone with her back to me, Agent Rosenow didn't hear.

The front doors of my apartment building stood out ever so slightly from the brick of the building, creating a vestibule entryway jutting toward the sidewalk. I eased around one side — protected, but still able to see what was going on. We didn't get a whole lot of wildlife in this area and this creature was almost my height. I supposed it could be a local tenant returning home after an overnight binge. But I didn't think so.

I was more curious than afraid. It was morning, I had an armed Secret Service agent less than five feet away, and I could easily duck into the apartment building if necessary. I moved my head from side to side, to try to get a better view.

When the intruder moved again, cracking shrubs as it pushed its way out, I grabbed Agent Rosenow. She started to say something about a delay when I pointed.

"Get behind me," she said.

I didn't argue.

The elderly doorman inside watched with interest. I could only imagine what he was thinking. Agent Rosenow had her gun ready, and held me back with her free arm. Not that I intended to rush out or anything; I'd had my fill of gun battles, thank you very much.

The elderly guy boosted himself up and started around the desk, clearly intent on coming to the front door. I waved him back.

"Come out," Agent Rosenow shouted to the shrubs. "Make yourself known. Hands up."

A wavering voice called back. "Put the gun away. I'm not going to hurt anybody."

I'd heard that voice before, but I couldn't place it. "He doesn't sound very menacing," I whispered.

"Come out now," she repeated, never taking her eyes off the bushes in the berm. "I won't tell you again."

"Okay, okay, just don't shoot."

At the moment the elderly guy pushed through the door. "What's going on?"

"Get back inside," Agent Rosenow ordered in a voice that brooked no disobedience.

He put his hands up and backed into the lobby, eyes wide. Making eye contact with me, he pantomimed holding a phone receiver and mouthed, "Should I call 911?"

I was about to answer him when our shadowy visitor stepped out from behind the shrubs, hands high, a sheepish expression on his face. "Milton?" To Agent Rosenow, I said, "It's okay. I know him. Sort of." I turned to the eager doorman and shook my head. He looked extremely disappointed.

Rosenow lowered the gun, still not taking her eyes from him. "Keep your hands up," she said as she holstered the weapon. As she patted him down, I stood next to her.

"What were you thinking, Milton?" I asked. "You could have been shot."

He spoke over his shoulder. "I didn't know you had a guard with you." She'd moved down to his legs. "I just wanted to talk to you, and I know you get in early. You're running late today."

"How do you know my regular schedule? Have you been watching me?"

His face colored. "Are you done yet?" he asked Agent Rosenow.

She stepped back. "Show me some ID."

As he complied, I pressed him again. "Why have you been watching me?"

"Petey won't give me the time of day. And I know something that could help you with your investigation."

Agent Rosenow looked at me with growing suspicion. "What investigation is he talking about, Ms. Paras?"

"None. Nothing," I said. "I'm not investigating anything."

Milton pointed. "Is she with the Secret Service?"

I nodded.

"Then I can talk in front of her?"

"I'd rather you didn't."

"It's about that meeting we had the other day," Milton said, "remember?"

I did a quick assessment of the situation.

If he started talking about the double murder, I had no doubt Agent Rosenow would run him in as a suspect. Milton was harmless, but it would cause Sargeant untold grief to have to deal with an incarcerated relative. Although the temptation to irritate Sargeant was almost too much to pass up, I took the high road. "Agent Rosenow," I said, "could you please give us a minute?"

She didn't look happy about it, but she stepped back inside the lobby with a glare directed at Milton that silently conveyed, "I'm watching you."

Milton coughed but didn't cover his mouth well enough. "Have you been drinking?" I asked.

"Got to find confidence somewhere."

"Not from a bottle." I thought about what Sargeant had said about Milton ruining his life. "What happened between you and Peter, anyway?"

"What did he tell you?"

"Not much."

Milton shifted his weight. He wagged his head. "Maybe some other time. Don't you want to know what I found out about the murders?"

"Metro Police and the Secret Service are working together. I'm sure —"

He brought his face closer to mine and

spoke in a hushed tone, keeping a hand cupped next to his cheek as though to prevent Agent Rosenow from reading his lips. It sure didn't keep the sickly sweet smell of liquor from invading my space. "I know who's behind all this."

Placing my hand on his arm, I said, "I think you should probably just go home and —"

Rather than shake my hand off, he placed his cold one atop mine. "Listen to me . . ."

"You're freezing," I said. "Come inside."

"I don't want her to hear."

"But you've been out here for so long."

"I'm used to being outside. Now listen to me." The cloudiness in his eyes dissipated. "You know that guy who bumped us the other day?"

I nodded.

"Him and another guy came to the restaurant where I work. Sat at the bar, then another guy came in. I've seen this guy before. He's some big shot."

"Who?"

Milton frowned. "I can't remember. I've been trying hard, too. But he's in the government. I know it. I just can't place him. But I will."

"That's not —"

"Would you listen!"

The sooner I let him talk, the sooner I could send him on his way. "Sorry. Go ahead."

"They all pretended like they didn't know each other, but I was watching them. Their body language was off. I know people. I've been screwed by more people than I can count. Something wasn't right."

"What happened?"

"The two guys got up and went out the front door. They headed east." He glanced from side to side as though making sure no one was listening. But the only sounds we heard were tree branches twisting in the breeze and the soft sounds of traffic from the street. "A couple minutes later, the government guy gets up, too. He goes outside, but he goes west."

My patience was wearing thin.

"I thought maybe I was wrong about them knowing each other, and so I went back to work. But a few minutes later, I took a smoke break behind the restaurant and I saw them again. All three of them. All together. Talking."

"What were they talking about?"

"I couldn't get close enough to hear anything. And I didn't want to be all obvious about checking them out."

"They didn't see you?"

He gave me a sad look. "Don't you get it? I'm invisible. I'm part of a clean-up crew in a restaurant — just like the million other busboys and dishwashers and scut workers in the world. Nobody sees us. They think we don't matter."

I thought about where I would be without the staffers on our White House team who were responsible for those unpleasant but very important jobs. "Of course you matter."

He waved my comment away. "My point is, they had no idea I noticed them. Now, why would the guy who bumped us the other day be meeting with a guy from the government if some big shot wasn't behind the killings?"

First of all, I had my doubts that Milton could actually recognize the guy who bumped us. I thought it was possible that the combination of his imagination and a desire to be part of the action were what made him see resemblances where none existed. But that didn't mean I wanted to shut him down. Milton seemed like a guy the world had kicked around. I didn't want to be another person who made him feel worthless.

"Just for a minute, let's say you're right and these three guys didn't want anyone to know they knew each other."

He nodded quickly, eager for me to believe him.

"What do you think this actually means? That the government was involved in killing Chief of Staff Cawley and the First Lady's assistant, Patty Woodruff? That's pretty far-fetched."

Milton shrugged. "That's the part you have to figure out. I held up my end."

"Listen, Milton," I said, "I'll mention this to the proper authorities . . ." The proper authorities being: nobody.

"If what I told you pans out, do you think you might be able to talk to Mr. Vasquez on my behalf? When he gets back, I mean."

My brain had been in hyper-drive for the past several seconds. Something Milton said had struck a nerve, but I hadn't been able to pinpoint it. Rather than answer him, I asked, "The other guy — the one who accompanied the guy who bumped us. What did he look like?"

Milton coughed again. I raised my eyebrows, wishing I could get him indoors. Except for his bright red ears and red nose, the man was pale gray.

"Let me think." Milton closed his eyes and rubbed his face. "He was uh . . . taller than me, and big. Like a big guy, you know?

Maybe thirty years old or so." I think he was surprised to see me paying close attention when he opened his eyes. "You want more?"

"Whatever you remember."

He scratched his forehead. "I didn't see the color of his eyes, but he reminded me of a pig because he had a lot of . . ." He brought his hands up to gesture. ". . . pudginess here, but his eyes were small and kinda walleyed."

I felt my pulse perk up. "Hair?"

"I don't know. Blond, maybe brown. Can't remember. Not a lot of it. I paid more attention to the other guy — the one who bumped us. The other guy wore a hat the whole time he was outside, too. So maybe I'm not remembering his hair."

Or maybe he was. "Anything else?"

Squinting, then closing his eyes again, he said, "No . . . wait . . . yes! The guy had one of those butt-chins."

I knew what Milton meant. A cleft. "Brad," I said under my breath.

"You know him?"

"Not really. But I may have met him."

"And?"

"And nothing."

Milton gave me a helpless look. "I thought this might be good information."

"It might be," I said, thinking it might actually be excellent information. "I will definitely have someone look into it."

"I think you and Petey should look into it yourselves."

"I've had enough personal involvement, thank you." I glanced back toward the street. Where was the car? I really needed to get back into the White House this morning.

Inside the lobby, Agent Rosenow must have read my mind. She took a quick look at her watch, then mouthed, "Five minutes."

"Well, I thought it was worth telling you at least," he said as he prepared to leave. "Petey told me not to show up at the White House anymore or he could lose his job. I wouldn't want that."

"What happened between you two?"

Milton shuffled his feet and stared at the ground. "I made a mistake. A big one."

I waited.

"It's bad," he said, not looking up. "I don't want to tell you."

Agent Rosenow came outside, saving Milton from my interrogation. "Your car is here," she said.

I gripped Milton's arm for a brief moment. "I'm sorry." I didn't know what else to say.

Mr. Silent Treatment, Agent Scorroco, was at the wheel. We were halfway to the White House when I snapped my fingers. He didn't even flinch. "Maybe it was Milton who showed up at my apartment last night," I said.

Agent Scorroco didn't answer. Didn't even meet my eyes in the rearview mirror.

"I should have asked him," I said. If Milton had been the intruder Mrs. Wentworth had spotted, maybe I wouldn't need bodyguards around the clock. I had no way to contact Milton to ask him, but I was sure Sargeant could.

"Does anyone know if Sargeant is in today?" I asked.

Bucky sent a scornful look across the room. "Haven't you had enough of him lately?"

I washed my hands and wiped them on a clean towel. "Too much." I gave a wry smile. "I need to check with him on a couple of things."

Cyan was preparing filling for one of our *vol-au-vent* options. "I saw him this morning when I stopped by Paul's office —" She wrinkled her nose. "It's going to take me a while to think of it as Doug's office. I stopped by there to pick up notes for tonight. Sargeant was in there complaining about something."

"So what else is new?" Bucky asked.

"Can you guys hold down the fort for a few minutes?" I asked.

Virgil had his back to me. "Easily," he said over his shoulder, "take your time."

Bucky, Cyan, and I exchanged a look. If there was one thing that had served to cement our relationship, it was our shared distaste for Virgil. "I don't enjoy working with him," I said, raising my voice a few notches. "It's hard to deal with a person who takes such pride in being difficult."

"Hey," Virgil turned, "you're still talking about Sargeant, right?"

I smiled and walked out the door.

Sargeant's office was in the West Wing on the second floor, an area of the White House I didn't visit very often. His door was closed and I worried for a minute that he wasn't there, until I heard murmuring inside. I knocked.

There was a two-second delay. "Come in."

I opened the door to see him hunched at his desk, staring at his computer monitor. "Oh," he said, looking up. "I was expecting someone else."

I left the door open and pointed to the seat across from him. "Do you mind?"

He waved me down without breaking his concentration from the screen. From my angle, I couldn't see what had him so enthralled.

"Maybe I should come back another time."

His head didn't move, but his eyes flicked sideways. I could tell it took effort to drag his attention away from his task, but he did. "What is it?"

"Milton came to see me this morning."

The veins in Sargeant's neck came into sudden sharp relief. "I told him to stay away from the White House."

"He did," I said. "This was at my apartment."

Sargeant's face fell. He put his hands up to his head, much the way Milton had earlier, and massaged his brow. "Just what I need. Did he say what he wanted?"

I started to answer, but Sargeant interrupted. "Don't tell me. Let me guess: He wants you to put in a good word for him here. He wants a job in your kitchen."

"Of course, but that wasn't the reason for his visit."

Sargeant looked up and I noticed weariness on the man's face. He had been pressed and crisp every single moment I'd known him. From the crease in his pants to the sharp corners of handkerchiefs forever peeking out of his breast pocket, Sargeant was always polished and alert. Like a bright-eyed squirrel, scheming to gather all the best nuts before his competition even knew they were there. The man who sat across from me now, however, looked rumpled and worn out.

Maybe I shouldn't have bothered him, but I plunged on. "I didn't think to ask Milton something this morning, and I have no idea how to get in touch with him. I figured you would."

Suspicion clouded those weary eyes. "What do you need him for?"

Without getting too detailed, I told him about the near break-in at my apartment and how the Secret Service was now keeping an eye on me and my place around the clock.

"Do they think whoever murdered Cawley and Woodruff is out to get you?" Sargeant's hands went to his throat. "Do they think they're out to get me, too?"

This wasn't going well. "There's no proof that anyone is out to get me. It could have been anyone. In fact . . ." I waited until I had his full attention, "it could have been Milton."

Sargeant might not be a nice man, but he

wasn't a stupid one. He understood my point immediately. I watched relief flood his features. "You think so? If it was Milton who tried to talk with you yesterday, then no one is actually after you."

"Exactly. And if no one is after me, then I have a good shot at convincing the Secret Service to drop their guard."

Sargeant's face tightened again. "It wouldn't be like Milton to try to get in your apartment when you weren't there."

He'd just pointed out the one weakness in my theory. "I didn't think so either, but when I talked with Milton this morning, I thought I smelled alcohol on his breath. Who knows what he might do when he's . . . impaired?" I hesitated, then added, "He did offer up a tidbit that might prove interesting."

Sargeant fixed me with a skeptical look.

"There's a chance, ever so slight, that the guy who bumped into you on our way to Lexington Place may be working with the guy who followed me the other night."

"Did you tell the Secret Service about this?"

"First thing this morning."

"And?"

"The agent I talked with said he would talk with Tom."

"Keep me apprised on that." Sargeant looked up, almost as though hearing the abruptness of his words. "Please." He pulled out a piece of paper and wrote himself a note in slow, precise handwriting. "I will attempt to reach Milton."

I started to get up. "I appreciate it."

He looked like he was about to say something but stopped himself.

"What?" I asked. "You've got more on your mind."

He didn't answer, but I could read it in his face. He got up and shut the door before returning to his seat.

"What is it?" I asked.

Placing both hands on top of his desk, he silently worked his lip. "Ms. Paras . . . Ollie . . ."

Uh-oh. He never called me Ollie. This was going to be big.

"From the day I began working here, you and I haven't exactly seen eye-to-eye on matters."

Understatement of the year. I nodded.

"Can we put aside our differences? Momentarily?"

"I would like to put aside our differences permanently."

At that, he gave me a funny look.

"After all," I continued, "we're both on

the same team."

He sniffed hard through one nostril. "Be that as it may, you and I have a tendency to get under each other's skin. I'm not saying anything that isn't true, am I?"

"What's your point?"

"It isn't a point so much as a request. A favor."

"What is it?" I asked warily.

He turned the computer monitor so we could both see it at the same time. "This is the preliminary list of guests for Secretary of State Quinones's birthday party. The one that Doug insists I manipulated."

I studied it. To me it was just a list of names. I recognized celebrities and a few not-so-famous people from dietary issues we'd worked around before, but otherwise it didn't look familiar. "What's the favor?"

"I will get to that momentarily. I've been back and forth on this issue a hundred times. You need to understand that I keep copies of every guest list I've ever been given. I use them to create spreadsheets to keep track of guests' religious observances, birthdays, known dietary restrictions . . ."

He must have seen my expression because he waved down my reaction. "I'm not second-guessing you. But you can appreciate how important it is to keep a document like this with all preferences in one place."

"Doesn't the social secretary cover all this?"

He heaved a sigh. "We've changed social secretaries three times in the past few years. If my job is to oversee protocol, I want to maintain control over our data."

"Smart move," I said. It was.

"I save every incarnation of every document that comes past me. I'm obsessive about it. The original list topped two thousand. Although it was pared down considerably, the Baumgartners were never taken off. I have seven different lists here — each one time-stamped and dated when I saved them. On every single one of them, Mr. and Mrs. Baumgartner are there, exactly where they should be. Yet here . . ."

He clicked on his e-mail. "A file was sent to the calligraphy department from my account and when I opened that file, guess what?"

"The Baumgartners are missing."

"Yes!" he said, eyes so wide I thought they might pop out of his head. "I have no recollection of sending this e-mail. None. I'd sent one about an hour prior, but I don't recall sending this follow-up. Yet the e-mail instructs the calligraphy department to ignore the prior list and use this one." His voice was hoarse as he whispered, "Who could have done such a thing?"

CHAPTER 12

"You think someone sabotaged the list and wanted to frame you?"

He sat back. "What other explanation is there?"

"Don't you log out when you leave your computer?"

His face reddened. "At night I do. But during the day, I see no need to constantly log off and log on. I mean, it isn't as though anything I handle is of national security proportions."

"You do handle sensitive personal information."

He threw his hands up. "Fine. I'm guilty. But who would want to get me into trouble? Who dislikes me so much?"

I bit the insides of my cheeks. "That's the million-dollar question, isn't it?"

"I asked Doug who it was who'd noticed the discrepancy and he told me it was Lynn, from the calligraphy department," Sargeant said. "That's who I thought was coming to visit me when you arrived. Maybe she can shed some light on this."

"Maybe."

"You don't sound convinced."

With about ninety individuals on staff at the White House, about ninety suspects came to mind. But the truth was that despite our differences — and the occasional personality clash — everyone here respected one another's work. If Sargeant was right about someone trying to get him into trouble, this was a work of a saboteur.

"What I mean is," I said, "I can't imagine how she would know who actually sent the e-mail."

He clenched his lips tightly.

"But," I said, "it's worth asking."

"Except she refuses to talk to me."

"Seriously?"

"I've e-mailed her twice, asking her to stop by."

"Did you visit her in person?"

"Of course not," he said. "I don't wish to discuss this in front of her coworkers. This is a private matter. I won't be fodder for office gossip."

Too late, I thought uncharitably. Chastising myself, I decided to take the high road yet again. "You know, Peter," I said, "sometimes you can be a little bit intimidating."

He sat up, as though I'd just paid him the highest compliment. "You think so?"

I pictured the mousy girl. "Lynn might be afraid to come talk to you."

"There's nothing to be afraid of."

"Did you tell her what you wanted to talk with her about?"

He shook his head. "I want to watch her as I ask the question. Determine if she's hiding anything."

"Lynn's what? About twenty-two? She strikes me as kind of shy and nervous. I'm not sure she'd have the self-confidence to walk in here on her own."

"Maybe you can talk with her."

"Me?"

"That favor I mentioned . . ."

"You just said you wanted to watch her as she answers."

"She won't even answer my e-mails, so it will just have to be you who talks with her. And report back to me."

I wanted to ask at what point this had become my problem, but I was again struck by the toll this had taken on him. His face was pale and slack. It looked like he hadn't slept since Doug had delivered the news. "You know," I said, "if you'd just taken responsibility right off the bat, maybe Doug would have considered investigating himself, once you explained."

I expected him to explode. To jump out of his chair and shout that he hadn't done anything wrong and to insist he shouldn't be forced to take responsibility for something he hadn't done.

Instead, he actually looked pensive. "That would have been the right move. At least with Doug. Paul would have believed me. He knows I take responsibility for my mistakes — though I've never made any at the White House."

Nothing wrong with this guy's self-esteem.

He sighed. "Now that I've argued my point, however, I am forced to prove myself. You understand, don't you?"

Unfortunately, I did. Too well. "Can I give you some advice, Peter?"

He sat back as though afraid of what I might say. "Go ahead."

"Own up to it —"

"But I didn't —"

"You left your computer vulnerable and that's actually worse," I said. "Take it from me. You're always eager to point out how much trouble I am . . ."

He gave a so-so shake of his head.

"But have you noticed that despite all the 'trouble' I've caused, I'm still here?"

He blinked twice. "You don't think they would let me go because of this, do you?"

I couldn't very well share what Paul had told me. Time for me to get back to the kitchen. "Who knows how decisions are made around here anymore? Doug is still an unknown right now. It's just smart politics to be careful."

He grumbled under his breath.

"What was that?" I asked.

"I hate it when you're right."

"Yeah," I said, "I know you do."

Tonight's dinner would be a nice, easy one. Although we were diligent at providing the tastiest and most interesting food for our guests, the kitchen remained relatively calm. This was not the sort of event that made the news. Not an official social gathering. Working dinners for the president and his guests didn't require the crazed, last-minute wildness of preparing a hundred perfect meals all ready to go at precisely the same time.

What was special about this gathering — at least for us in the kitchen — was that we hoped to gauge reactions to a few new items we were considering for the secretary of state's birthday party next month. Pastry-wrapped asparagus with prosciutto topped my list. Now that the event's location was set and its invitation list no longer in flux, I hoped to get cranking on finalizing the menu.

"Where's Virgil?" I asked when I got back.

Bucky gave me a baleful glare. Cyan giggled. "He's upstairs, in the residence."

"Mrs. Hyden and the kids aren't here. The president is taking lunch in his office. What's Virgil doing up there now?"

"I'm ready for my close-up, Mr. DeMille," Bucky said, striking a pose. "He's walking a photographer through some of the rooms to get 'inspiration' for yet another magazine spread."

I hated to point out the obvious. "Shouldn't the magazine be focusing on photos of him working in the kitchen?"

"You'd think, wouldn't you?" Bucky asked.

Cyan wore a mischievous grin. "He prefers photographers and feature writers to capture 'his full essence.' "

"He said that?"

Cyan laughed again. "Word for word."

I was not a person to look a gift horse in the mouth. "While he's gone —" I said.

Bucky turned. "You've got some dirt on him?"

"Sorry, no," I said, "but I do want your

opinions on a matter that just came up, which I'd rather not discuss in front of Virgil."

"Ooh, Ollie, what is it?" Cyan crossed the room to peek around the corner. "The coast is clear."

I beckoned them closer. Keeping my voice down, I told them about the guest-list problem and how I believed Sargeant wasn't responsible. "He's asked me to help him find out who might have done it."

"Oh, ho!" Bucky said loudly. "Sure, he comes to you when he needs help because he knows that you find answers. Whenever you've been in trouble in the past, though, he's always first in line with a rock in his hand."

"I know, but —"

Cyan winced. "I'm with Bucky on this one," she said. "He's been nothing but trouble for you from day one. Let him figure this out himself."

"Who do you think has it in for Sargeant?"

Bucky rubbed his chin, pretending to study the ceiling. "I don't know. Maybe . . . everyone?"

"I know he's been a problem, but I'm stuck working with him —"

"And you feel responsible," Cyan finished for me.

I winced at her spot-on analysis. "Sort of."

Bucky leaned in. "Listen, maybe this is just the thing to get him out of here. You don't *know* he didn't make this mistake. Maybe he's hoping you'll poke around so that he can turn the tables and blame *you.*"

I started to protest, but Bucky also had a point.

"Call me insensitive, but all we need are a few mistakes blamed on him and we'll be saying bye-bye to our sensitivity director."

"So you two think I should let this drop?"

Cyan gave me the look. "That's a no-brainer."

Five minutes before serving time, we were experiencing the last-minute jitters that always occur right before an event, no matter how small. With only twelve diners tonight, the craziness was down to a minimum, but Virgil, unfortunately, was still his wild self.

"What is wrong with you?" Virgil screamed.

The object of his outburst was one of the young Service by Agreement assistants we'd brought on for the night, Samantha. She cowered under the chef's glare. In her early twenties, with chubby red cheeks and curly maroon hair pulled back in a severe bun, she'd been stuck working next to Virgil all night.

"Haven't you learned to pour without spilling all over the dinner plate? How did you ever land this position with such inferior habits?" Poor Samantha had done the unforgivable. Hands shaking as she'd drizzled béchamel sauce over a sampling of shrimp, she'd allowed an errant drop to land on the edge of one of the dinner plates. "Don't they teach you anything in school? You're not four years old anymore. You're accountable."

"Yes, Chef," she said meekly as she reached for a hand towel with the clear intent of wiping the offending plate clean.

"Don't use that!" he screeched.

Startled, she jumped back, but because her left hand had been gripping the plate, the dish jumped along with her. Food leapt overboard. Most of it landed on the countertop, the rest went *splat* on the floor.

Samantha's lower lip trembled. "I'm sorry," she whispered, "I didn't mean —"

"Look what you did." Virgil lifted the plate and banged it onto the countertop in emphasis. "You ruined a perfectly good dinner. Now we have to prepare a replacement, which means our diners will be required to wait. This is unacceptable. Do you hear?"

Fat tears shimmered in Samantha's eyes, swiftly breaking free to run down her reddening cheeks. She looked like a trapped animal right before the hunter sliced its neck.

I took the plate out of Virgil's hand and spoke quietly. "This is President Polk's china. Its pieces are irreplaceable."

Virgil waved dismissively. "It was her."

Still holding the plate, which I inspected for damage, I addressed Bucky. "Let's get this taken care of. Can you get a new dinner together quickly?"

"I'm on it."

Butlers collected the remaining eleven plates and waited for Bucky to re-create the dish. I turned to Samantha. "Take a moment, collect yourself. Go splash cold water on your face. Then come right back and I'll have a job for you."

Those big eyes seemed to grow wider, but she nodded and ran out of the kitchen toward the nearest washroom.

"Virgil," I said the moment she was gone, "this kitchen is not the place for such behavior and I will not tolerate it."

"That's your problem. You have no passion for what you do. If you did, you wouldn't allow substandard meals to be served to your guests. If I hadn't caught her spill —"

"Then we wouldn't be having this conversation right now," I finished. "Because if anyone else: me, Bucky, Cyan . . . one of the butlers . . . had noticed it, we would have either pointed it out to her in a civilized manner or we would have corrected the problem ourselves."

"That's no way to run a kitchen," he shouted. "These underlings need to know who's boss!"

I pulled my lips tight and waited for my temper to quiet. "You're completely right," I said.

"I know I am."

"People do need to know who's boss."

He blinked.

"I am the boss," I said. "Go home."

"But . . ."

"Immediately. Take off your apron and leave. Come back when you're ready to work well with others."

"You can't —"

"Do you need an escort to show you the way out?" I asked conversationally. I nodded to Bucky, who moved closer to the phone. "We have a dinner to finish serving, and right now you're in the way."

"You can't do this."

"Watch me."

As my second-in-command picked up the receiver, Virgil yanked off his apron and slammed it onto the countertop. "Fine. I'm out of here!"

He stormed out of the main kitchen into the back area, where most of us kept our coats. Not one of us turned as he stomped past us. Not one of us wished him a good night.

The moment he was gone, Bucky said, "I swear that guy is the biggest diva I've ever met. He's even worse than I was."

CHAPTER 13

Dinner was served and enjoyed. Empty plates were returned to the kitchen for us to analyze. We made our notes, cleaned up, then sent Samantha home with our thanks for her help and a promise that we'd call her again.

Then came my favorite time: Bucky, Cyan, and I basked in the glow of a job well done. Bucky gave the countertop a final blast with cleaning solution, then wiped until it sparkled. "You realize you got lucky," he said.

Cyan, transcribing our notes into a computer document, perked up. "You mean because just about everyone tonight joined the clean-your-plate club? Luck has nothing to do with that. It's our incredible talent that made this happen. If these weren't fancy schmancy White House people, I'd have guessed they all licked their plates clean."

I laughed. It felt great to have created a meal that had been so universally enjoyed. Except for one diner's plate that came back with the asparagus virtually untouched, the food had disappeared. To us, that indicated an unqualified success.

"That's not what I meant," Bucky said. "You're lucky you reamed out the First Lady's pet chef while she was out of town. He can't go crying to her tonight. He's going to have to wait until she gets back."

"And by then he'll probably have lost his steam," I said, "right?"

"Right."

"Just like Cyan said a minute ago: Luck had nothing to do with it."

Bucky's eyebrows shot up. "You planned it that way?"

"I didn't plan to reprimand him tonight, if that's what you mean, but I suspected the pressure would get to him. It always does. And I was completely aware that the First Lady was out of his reach." I smiled. "You heard of picking your battles? Well, tonight I chose wisely."

Bucky grinned. "There's hope for you yet."

One of the White House pages showed up in the doorway. "Chef Paras?" she said.

I looked at Bucky and Cyan. "I hope I

didn't speak too soon."

"The secretary of state would like to speak with you upstairs."

My hand flew to my forehead. I'd totally forgotten about Secretary Quinones's plan to give me a gift for rescuing his father-in-law. "Do you need me up there right now?"

"What's going on, Ollie?" Cyan asked.

"It's nothing. I should be back in a minute," I said. Quickly washing my hands and drying them, I untied my apron and brushed crumbs off my smock. "Do you think I need to change it?" I asked.

Cyan squinted. "For meeting with the secretary of state? With the president there? With a bunch of other really important people around you? With that splotch of grease across your chest? Yeah, I think maybe you should change."

I held a finger up to the page, who looked terrified to be making a top official wait. "I'll just be a second."

"I'm sure he'll understand. You work in a kitchen, after all —"

By the time she got the sentence out, I was through the door with a new smock in my hand. Less than a minute later I had donned fresh clothing and was making my way back to the kitchen. "See," I said, "that didn't take —"

A stranger stood in the center of our kitchen. "Ms. Paras?" he asked. Wearing a charcoal suit that contrasted his fair skin and hyper-blond hair, he was about my age and very tall. I didn't recognize him. Astoundingly handsome, with expressive blue eyes and a tentative smile, he reached out to grasp my hand. Thank goodness he couldn't see Cyan's thumbs-up of approval from behind.

"My name is Ethan Nagy. I'm assistant to Secretary of State Quinones."

I was sure I must have seen this man on TV at some point, but he didn't look at all familiar. That wasn't unusual. We didn't always get to know all the assistants of all the cabinet members.

"It's very nice to meet you, Mr. Nagy."

"Ethan, please. Secretary Quinones would have liked to have come down here himself . . ."

"I'm sure he has much more important things to do."

A wider smile this time. "Thank you for your understanding. Secretary Quinones wishes to express his profound gratitude for your help in rescuing his wife's father."

"He already thanked me once," I said. "Really, it was just luck that I happened to be there."

Ethan turned his head a little bit. "I don't think luck had anything to do with it," he said, echoing the words we'd said in this kitchen just moments before. "From what I understand, you have a history of getting involved in unusual circumstances."

"The media often blows stories out of proportion."

"Maybe so," he said. "We've certainly had issues with the media running with stories that are only half-true. I think we all know, however, that you've proven yourself to be an asset to the First Family. It seems you're an asset to Cabinet members as well."

"That's very kind of you to say . . ."

Nagy reached for something in his breast pocket. "The secretary didn't know what would be a proper gift for a chef who also sleuths, but he wanted to give you a remembrance of your good deed."

Ethan drew out a long, narrow box. A bracelet? I hoped not. That would be too personal, too weird.

When Ethan opened the brown leather case, I breathed a sigh of relief. A silver pen. "It's lovely," I said as he placed it into my hand.

"It's engraved."

I twisted the pen to see the words inscribed there. "Olivia Paras, White House

Executive Chef." No mention whatsoever of the secretary of state, his father-in-law, the purported rescue, or my amateur sleuth tendencies.

"Thank you."

Ethan seemed to be studying my reaction. "I . . . that is, Secretary Quinones . . . thought it best to make a gift you might actually use. One that we hope will remind you of his gratitude."

That reminded me. "Did you ever find out how Mr. Bettencourt disappeared? I mean, what actually happened that day?"

Ethan shook his head. "It's still being investigated, and unfortunately, we can't share what little we've heard. I can tell you that Mrs. Quinones is blaming herself. She is inconsolable, recognizing the danger and how lucky she is that her father was returned safe and sound." He glanced at the pen in my hand. "Which is why she wanted to do this for you."

"That's very thoughtful," I said, smiling up at him. Not knowing what else to say, I added, "I love it."

Cyan had sidled up next to me. "What a perfect gift, Ollie. You're always digging for a pen to scribble notes. Now you have your own. One that nobody's going to borrow."

Ethan gave me a quizzical look. "Ollie? Is

that a nickname?"

"That's what everyone calls me."

"Ollie," he repeated. "I like that."

Cyan nudged me. Like I couldn't read her mind.

"Thank you very much," I said in an effort to end the conversation and get back to work. "I'm very touched. I will be sure to send Secretary Quinones and his wife a thank-you note."

"There's no need for you to thank them," Ethan said, "but if you insist . . ."

"I do."

"You can send it care of the secretary's office." He pulled out a business card. "That's my card, and my phone number. The address is the secretary of state's office." Pointing, he added, "That's my personal cell phone number, too. In case you have any questions, or anything."

Another nudge from Cyan.

"Thanks," I said again. "If I have any questions, I'll be sure to contact you."

"I'd like that."

He smiled again, shook my hand again. Said how nice it was to meet all of us, and was finally gone.

"Oo-ooh," Cyan sing-songed the moment he left, "Ethan likes Ollie."

"He does not," I said.

Bucky scratched his head. "He was certainly flirting with you. Of course, the last thing you need right now is another 'connected' boyfriend."

"Yeah." I returned the pen to its box and put it in the drawer by the kitchen's computer.

"You're not going to just tuck it away, are you?" Cyan asked.

"I'm afraid it will get all sticky and gloppy if I use it. This isn't exactly a tidy environment, you know."

"Take it home, then," she said. "Just think how cool it is to have something like that. Kind of like a trophy. You should have quite a collection by now, except I bet you didn't save a single thing from any of your other adventures."

I thought about that. I had managed to amass a few precious items over the years: a copy of a competitor's video that helped me win the job of executive chef, a fake bomb that Gav had used to instruct me on recognizing such devices, one of the commemorative wooden eggs handed out at the Campbells' last Easter Egg Roll, and a handmade thank-you note from the Hydens' son, Joshua. "Good idea, Cyan," I said, "but maybe instead of hiding this one away, I'll actually use it. After all, this wasn't really all that much of an adventure. I didn't really face any danger this time."

"Well then, maybe this one is a lucky charm."

CHAPTER 14

Virgil was in an uncharacteristically chipper mood when he returned the next morning. Because the president was already in the West Wing, Virgil was using our kitchen to prepare breakfast instead of doing so upstairs. What was most unusual was the fact that as he worked he whistled. The noise was shrill, the tune unrecognizable. Too bad it was Cyan's day off. She'd be surprised to see the chef in such good spirits, especially after last night's confrontation. A happy demeanor from him was a rare occurrence in this kitchen. I wasn't about to do anything to spoil it.

Bucky apparently held no such compunction. He glared at him from across the room. "What is that ridiculous noise?"

"Don't you recognize it?" Virgil asked with affected innocence. "It's 'Leavin' on a Jet Plane.'"

"Sounds more like the *Howdy Doody* theme."

"The what?"

Bucky turned his back. "Never mind."

"Want to know why that song is in my head?"

"No."

Leave it to Bucky to deliver total honesty.

"Why, Virgil?" I asked.

Bucky twisted around to glare at me.

I glared back. Taking the high road never hurt anybody. Did it?

"I *am* leaving on a jet plane. This afternoon." Virgil wiggled one hand. "Well, not exactly a plane. I'll be on a helicopter."

"Today?" I asked. "You haven't cleared any time off with me."

A butler arrived to accept the freshly plated breakfast. "Thank you, my good man," Virgil said to him as he returned to the countertop to clear his work area. "That's the beauty of this. I'm not taking any personal time. I'm off to Camp David to cook for Mrs. Hyden and the kids." He tossed a drippy whisk into the sink, and spun to face us. "Now that I'm finished with breakfast, I'm out of here. Have to get home and pack a bag, you know."

Anger bubbled up. "Exactly when was this decided?"

"Doug and I had a little powwow," he said as though that explained everything. "I think I'm going to like him better than I did Paul."

I was close enough to Bucky to hear him mutter, "You would."

Untying his apron, Virgil graced us both with a beaming gloat. "I guess I'll see you when I see you."

Bucky waited until he was gone. "He has to be blackmailing Mrs. Hyden. How else do you explain her bringing him on?"

"I just think our newest chef is adept at putting on the right face for the right people. Unfortunately for us, he's going to be alone with her and the kids for as long as this murder investigation continues."

"They don't even have any suspects, do they?" he asked.

"Not that I've heard."

"I wish they'd get moving on that. The sooner the better."

"You and me both." I turned to our computer. "Looks like we're off the hook for lunch. The president will be in meetings all day and the Navy Mess is handling it."

"Leaves us more time to work on the birthday party planning."

"So let's get to it."

Bent over the countertop, where we'd

strewn far more papers than we needed, Bucky and I were deep in discussion as to whether we should serve a version of beef Wellington when Peter Everett Sargeant popped in. "Ms. Paras," he said, "do you have a moment?" I looked up to see him gesture. "I'll be out in the hall."

Bucky stared after him. "Did he actually say 'Ms. Paras, do you have a moment?' When did Sargeant get so polite?"

I straightened and stretched. "He wants that favor, remember?"

"You didn't try to fix things for him, did you?"

"Not yet."

"Ollie, don't. Whatever trouble he's gotten himself into, he probably deserves it. Would he lift a finger to help you if you asked?"

"You may be right."

"I am right." With a stern look, he added, "Don't mess up this chance. If he gets himself into deep enough trouble, we might be rid of him for good."

"Wishful thinking, Buckster."

"Don't blow it."

Sargeant was pacing the hall when I got out there. "Have you talked with that calligrapher Lynn yet?" he asked.

"Peter, we had a dinner to deal with last

night and it's not even lunchtime. Plus, it's Sunday. Chances are she doesn't even work today."

It was as if the thought hadn't even occurred to him. This was not the sensitivity director I knew and despised. His eyes were bloodshot, his breast pocket handkerchief droopy. "What's wrong?" I asked.

"Nothing. Everything. I just wish I could put this issue to bed. But that isn't why I wanted to talk with you."

That was a surprise. "What do you need?"

"I spoke with Milton. I think he was more than a little embarrassed. It took some coaxing, but he did admit to hanging around your apartment two nights ago."

"He did?"

"My lowlife nephew admitted to creeping around your apartment. Doesn't that bother you?"

"Not as much as it would if that guy who followed me on the subway was shadowing me. Milton is harmless, isn't he?"

Sargeant's lips were set in a thin line. He breathed deeply through his nose. "To you, yes."

"What did he do to you to make you hate him so much?"

My question clearly took him aback. "I don't hate him."

"You give a mighty fine impression of it."

Whatever he might have been willing to say disappeared as his face closed up. "Will you talk to this Lynn person?" he asked.

"I'll do my best."

His mouth twisted. "Well, that's something, at least."

Back in the kitchen, Bucky pointed upward. "Doug wants to see you the minute you're back."

"What now?"

Bucky shook his head "It's always something."

Doug was on the phone when I knocked at the jamb of his open door. Mouthing, "Just a minute," he indicated I should take a seat. "Count me in. I haven't gone out with you guys in a while," he said into the phone. "Thanks, Wyatt. Talk to you later."

When he hung up, I asked, "Wyatt Becker?"

Doug didn't seem to mind my nosiness. "Yeah. He's getting a group together to go camping. We used to go every few months. Now we're lucky if we make it once a year."

"I didn't know you and Wyatt were friends on the outside."

"Hard to make friends anywhere else when we spend so much time here."

"True enough. You wanted to see me?"

He pulled out a pad of scribbled notes. "It's about Virgil."

"Is he really going to Camp David?"

"I thought it best."

"Why?" I asked. "That's just avoiding the problem. We need to work this out."

"Not until both of you cool down. You can't constantly harass the new guy, Ollie."

"*Me?* If anyone is harassing people, it's Virgil. He's wild, unpredictable, and downright mean to our kitchen assistants. He doesn't need time to regroup. What he needs is to be taught manners. He's not going to learn that up at Camp David."

"It's for the best."

"Just the opposite."

Doug stared at me. "Paul didn't tell me you were this argumentative."

"Paul understood people. He knew how to facilitate cooperation. You could have learned a lot from him."

His eyes narrowed. "What are you saying?"

I had clearly overstepped my boundaries. Quieting the fury roiling in my gut, I stared back. "Paul let me run the kitchen the way I knew best. I came to him with problems if there were any. Virgil needs to respect the chain of command. That's how we've always functioned around here because that's the way it works best. Paul would have told Virgil to try to work things out with me first. If that didn't resolve the issue, Paul would have set up a meeting with the three of us to talk things out."

Something behind Doug's eyes shifted. I recognized it. He knew I was right. The question was, would he admit it so we could move forward, or would he dig in his heels and refuse to back down?

"I'm not going to tell him he can't go," he said finally.

"I think that's a mistake."

Doug's eyes went flat. "Thank you for stopping by, Ollie."

My hands worked themselves into fists as I made my way back to the kitchen. Bucky looked up as I walked in, and took a step back. "Whoa. What happened?"

I didn't often lose my temper. At the moment, I wasn't out of control, but I was having a hard time keeping a handle on my emotions. "Can't we ever catch a break around here?"

Bucky didn't say a word.

"Our job is to work as a team to prepare all the White House meals, right?"

He nodded, looking afraid.

"So then why, I ask, do we need a chef dedicated to handling the First Family's daily meals? On his own? That is detrimental to the team spirit, if you ask me. Of course," I grumbled, "no one's asking me. But fine. I could have dealt with Virgil if Doug had stayed out of this mess. But no." I shook a finger. "Paul wouldn't have interfered."

Bucky still didn't interrupt.

I took a breath. "Virgil's going up to Camp David, with Doug's blessing. How does that look? Like we both said — you know that Virgil has the First Lady's ear."

"You've got some capital with her, too, you know. Especially after Virgil bailed when Josh was in danger."

"Yeah." Bucky was right about that, but I didn't want to stop. I needed to keep up my tirade. I needed to vent.

"Doug's just new in the job," he said. "He's bound to make mistakes."

"Are you trying to make me less angry?"

Bucky smiled. "Is it working?"

"No," I said. "Yes."

"We'll get through this, Ollie. We always do."

"Yeah." I wasn't convinced.

"At the risk of sending you into another downward spiral — what did Sargeant want?"

"Actually, Sargeant brought good news."

"There's a first time for everything."

"I told you about his nephew, Milton. It seems as though he's been loitering around my apartment the past couple days."

"And that's good news?"

"Better him than whoever killed Cawley and Woodruff."

Bucky grimaced. "Good point."

"That reminds me," I said, picking up the phone. "I need to see if the Secret Service is willing to call off the guard."

I left a message for Tom to call me at his earliest convenience. I didn't want to be a bother, but I also didn't want to have to deal with the Secret Service watching my every coming and going.

Bucky and I worked side by side. As cranky as Bucky could be, he was silent most of the time and I preferred a calm, quiet kitchen over one with a raging lunatic chef ordering everyone around. As soon as Virgil got back, he and I were going to have a chat. Before then, I just needed to figure out exactly what I wanted to say and the optimal way to word it.

After about an hour of mulling and after multiple rehashings of my conversation with Doug, I asked Bucky, "Do you know Wyatt Becker, the social aide?"

He shook his head. "Should I?"

"He's been here enough. You've probably seen him."

We worked a little longer.

"Was there a reason you wanted to know?" Bucky asked.

"Oh, yeah," I said, half surprised by the question. "I just . . ."

He waited.

"You'll keep this confidential?"

Bucky cocked one eyebrow, as if to say, "Don't I always?"

"Sargeant and I have been working with Wyatt Becker."

"From the look on your face, I take it you don't much care for the guy."

"That obvious, huh?" I asked. "I met him once, and my impression is that he's the worst kind of wimp."

"There are levels of wimp?"

"Wimps can be pleasant enough, given the right circumstances. But this one is totally stuck on himself."

Bucky nodded. "Okay, got it. What does he have to do with you?"

"He's been assigned to help me and Sargeant work on this event. But I can't stand the guy."

"You?" Bucky said, bringing his hands to his chest, "Be still my heart. Except for

Sargeant and Virgil, I thought you liked everybody."

Gracing him with a mock withering glare, I went on, "There's something so smug about this guy. He keeps telling us about how he saved the day here, or prevented calamity there. But all he does is sneak around, promise what he can't deliver, then hide out of sight until the storm passes."

"Maybe he's been taking lessons from Sargeant."

I laughed. "Good one. Big difference, though. At least with Sargeant you know exactly where you stand. He has no compunction letting me know he can't tolerate me. I'm able to deal with that. It's real. It's tangible. This may sound weird, but with Sargeant there's no pressure. Nothing I do for him will ever change his opinion of me, so I don't worry about it."

"Sounds like you're going soft on him."

"Maybe I am."

"Don't let the wimps and bullies get to you," he said. "I've been around this place a long time. I've seen people come and go. Sure, there are exceptions, but for the most part, those of us who put our heads down and do our jobs well are recognized. Those that don't are found out soon enough."

"I hope you're right."

"Yeah," he chuckled. "Except that doesn't apply to you."

"What do you mean?"

"You never keep your head down."

"Ha-ha."

The phone rang next to me and I picked it up. "Ollie, it's Tom. Got your message. I'd rather do this in person," he said. "Can you stop by my office in about ten minutes?"

I looked at my watch. "I'll be right there."

When I hung up, Bucky said, "Uh-oh."

"What?"

"From the look on your face and the tone of your voice, I'm worried."

"Don't be." I pulled out my pen and began writing a few notes. "Just a quick trip over to Secret Service. I have no idea how long I'll be, but here are a few ideas I wanted to talk with you about regarding the party. Given how today is already scattering, I'm afraid if I wait much longer, I'll forget something."

"You're using your new pen. Any particular reason?"

I looked at him, deadpan. "To write with?"

"Or because it reminds you of Ethan Nagy's visit here? Cyan is convinced he wants you to call him."

"Cyan's got stars in her eyes." I held up the pen. "This is a nice remembrance of doing a good deed. They didn't need to give me anything, but I take my positives wherever I can."

"So you're not interested in Nagy?"

"Why, are *you* trying to set me up now?"

He gave me a shrewd look. "Not if you're already seeing someone."

I felt the blush rise to my cheeks.

He grinned. "I knew it."

"I don't know what you're talking about, but I need to get over to Secret Service, pronto."

"I'll hold down the fort."

I started off but stopped at the doorway. "Not that it matters," I said, feeling lame even as I asked, "but who exactly do you think I'm seeing?"

Bucky smiled enigmatically. "Get going. You don't want to be late."

There was no way Bucky knew about Gav. No possible way. As I made my way to the Secret Service office in the West Wing, I argued with myself. Gav and I had something, clearly, but we hadn't yet defined exactly what that was. A tight friendship? Something more? And who the heck said it needed to be defined immediately anyway?

The only thing stopping us at this point was his reluctance to move forward. Based on what he'd told me about his two prior relationships, I understood his fears completely. But I didn't know what I could do to help him see that what we had was different. That he wasn't a jinx.

Tom was waiting for me. "Come on in," he said, "and shut the door."

I complied and sat down.

"If I get this straight, you want us to cut your Secret Service detail, correct?"

"That's it in a nutshell. Mrs. Wentworth, my neighbor —"

"I remember Mrs. Wentworth."

I felt the blush creep up again. Of course he did. "She saw someone hanging around my apartment."

"I know."

"I found out it was Milton Folgate, Peter Sargeant's nephew."

The look on Tom's face would have been comical in a different circumstance. "I heard he showed up yesterday morning to talk with you. What's going on here, Ollie? Why is he bothering you?"

"Mostly he just wants a job at the White House, and he thinks I have some pull."

"Hello? Reality check. You don't get hired by the White House when you're caught stalking the staff."

"Yeah, well . . . He also wanted to share that information about the double murder."

Tom looked at me. "What information?"

"I talked with one of your agents here yesterday," I said, then explained about the guy who had bumped into Sargeant that morning, and about Milton shouting after him.

Tom nodded. "I remember that from your statement. But no one here said anything about this yesterday. Go on."

There had been a lot of bad press over the past few months about mishandlings by the Secret Service, and I wondered now how much of that was based in fact. Tom should have been apprised immediately. "Milton swears he saw him again. With another guy. When I asked him to describe this other fellow, it sounded a lot like Brad, who'd followed me on the Metro."

Tom blew out a breath as he wrote a note on the pad next to him. "Why is it always —"

"Me?" I shook a finger at him. "Don't say it."

He looked up. "Fair enough. Is that it?"

"The two guys met a third guy."

"Description?"

"Not much. Just that Milton knows he works for the government. Unfortunately, he can't remember where he's seen him before."

"That's not much, but every little bit helps. He told you all this yesterday?"

"Yeah, but he'd been drinking. I could smell it on him. I can't promise that anything he said is worth anything."

"Probably not."

"So," I asked, "since it was Milton hanging around my place, can we dispense with the armed escort?"

"I'll consider it."

My face must have fallen because he added, "I can't make that decision right here and now without giving it careful consideration. There's no doubt in my mind that whoever Brad was, he was somehow involved in the murders and possibly also in Mr. Bettencourt's disappearance. If this Milton fellow is right and Brad is connected with your 'bump guy' from the day of the murder . . ." Tom stopped, looked up and closed his eyes. "I'm starting to sound like you. We don't have any evidence that the bump guy is in any way connected, yet I'm starting to see conspiracies."

"If Milton saw him with Brad, that's something."

"You said that you never got a clear look at the bump guy's face and that you didn't believe Sargeant or Milton did either. How can he be so sure he's seeing the same person now?"

"Good point. No idea."

"Everybody wants to help the Secret Service."

"Take it as a compliment."

"Not when they think we're falling on our faces."

I stood up. "You'll let me know?"

"Yeah," he said.

Just as I got to the door, he said, "Ollie . . ."

I turned.

Tom played with the pen in his hand. He readjusted himself in his seat. "Are you and Special Agent Gavin . . ." He spread his hands in question.

I had no idea how to respond to that. Of all the people in the world, Tom deserved a straight answer, but I didn't have one to give. I hesitated.

"You can tell me it's none of my business," he said.

"No, it's not that." I searched for the right words. "It's just . . ."

He waited.

"The truth is, I don't know," I said. I didn't want to be disloyal to Gav by sharing personal information, but there was precious little to share and this much, I was sure, would be fair game. "He's a friend."

Tom stared down at the pen again. "He's a good man, Ollie."

"He says the same thing about you."

Tom gave me a sad smile.

"The thing is . . ." I wrapped my fingers around the doorknob. ". . . you're both right."

CHAPTER 15

With no word from Tom, I was still under Agent Scorroco's conversation-less guard on the way home. Just as I was about to alight, however, he said, "I won't be here tomorrow."

"Day off?" I asked.

"No, ma'am. The Secret Service has eliminated the need for your coverage."

"This is it, then? I'm done?"

"That's what I've been told, ma'am."

"Nobody told me."

"I'm telling you."

"Yes, of course. Thank you."

He gave a brief nod and pulled away the moment I shut the passenger door. "Well, wasn't that fun?" I said aloud. Delighted to be on my own, I grabbed my cell phone and dialed Gav. He answered right away.

"Hey," I said, "guess what?"

"You no longer require an armed escort to and from work?"

"It's hard to be mysterious around you."

He laughed. "What's up?"

"It's a Sunday night, I'm free as a bird, and I'd love to cook you dinner. What do you say?"

He hesitated. "Tell you what: Let me *take you* to dinner. Somewhere near your place."

We agreed to meet at a seafood restaurant about a mile or so from my building. An easy walk on a spring evening. I had about an hour to get ready, so I immediately dashed into the shower. I usually wore my shoulder-length hair in a ponytail to keep it out of my face, but tonight I expended a little effort with the blow dryer and a styling brush to add bounce. When I was finished, I picked up the curling iron and gave myself a critical glance.

I kind of liked the sleek look. It was younger, more fun. Okay, I thought, done with the hair. Next, makeup. Except for mascara, I generally went to the White House each day wearing nothing on my face except moisturizer and sunscreen. Tonight I added a little eyeliner, dusted on some mineral powder and even a little blush. I decided to wear my favorite black pants, a new fuchsia top I'd recently picked up, and silver earrings. A last look in the mirror and I was quite pleased. Best of all, I was done with plenty of time to spare.

I hoped to get to the restaurant before Gav did. He'd offered to pick me up, but I knew he'd be coming from work — possibly running late — and now that I was out from under the watchful eye of the Secret Service, I craved being outdoors by myself. Plus, it wouldn't be dark for at least another half hour.

I pushed through the restaurant's revolving doors into the dimly lit bar area. Fairly quiet in here tonight, there were three couples at high tables and a group of men chatting amiably at the bar. I glanced around, but didn't see Gav.

"Hey," he said from behind me.

I spun. "You scared me."

"Good. That'll teach you to be more observant." He stepped back. "You look wonderful."

His words warmed me from my head to my toes. "Thank you."

"Come on," he said, "our table is waiting."

As we were seated, the hostess handed us menus and told us our waitress would be with us momentarily. "I'm off duty tonight," Gav said, as he perused the wine list. "Would you like to share a bottle?"

Surprised, I was nonetheless pleased.

"Absolutely. What did you have in mind?"

He studied the wine list as I studied him. There were tiny crow's-feet at the corners of his eyes, and the brackets around his mouth had deepened since we'd first met. But he was a very handsome man. Tall, distinguished looking. Smart, too. I felt a little flutter in my heart as I took him in. So serious. Even about picking the right wine.

When he looked up, he didn't seem surprised to catch me watching. Instead, he smiled, and the flutter in my heart beat a little faster.

"You know wines?" I asked.

"A bit. I have a couple of favorites. I can't always find them."

The waitress came by to recite the evening's specials and ask us about drinks. Gav ordered a vintage that seemed to impress the waitress. She pointed to the wine list. "This one, right?" she asked as though she wanted to make sure.

When the waitress brought it and went through the customary showing, offering, pouring, Gav smiled his approval. "You're in for a treat," he said to me.

The moment she left, he lifted his glass. "To . . . first dates?" he asked. "This is actually our first real date, isn't it?"

My stomach was now in the midst of full-out flip-flops. "First dates. I like that," I said as our glasses clinked. "Although I feel as if I've known you forever."

"If anyone would have told me I'd be here, clinking glasses with that little upstart from the kitchen . . ." He let the thought hang, but he was smiling as he sipped his wine.

I sipped, too. "Oh," I said as I savored the taste, "that's wonderful."

"One of my favorite whites," he said. "I'm usually more of a red man."

"I thought you might be."

"Did you, now?" He placed his glass down and set his elbows on the table. "Are those your superior deductive skills at work?"

"You know it." I took another sip. "This really is an extraordinary wine."

"I'm glad you like it."

"What I like," I said softly, "is being here with you."

"I want to talk about that," he said.

I put my glass down.

The waitress took that as a signal. "Are you ready?" she asked.

"I don't think he is." I shot a meaningful look at Gav that had nothing to do with ordering food.

"I'll give you a few minutes, then."

Gav gave me a shrewd stare. "Still the

smart aleck, aren't you?"

"You bring out the best in me."

"Do I?" He placed his menu on his lap and leaned forward. "Or . . ." he hesitated, "am I making things worse?"

"What?" I said too loudly.

He shushed me.

"What can you possibly mean by that?" I asked.

"I'm older than you are."

"So?" I said, then added, "Not by much."

"I've been single a long time."

I tried reading the look in his eyes, but I was coming up short. "And you don't want to give that up?"

He laughed, but it was a sad laugh. "Hardly."

"It's me, then."

"You know it's not you, Ollie."

My menu was open in front of me, I leaned forward, too, pressing it to my chest. "That's exactly the problem."

I could tell I'd confused him.

I sighed. "Whatever is stopping you from moving forward *should* be about me. If it isn't, then why not? If you really wanted to be with me, if you wanted this to be a relationship instead of just a first date, you would." I leaned back and pretended to read the menu. "It's that simple." So attuned to

Gav, his mood, whatever he was about to say next, I had no idea whether I was looking at appetizers or entrées.

"It's not that I don't want to be with you."

I looked up. "When I really want something, nothing can stop me."

"I know that."

"But?" I went back to reading the menu. Still not seeing it. "There's a 'but' hanging there. What is it?"

"You scare me."

That caught my attention. I glanced up. The look on his face said he wasn't making a joke.

"You are like no one I've ever known before. Willing to stick your neck out — sometimes quite literally — for the greater good. You're brave, strong, upbeat."

"There's something wrong with that?"

"Ollie." He said it so softly it made the hairs stand up on my arms. "You know better."

I wasn't angry and I didn't want him to misconstrue. "I told you I'd be patient. I don't intend to go back on my word."

The waitress reappeared. "Ready?"

Gav handed her the menu but held his hand out to me. "Ladies first."

"Uh . . ." Caught unawares, I quickly scanned the menu. "I'll have the trout."

Made with cannellini beans, garlic, sun-dried tomatoes, and arugula, it sounded like an interesting combination.

"The swordfish special for me," Gav said, "but could you substitute another vegetable for the asparagus?"

"Brussels sprouts or spinach?" she asked.

"Brussels sprouts, thanks."

"You don't like asparagus?" I asked when she left.

He made a face. "Had it once as a kid. Never recovered."

"You've never tasted my asparagus."

"That's true enough."

"I bet I could make a believer out of you."

"I'd like to try." His eyes grew serious. "Now, what were you saying about not going back on your word?"

"Gav." I played with my wineglass. "You need to understand something: I want to wait for you. I'm happy to do it."

"Then what is it?"

How could I feel this much emotion for this man when we'd both just agreed this was our first date? I could feel how right we were together. How good. But there was one major stumbling block.

"You."

"I don't —"

"There's something else holding you back,

260

Gav." I paused, hoping he'd jump in and deny, but he simply waited for me to continue. "It isn't just you believing yourself to be a jinx to people you care about. There's more. I think we have something special here, but I'm wondering if you really *want* to move forward. If maybe you're having second thoughts."

He was silent for a long moment. Too long. My words had touched a nerve. I could see it in the way he blinked, looked away, then tried to smile.

"Deductive skills, Ollie. You really should have considered a job with the bureau."

The tone was light, but his words cut me. I tried to mask my reaction by taking another sip of the wine.

He asked, "What do you want from me right now?"

"Honesty."

His mouth curled in a way that told me he knew I'd say that. "Then you will have honesty. But not here. Not now. Let's talk the way we usually do. Like friends. Like colleagues. Like brothers in arms. Tell me what's new. What's going on. Then later we'll talk about us."

"Later as in tonight? Or later as in a year from now?"

"Tonight. I promise we'll talk. I'm uncomfortable having this discussion in the middle of a restaurant."

I sat back, but my stomach had other ideas. Dinner, no matter how tasty, would be wasted on me tonight. What did he have to share that couldn't be discussed here? "Okay."

"Now, how's the kitchen? Anything new?"

Without veering into a discussion that could compromise the Hydens in any way, I told him about Virgil's most recent meltdown. "Doug doesn't seem to have a handle on the position the way Paul did," I said. "He sent Virgil off to . . ." I couldn't very well say "Camp David," so I used the escape's former name. ". . . Shangri-La to let him cool down. That's hardly an effective way to deal with the problem."

We stopped talking when our food arrived, but jumped right back in the moment the waitress was gone. Shop talk had calmed me enough to appreciate the steaming trout on my plate. "This smells heavenly."

"I'm not impressed with Doug," he said. "He's got a long way to go."

"How much rope will they give him? Any idea?"

Gav sliced off a bite of his swordfish. "I'm not always privy to staffing information."

"Only when it involves security?"

"Something like that."

"Since this is our official first date," I said, "I guess we should try to get to know each other better."

Gav's mouth twitched. "What do you want to know?"

"For starters, where did you grow up?"

"Foster homes, mostly."

I'd expected him to name a city, or a state, even a region. I hadn't expected that. Rendered speechless, I didn't know how to follow up.

"I've made you uncomfortable."

"I just don't know what to say next," I said. "I'd love to know why you were in foster homes and anything else you care to tell me, but I don't want to pry."

He almost smiled at that. "Come on. My Ollie always wants to pry."

His Ollie? I liked the sound of that. The trout on my plate suddenly tasted a whole lot better. "Okay. Tell me everything."

"An abridged version tonight, is that okay?" He shrugged as though his story was of no consequence. "I was three when my mother left me with the babysitter and never came back." He waved his fork, "Yes, Doctor Freud. Tie that in with what you already know, and I do have issues with the important women in my life leaving me."

"I wasn't going to say . . ."

"You didn't have to. Your face gives you away. As a detective, you'd be great. As a spy . . ." He frowned. "Not so much."

"Thanks."

"Where was I? Oh yes. I got thrown into the system pretty young, but I got lucky. Most of the foster homes I lived in were good ones."

"Most?"

He shifted his shoulders as he cut another piece of fish, but instead of bringing it to his mouth, he stared at it. "The last one was rough. Fortunately I didn't have to stay long. The day I turned eighteen I joined the military. Did my stint there, got out, got my degree, had a life for a while . . ."

He didn't have to expand on that part. I remembered.

". . . and eventually started working for the government."

I'd stopped eating to listen.

"That's the short version. I can't imagine you ever wanting to hear the long one. But if you're asking about where I grew up geographically, I'm a Midwestern kid, just like you. Born just a little farther south. Indianapolis." He popped a bite of fish into his mouth.

"I didn't know that about you."

"About the foster homes? Not too many people do. No reason to tell anyone. People make assessments. Judgments based on what they think they can deduce. Unfortunately, many of them are right."

"That's why you didn't tell me?"

"I just did." His gaze softened. "Of everyone I've ever met, you're the least likely to judge a book by its cover or a person by their upbringing. You see things clearly the way they are. I admire that about you." Focusing on his plate, he speared a brussels sprout and turned the tables on me. "I know you're from Chicago and that your mom and grandmother raised you, but what about your dad?"

"That's kind of a big story, too."

"If you don't want to talk about it —"

"No, no. That's not it. I do." I smiled up at him. "My dad, Anthony Paras, is buried in Arlington."

Gav's eyebrows came together. He started to reach for my hand, but stopped himself. "I'm sorry."

"It's okay. He died when I was very young. My mom never really told me how. Just that he died in service to our country."

"No specifics?"

"None."

"I'm surprised you haven't dug deeper."

I took another sip of wine, admitting to him what I hadn't told anyone else. "I know there's more to the story. I also know that I've made enough friends around Washington, D.C., that I might be able to find out if I tried hard enough."

"So what's stopping you?"

"My mom always gets this funny look on her face whenever I bring up Dad's death."

"I'm surprised that hasn't made you more curious."

"Are you kidding?" I asked. "I'm crazy curious. But my mom doesn't want me to dig."

"Have you ever asked her why?"

I swirled my wineglass. "You've never seen the look."

"That's hard for you, isn't it?"

I didn't answer. I just nodded.

"You're a good person, Ollie."

I glanced up to see him looking at me with a sad expression.

As the waitress cleared our plates, she asked if we wanted dessert. "No, thanks," I said, then asked Gav, "You?"

"Maybe next time." The minute she left, he whispered, "I have a bit of a sweet tooth."

"You should be hanging around with our pastry chef, Marcel."

He gave me a wry smile. "He's not my type."

Out in the parking lot, I looked for a government-issue car. Couldn't find one. Gav pointed and clicked his remote and a car in the next aisle beeped hello. "You really are off duty," I said as we made our way toward it.

"I don't have to be back until Tuesday."

"Must be nice."

"There's probably no chance of you getting tomorrow off, is there?"

For a half second, I considered it. I had no idea what Gav had planned, but it didn't matter. I wanted to spend more time with him. Growing up, I could tell a boy liked me if his eyes sparkled. And right now Gav was looking at me exactly the way I'd been wishing he would.

"Tomorrow?" I repeated weakly, wishing for one wild moment that I could throw off my responsibilities and just run with it. Just for a day. But one of the things that tied us together was our dedication to duty. "With Virgil at Camp David and meetings for the secretary of state's birthday party on my agenda, there's no chance."

"Figured. But worth a try."

We'd arrived next to a silver Honda Civic. "This yours?"

"Flashy, huh?" he asked as he held the door open for me.

I slid into the passenger seat. "It's nice. If you drove a Corvette, I might be worried."

"Nothing wrong with Corvettes," he said. "Lots of my friends drive them." He held the door for a moment. "Just not *my* style."

When he shut the door, I whispered, "I'm glad."

He got in and started the car up. "Straight home?"

I was eager to have the talk he'd promised. "Sounds good."

He eased the car out of the space. "I get the impression you're pleased to have lost your Secret Service detail."

"You know it," I said. "The minute I found out it was Milton — Sargeant's nephew — shadowing me, I asked to have them released."

"I'm not thrilled, you understand. I think they should have kept you under guard until all of this is over." He turned toward the exit. "What did Milton want?"

I told him about the man's assertions that he'd seen Brad and bump guy together and that he'd also seen them in the company of an unnamed government official. "The thing is," I said now that I'd had a chance to mull this over, "if he's right and bump guy is tied to the murders and we know Brad is tied to Bettencourt, then does that mean that the murders are connected to Quinones? Could he be in danger?"

Gav gave me a sharp look. "Geez, Ollie."

I didn't understand. "Are you angry?"

He stared ahead, then pulled over to the side of the road. Why did I seem to always have this effect on the men in my life? But when Gav looked at me, it was very different from Tom's reaction. "We've been getting reports that suggest that Secretary of State Quinones may very well be in danger. These reports came through reliable, but secure — very secure — sources. How does information like this just happen to fall into your lap?"

"I don't know."

"I wish I had your gift."

I laughed. Not happily. "We've had this conversation, remember?" I thought back to when I first realized Gav had faith in me. "Hardly a gift. Feels more like a curse."

"Can we get some of that to rub off on me?" Even in the darkened car, I could see his face color. "Sorry, that came out wrong."

This time I laughed for real.

He pulled back into the light Sunday evening traffic. "So what happens now?" I asked.

"You'll probably hear Quinones on TV in the next day or so. He's been instructed to make a big deal about how he's received death threats . . ."

"Has he?"

"No," Gav said. "Nothing quite so obvious. The intelligence we've gathered suggests he's a target, but we don't know exactly who is after him. Your friends Brad and bump guy are undoubtedly working for a higher up."

"Foreign power?"

"Hard to say. Quinones will address the media soon to let them know about his new protective detail. We're hoping that not only stalls whatever they may be planning, but also buys us time to find out who they are."

"And you think that whoever killed Chief of Staff Cawley and Patty Woodruff is now aiming for Quinones?"

"We do. I know you said you didn't see bump guy's face, but I'd like to have you take another look at mug shots to find Brad."

"You know I did that already at the police station. Came up empty."

"We have additional photos the police don't. People we're watching but who may not have criminal records. Yet."

"Like . . . spies?"

"You should still be guarded," he said, not answering the question. "Even if bump guy doesn't know who you are, it's clear Brad does."

"But he doesn't know where I live."

Gav took his eyes off the road long enough to give me a hard stare. "You think that will stop him?"

I didn't like the way this conversation was going. "I'm sure I'll be fine."

Gav turned into the parking lot and found a spot near the back. He shut off the car. "Time to talk."

My heart trilled a weird beat, but I unlocked my seat belt and nodded. "Want to come up? No more guard on duty, remember? The coast is clear."

"I don't know . . ."

"It's going to get chilly in here soon and if we do a lot of talking, we're going to fog up the windows. How would that look?"

He smiled. "You can be very convincing."

CHAPTER 16

We walked to the front door, past James snoozing at the front desk. "Not much of a guard," Gav whispered.

"I know. But he's such a sweetheart and truly loves his job. It's not like we get a lot of excitement around here."

Gav's eyebrows shot up.

"Okay," I amended, "we get some."

We rode the elevator in silence. Gav studied the digital readout as we made our way up. I wondered what he was thinking.

When we arrived at my floor, the first thing I noticed was that Mrs. Wentworth's door was shut. I was about to comment, when I noticed something else. Mine wasn't.

I started to point, but Gav was already pushing me behind him. He reached under his jacket and slid out his gun, creeping forward. Silently, he signaled for me to move far, far back in the hall. I knew not to make a sound, so I mouthed, "Be careful," to his back.

He nudged the door open wider, leading the way with his semi-automatic. He didn't call out the way police do on TV shows. Instead he surveyed what he could see carefully, then disappeared inside.

I'd been holding my breath, but it wasn't until little sparkles began to dance in front of my eyes that I realized it. Keeping as quiet as I could, I waited, listening for any sound, any hint of what was going on inside. But all I heard were the creaks and groans that my building normally made and the breathing I tried hard to keep silent.

A glance at my watch told me nothing. It felt as though he'd been in there for twenty minutes, but in truth it couldn't have been more than two. I waited, growing more impatient by the second, reassuring myself that nothing was wrong. That I'd forgotten to lock up before I left.

But I knew better.

In my gut I knew it couldn't have been Milton. He'd had his say, and I knew he wouldn't come sneaking around again. More to the point, he wouldn't have broken in.

My gaze traveled again to Mrs. Wentworth's door. Still shut. Usually when she heard the ding of the elevator, she cracked it open to peer out. Had someone come by to break into my apartment? Had she seen the person? Had he hurt her?

Torn between not wanting to make noise and needing to find out if Mrs. Wentworth was okay, I started for her door.

"Ollie." Gav didn't whisper. He'd reappeared in my doorway with a grave look on his face. "You better come take a look."

"Let me check on Mrs. Wentworth first," I said. "She should have popped out by now."

I watched Gav's realization dawn. He started toward me. "Let me do it."

Behind us, the elevator whirred to life. It was a noise I barely ever noticed, but tonight in the tense quiet, the machinery humming was ominous. Loud.

"Get behind me," Gav said again.

"It could be going to another floor."

He grabbed my arm and in four long strides was next to the elevator doors, pushing me to stand behind him, holding me back with one hand. In the other, his gun was low, but ready.

"Be careful," I whispered.

He didn't answer. He didn't move. I could practically feel the tension vibrating off his taut body.

Again, I held my breath.

The whirring continued, then stopped as

the elevator dinged its arrival. On my floor. "Shh," Gav said softly, barely breathing the sound. Like I would have moved.

The hand that had been protectively holding me back dropped to his side, then came up in a double-grip on his gun just as the elevator doors opened. He flattened himself against the wall, waiting for the intruder to alight.

Mrs. Wentworth and Stan nearly jumped out of their skins when they saw the two of us skulking there. "Heavens!" Mrs. Wentworth exclaimed. "What on earth are you doing there?"

Gav surreptitiously slid his gun under his jacket. "My apologies," he said.

Instant relief for me. Not so much for the elderly couple. "Mrs. Wentworth! Are you all right?" I asked, moving toward her.

It took her less than a heartbeat to assess the situation. "What's going on?" she demanded.

Stan held Mrs. Wentworth's arm, pulling her close. All the blood had drained from his face. "What happened?" he asked, looking from me to Gav and back.

"I do apologize," Gav said. "Let's get you into your apartment."

Mrs. Wentworth gave him the eagle eye. "Not until you tell us why you felt the need to scare the daylights out of two old people coming back from a date."

Gav knew as well as I did that it was useless to argue with her. "Ollie's apartment was broken into this evening."

Her hand came up to her throat. "You weren't home, were you?" Before I could answer, she asked, "Was it a robbery?" To Gav, "Or something more up your alley?"

"I don't know what you mean," he said as he guided them both to Mrs. Wentworth's apartment. "Ollie hasn't gone in yet, and I want her to take a look before we call the police. Can you sit tight for a while? We'll come let you know when it's clear."

Grudgingly they allowed themselves to be safely tucked away.

"Come on," Gav said as we pushed through the door, "take a look."

For the second time in as many days, I wandered through my own home in the wake of a potential break-in. At first glance nothing looked out of place. I made my way into the living room, then the kitchen, looking for signs of a robbery. Maybe I'd watched too many TV shows, but I expected my sofa cushions to be sliced open and tossed on the floor, the kitchen chairs to be upended, and every drawer pulled out. But the place looked completely normal.

"Maybe I left the door unlocked?" I said.

Gav motioned for me to follow him. "I'm sorry for invading your privacy, but I had to look in here."

"Here" was my bedroom. Almost as I'd left it. Almost.

"I never leave my drawers open," I said, walking over to them and peering in. Nothing seemed to be missing but the fact that a stranger had been pawing through my underwear gave me a sick feeling of violation. I swallowed as I poked around. The little bit of jewelry I owned was still exactly where I'd left it. "I can't tell for sure, but I don't think anything is missing."

"What about in here?" Gav stood in the hallway, ever reluctant to invade my space. I followed him into the second bedroom.

"Oh," I said, "they can't have taken that."

Gav waited.

I indicated the only clear and dust-free spot on my desk. "My computer. It was old — like, should have been replaced five years ago old. It's clunky, slow, and can't be worth much, even for parts." My voice rose, as though explaining its lack of worth would somehow magically bring it back. "Why would anybody steal it?" Ripped away from its printer and monitor, my trusty desktop tower was glaringly absent. I stepped closer to my desk. Whoever had taken it had also taken all my notes and papers. I tended to leave my desk area messy, with piles of to-dos and have-dones that I cleared out about twice a year. My last purge must have been at least four months ago.

"Maybe it wasn't the computer. Maybe it's what's on it."

I made a circle of the room, fighting anger against an unknown enemy. I wanted to lash out, to grab whomever it was and demand they return my property — now.

"Do you think it was that Brad?"

Gav didn't answer.

"What did they think they were going to get?" I asked, trying to tamp down my growing irritation. "I use it for recipes and e-mail. I'm no big shot with access to classified information. There's nothing particularly confidential about how to prepare spinach, or notes I've made for the secretary of state's birthday party."

Gav waited a moment for me to calm myself before he spoke. "Secretary of State Quinones's birthday party," he said as though thinking aloud. "Did you keep notes about what happened that day when you and Sargeant discovered the murder?"

"Not on the computer. I did jot down a few impressions on paper . . ." I looked around, trying to remember where I'd left them. ". . . and a few about Brad — a description and a loose sketch — after I got home that night. I did that right after you left. Just to jog my memory if the need ever arose." Whoever had taken my computer had taken every scrap of paper around it, too.

"Are they here?"

My shoulders slumped. "Nope. Gone."

Gav didn't comment. "Anything else missing?"

I let out a little squeak of disappointment. "My date book." Frantically, I started opening drawers and rummaging through them. "I keep all my important information in my date book."

"You don't keep your calendar on your cell phone?"

"I keep all the White House dates on my phone and on the computer at work," I said, "but I'm talking about my personal date book. I keep that separate. Call me old-fashioned, but it's nice to be able to open it up and see a week at a glance."

"Think, Ollie. What could the thieves learn from your date book that they don't already know?"

I'd gone through every drawer. Disgusted by the loss, I folded my arms and frowned at the floor. "Not anything important. I have dry-cleaning to pick up. A dentist appointment. An annual physical. Stuff like that. A couple of upcoming local foodie events I thought about attending. Now I'm going to have to call around and try to re-create it all."

Gav was making notes in a book of his own. "Can you remember what you had planned for the upcoming week?"

"Why?"

"Can you?"

"Sure, but I don't understand why you need to know."

"Give me whatever you remember," he said.

That's when I understood. "You think they want to know where I'll be, don't you? You think they're targeting me."

He looked up, eyes clouded with worry. "The idea crossed my mind."

I leaned my back end against the desk's edge. "Oh geez." Outwardly I remained calm, but inside I was seething with fury and no small amount of terror. "I have a backup service for the computer. I can get all my files restored as soon as I have a place to put them."

Gav watched me.

"What do I do?" I asked.

"For starters, you don't circumvent your bodyguard. We're going to get them back here to keep a close watch over you."

That made sense. My stomach felt weak and wobbly; my legs, too. I leaned forward to place my hands on my knees.

Gav stepped closer. "You okay?"

From this lower position, I could see under my printer. Something shiny stared back at me. "Hey, what's that?"

Before Gav could stop me, I reached over and grabbed it.

"Wait —"

"They stole my notes but left my pen," I said, holding up the gift I'd received only the day before. "Probably because it's inscribed. Too easy to trace." I thought about it. "Or they just missed it."

Gav paid no attention to the pen. He was glaring at me. "Have I taught you nothing?" I opened my mouth, but he interrupted. "You must never touch anything suspicious."

"This isn't suspicious, this is my pen."

"Ollie." His voice was a warning. "What do you remember from our discussion in the briefing room?"

He was referring to shortly after we'd first met and I'd been the beneficiary of a one-on-one tutorial on bombs after skipping out on a group lesson.

I smiled up at him. "That I thought you were cute?"

His eyes narrowed, but I could tell he was amused, if only for a moment. "You've just walked into a crime scene," he said. "Everything is suspect. You can't pick things up willy-nilly."

"Willy-nilly?" I parroted, hoping to bring a little levity into the conversation. When he didn't smile this time, I ceded the point. "You're right. Completely. I should have been more careful. I'm actually kind of embarrassed to have made that mistake."

"Are you? Or are you just embarrassed that I caught you making it?" This time he did smile.

I began to shake. The knowledge that intruders — possibly killers — had been here finally sunk in. Annoyed with myself for my vulnerability, I tried to apologize. "I'm not usually this weak," I said. "I was fine until —"

"You're not weak, Ollie, you're strong."

I remembered being little, maybe eleven years old, and getting picked on, badly, on the way home from school. I was fine going up the stairs to our house. I was fine walking through the door. I was fine until I saw my mom coming around the corner to greet me. That's when I lost it. I felt like that now. If I'd been alone, handling this myself, I'd have kept it together. But now, I trembled like a kitten in a storm.

"It's okay," he said as though reading my mind. "I'm here."

I wanted to press my face into his chest and not look up, not see the evidence of killers cruising my property. But I wasn't eleven years old anymore and that wasn't my style. I took a deep breath, let it out, and took a step back.

He watched me closely.

Making a slow circuit of the room that seemed naked without all my papers and without my dusty computer tower, I said, "Okay, let's do this."

"That's my girl," he said.

"Feeling sorry for myself isn't going to catch these guys. What now?"

"We call the police."

Two officers arrived shortly, and though they talked with James at the front desk and asked me typical questions, they warned that this crime would likely go unsolved. "Unless we get lucky and the intruder left a fingerprint, and it matches one in our database . . ."

"I understand," I said.

They both eyed Gav, who stood next to

me but didn't say a word.

"You live here too, sir?" one of them asked, eyeing the bulge in the side of Gav's jacket.

"No."

"You have a permit to carry a firearm?"

Gav pulled out his Secret Service ID. The two officers nodded in sync when they saw it. The other one asked, "Is there some sort of security concern —"

"Ms. Paras is a White House employee," he said.

That seemed to satisfy them. For the moment.

As they prepared to leave, one turned back and pointed to me, "Hey, weren't you in the station the other day? Because you found that old guy who got lost?"

I glanced at Gav, whose face was expressionless.

"That was me," I said. "I went over some mug shots, too."

The cop grinned as he trundled out the door. "I knew you looked familiar. Have yourself a good night."

The minute they were gone, Mrs. Wentworth popped in, Stan following close behind. "What happened? What did they steal?" she asked.

As I tried to assure her that very little was

missing, she shook her head. "It's not your things they were after, Ollie. It was you."

"I agree," Gav said. "We're bringing back her security detail. I'll call them now."

Mrs. Wentworth gripped Gav's arm to stop him from walking away. "Maybe you should stay here tonight." Her knobby hand tightened. "Don't you think that would be best?"

Gav gave me a sideways glance. "You're lucky to have neighbors who look out for you," he said. Placing his hand gently over Mrs. Wentworth's, he smiled down at her. "As tempting a suggestion as that may be, it would be better to have several agents here guarding her rather than just one."

Before he could turn away again, I stopped him. "I'm not arguing the security detail, but how are you going to explain it?" I asked. "I mean . . ."

"She means that if you order the guards, then everybody will know you two are seeing each other socially," Mrs. Wentworth said, wagging her eyebrows.

Stan, who had been silent up until now, piped up. "You mean he's supposed to be a secret?"

Mrs. Wentworth jabbed him with her elbow. "They're keeping this relationship under wraps." Another eyebrow wag directed to Gav. "Aren't you? It won't be long before everybody figures it out."

If my apartment hadn't just been broken into, I might have enjoyed the interchange. "Gav," I said, placing my hand over his, "let me do it."

I watched indecision work across his face. "I'll call Tom," I said.

Mrs. Wentworth shot Stan a look, which he clearly didn't understand. "Uh-oh," she said. "Let's head back now, honey."

When they were gone, Gav put his phone away. "You're right. Better it comes from you. At least for now. But I'm staying until I know you're safe."

Tom was surprised to hear from me so late on a Sunday night. I told him what was up and he was immediately solicitous. "Are you okay? You weren't hurt, were you?"

"I'm fine. I wasn't here when it happened."

"Where were you?"

I hadn't expected that question. "Out."

"By yourself?"

I didn't feel like answering that. "I just wanted to let you know. What's next is up to you. I'm not asking for a guard detail, you know that."

"But you're going to get one. It was smart of you to call me before things got any worse. Seems like you're making some good decisions lately. What's changed?"

I pulled my cell phone away from my ear and gave it a dirty look. Gav watched, confused. Back into the receiver, I said, "I'm so glad you approve. Now, before I hang up, is there anything else you need from me? Will the guard come upstairs so I can meet him or her? So I know who's safe to let in?"

"I didn't mean that the way it came out, Ollie."

"It doesn't matter."

"Yes, it does. I'm sorry. I guess I was trying to ask something without asking it."

I didn't bite, but he asked anyway.

"Your friend Gav seems to take a special interest in your comings and goings. I'm just wondering if he's giving you advice. It's good advice, I mean. It's just not like you to . . ." He blew out a breath. "This is all coming out wrong."

"It was my idea to call you," I said. That much wasn't a lie. "So I guess there's hope for me yet, huh?"

"Again, I'm sorry. The agents should be there in less than twenty. I'll have them call your cell when they arrive."

"Thanks, Tom."

When I hung up, Gav looked at me expectantly. "What was the look for?"

287

"Old wounds."
Gav looked sorry he'd asked.

CHAPTER 17

Monday morning dawned as I rode in the backseat of a Secret Service vehicle. To the best of my knowledge, it was the same one assigned to me before. Either that or it was decked out identically, with its hard black seats, worn chrome trim, and bulletproof windows. Agent Scorroco was again my driver, but the big difference was this time two agents were assigned to stand sentry outside my apartment all day while I was gone.

As the dark sky turned from inky blue to gray, I thought about how hard it had been to sleep last night. In an effort to keep our secret safe, Gav had waited in his car in the apartment's lot until my security detail arrived. Before he'd left, he'd put his arm around my shoulders and said he wished we could have gotten that chance to talk. He promised we would. Soon.

When he was gone, I'd wandered back to

the space where my computer had been. Empty. Exactly how I was feeling right now. Gav had moved quickly to protect me. He'd done everything in his power to ensure my safety and he'd even been willing to expose himself by ordering the guard until I'd offered to do it.

So why did I still feel left out of his life?

Staring out the windows, sitting in the backseat of this utilitarian sedan with a driver who didn't talk, didn't help my frame of mind. All it did was make me feel more alone.

As soon as I arrived in the kitchen and checked the day's schedule, I realized Peter and I had a meeting planned at eleven regarding the secretary of state's party. Not for the first time did I think how odd it was to be planning such a festive event while the White House was in official mourning for its murdered staff members. But events of this magnitude didn't plan themselves and if we expected to have everything in place a month from now, we needed to keep moving forward.

With an eye on the schedule, I tapped a finger against my lips. A Cabinet breakfast had been scheduled for nine, which meant I could be free to visit the calligraphy department by nine-thirty. Despite Cyan's and

Bucky's warnings, it wouldn't kill me to go talk to Lynn on Sargeant's behalf. Sargeant wasn't a nice man, but he wasn't a careless one. If the Baumgartners' name had been accidentally dropped from the guest list, I knew it couldn't have been his fault. And if there was one thing that kept *me* moving forward, it was curiosity when pieces of a puzzle didn't add up.

Bucky arrived just a few minutes after I did, Cyan shortly after that. We were preparing breakfast for the president's Cabinet, a task the three of us had handled more times than I could count. I let myself get lost in the moment. Our team worked together in a companionable, easy silence. Comfortable with one another, good at our jobs, and confident that our teammates had our backs, we had produced hundreds — thousands — of meals that had been served to world leaders. Most important, we'd done all this by ourselves. It felt so good to have Virgil gone. I bit my lip. Who knew what trouble he was stirring up for us during his stint at Camp David?

As I pressed shredded potatoes into the bottom of a skillet with a spatula, I thought about Henry, who'd made his famous hash browns a staple in the White House. It was due to Henry's leadership that Bucky, Cyan, and I worked so well together. He had been teacher, mentor, and almost surrogate dad to all three of us. I turned the hash browns so that they'd be brown and crispy on both sides, considering where I might be falling short. What could I do to foster the same sort of collegiality Henry did, with Virgil in the mix?

It wasn't enough to complain that Virgil didn't fit in with the rest of us. While it was true that I'd worked hard to make him feel welcome, I had to admit to having concerns about being muscled out for the top job. Could I have unintentionally projected my unease and alienated him?

As breakfast was completed, plated, and gone — sent to the president and his advisors via the hands of our trusty butlers — I vowed to do a better job in creating a more cohesive team. It wouldn't be easy, but I pledged to plan while Virgil was gone.

Warmed by the feeling of trying to make the world a better place, and remembering that Sargeant had stepped out of his comfort zone to talk to Milton on my behalf, I set out for the calligraphers' office to talk to the elusive Lynn. Sargeant and I had never gotten along, but if I could smooth out our working relationship, it could benefit us both. Just like I hoped to do with Virgil.

Flush with confidence and brimming with good cheer, I made my way to the East Wing and up to the calligraphers' office. It was a sizeable room, filled with desks and hunched-over artists working at slanted top desks. Bright adjustable lamps illuminated each individual workspace. "Hello," I said to four backs.

They all looked up. The head of the department, Emily, waved a pen at me. "Hey, Ollie, what can I do for you?"

"Could I have a minute of Lynn's time?" I asked.

The girl's head jerked up. "Me?" she squeaked, pointing her pen to herself. With a panicked look at Emily, she raised her shoulders. "What did I do?"

"Nothing," I said. "I just need to ask you about invitations."

Emily waved Lynn toward me. "Ollie's great," she said. "Please do whatever you can to help her out."

Lynn put down her pen and followed me out into the hall. "You're the chef, aren't you?" she asked. "I don't understand what you need from me."

"I'm acting as liaison for the secretary of state's party, but I'm not completely in charge, thank goodness," I said with a smile to put her at ease. Skittish, she was like a malnourished, abandoned kitten. With pale hair, close-set eyes, and petite features, she was also just about as unimposing. "Mr. Sargeant has a question. About the guest list."

She blinked those teeny eyes. "What does he want? He scares me."

He scares a lot of people, I thought. "Nothing to be afraid of. There's a problem we can't figure out and we need your help. Do you have any idea how Mr. and Mrs. Baumgartner got dropped from the guest list?"

"They're not missing now," she said quickly. "We added their names back. Right away. Not a single person is missing from the guest list. We double-and triple-checked. We made sure."

Lynn seemed to think I was looking to point the finger at her. "Great," I said. "What I can't figure out is how Sar— Mr. Sargeant skipped the Baumgartners' name when he sent you the list. He can't remember making that adjustment, but clearly the file was changed. I'm working backward to figure it out."

"What do you mean?"

"Let me just get a couple of things straight. It was you who noticed that the Baumgartners were missing, right?"

Her pale face colored and she looked

away. "Well, kind of."

"Kind of," I repeated. "If you didn't notice, who did?"

Her cheeks were bright red and she stammered as she explained, "I like to get in super early to get my work done in the quiet," she said. "I work better when I'm all by myself."

I waited.

"I'm just a calligrapher. I do the invitations and cards and whatever they assign to me. I don't go looking for why we're sending them and I really don't pay attention as to who gets what. I just make sure that my work is good."

"Go on." By her own admission, she didn't pay attention to guest lists. Why had she done so this time?

"When I came in the other morning, there was a sticky note on my overhead light. It read that I should cross-check the guest list for the secretary of state's party against the current one. I thought Emily left the note for me, even though it didn't really look like her handwriting." She lifted her shoulders. "So I cross-checked. We print out hard copies of every guest list. It's not a real green way to do things, but it makes it a whole lot easier for us calligraphers."

"I understand," I said, just to keep her talking.

"When I compared the two — line by line — I saw that one of the names was missing. I went to Emily and told her she was right about a discrepancy. Except she didn't know what I was talking about. She hadn't left the note for me to find. Either way, we made sure to fix the problem."

"So who left the note?"

"Emily asked around, but nobody owned up to it."

"That's odd."

Lynn's cheeks still burned bright red. "Emily gave me credit for finding the mistake. I guess this would have been a really bad one if that Baumgartner couple hadn't gotten an invitation, but it really wasn't me. It was like a guardian angel came in and left it to make me look good."

"You did double-check," I said, "that's what counts. If you hadn't, there would have been problems. So take credit for that."

"That's the same thing Emily says."

"She's right." Lynn's admission still didn't explain how Sargeant's file had been changed. "Can I ask you about the file you received? The one where the Baumgartners' name was missing?"

"What about it?"

"Was there anything unusual about its delivery? I mean, did it seem as though perhaps someone other than Mr. Sargeant sent it to you?"

"I don't get files from Mr. Sargeant. Emily gets all that stuff and assigns projects to us, but she keeps us updated on what the whole department is doing. According to Emily, Mr. Sargeant put a message in the latest e-mail that noted this was the revised final. That's why we planned to use it." She bit her bottom lip. "Until I found that sticky note."

"Thanks, Lynn. You've been a lot of help."

Her expression perked up. "Really?"

She'd actually created more questions than provided answers. There was a fishiness to this story I couldn't put my finger on. "Yes, thanks a lot." As she turned to leave, I stopped her. "Has anybody else asked you about this? I mean, other than Mr. Sargeant and Emily?"

"Nobody."

"Thanks, Lynn." I hesitated, then added, "Let me know if anyone does."

"Sure thing."

"What's wrong?" Cyan asked when I got back.

"Nothing really."

Bucky snorted. "Like I've said before, you should never play poker. Your face gives you away every time."

"It's just —"

They waited. I hedged.

Cyan smirked. "It isn't even noon yet, Ollie. All we've done is prepare breakfast. It's a little early to get into trouble, even for you."

"Remember I told you about Sargeant's problem? The mistake on the guest list? A mistake he swears he knows nothing about?"

Bucky frowned. "You couldn't leave it alone, could you?"

"It just doesn't make sense." From the looks on their faces, I knew I was losing them. "There's no reason to let him be hung out to dry for a mistake he didn't make, right? I admit Sargeant is hardly my best buddy —"

"There's an understatement," Cyan said. "He's always had it in for you. If there was a chance to get you fired, don't you think he'd jump all over that?" When I didn't respond, she said, "He would. And you know it."

"Let me guess . . . you're getting involved and asking questions on his behalf because no one else on staff would lift a finger to help him." Bucky gave a deep, resigned sigh.

"Even when there aren't life-threatening issues involved, you can't stop yourself from snooping around, can you?"

"The problem is that I keep coming up with more questions than answers."

Bucky and Cyan exchanged a look. "So what else is new?" Cyan asked. "Just let it go, okay? For your own sanity as well as ours. Like I said before, for all you know Sargeant is setting you up."

There was no sense continuing this conversation. Picking their brains wouldn't work. At least not where helping Sargeant was concerned.

"You may be right." Just to change the subject, I moved toward the computer. "What's next on our agenda?"

Bucky sidled up next to me and indicated a new addition to our schedule. "We're hosting Secretary of State Quinones for lunch today. He and President Hyden are having a private meeting this afternoon."

"In addition to the Cabinet breakfast meeting?"

Cyan nodded. "After the news conference."

"Whoa. What?"

"While you were out sleuthing, we got an update from Doug. We're on the hook for a late lunch for the president, secretary of

299

state, and assorted others. The full slate is on one of the document tabs."

I studied the information there. "We changed the president's lunch from soup and salad to cheeseburgers and fries?"

Bucky shrugged. "You can always tell when the First Lady is out of town."

"Speaking of that," Cyan said, "any idea when she and the kids are coming back?"

"You mean when is Virgil coming back, don't you?" Bucky asked. "The longer he's gone, the better. I like it quiet. Like this."

Cyan had pulled out a tray of seasoned ground beef and begun shaping it into patties. "I do, too. If there was some way to engineer Virgil getting fired, I'd be in on that plan. Even more than I would to get rid of Sargeant."

I looked up. There was no way either Bucky or Cyan would have played fast and loose with the guest list, was there? How would they have gained access? I was convinced that whoever had dropped the Baumgartners' name had also left that sticky note for Lynn to find. The culprit apparently wasn't interested in ruining the party — just in ruining Sargeant.

Bucky was back to concentrating on his task. Cyan was back to humming.

No way. I trusted these two. They might

not shed a tear if Sargeant got the boot, but they wouldn't be party to an underhanded scheme to make it happen.

After the glorious lunch we served — bacon-topped cheeseburgers, crispy hot fries, and a side salad that no one had requested but that we'd added to inject a little extra nutrition into the mix — we cleaned up the kitchen again. Soon it would be time to start all over again for dinner. "The president's dining alone tonight, isn't he?" I asked. "No changes, right?"

"None that we know of."

I meandered over to the computer and clicked in to watch the live broadcast of the press briefing going on upstairs. Cyan watched over my shoulder. "Why are you so interested?"

I didn't want to tell her that Gav had predicted this media event and that I wanted to see how close his prediction came to the real thing. "Ever since I met him and he gave me that present for helping with his father-in-law, I've felt protective of the family."

"That's so like you."

"His father-in-law was just a lost soul," I said. "And his wife —"

"You met her?"

"I only caught a glimpse of her at the

briefing after her father came back. She seemed so fragile."

Bucky had been listening in. "You got all that from a glimpse?"

I wiggled my finger at them both. "Be very afraid," I bantered back. "You should see what I come up with after I've known people for a while."

Secretary of State Quinones was about to begin speaking. A large, boisterous man, he had full, pink cheeks and deep lines at the corners of his eyes. He rarely shied away from the camera and was usually seen smiling, laughing, and talking. Always in a loud voice. Always a gregarious demeanor. From what I'd heard, his approach was often first met with criticism overseas, but once heads of state got to know him, they fell under his spell. In the short time he'd held the position, he'd made enormous strides. People referred to him using words and phrases like *genius* and *one of a kind.* Local pundits said he was that rare combination of brilliant strategist and all-around great guy.

Today, however, he wasn't smiling. "My friends." He gripped the lectern with meaty hands and made eye contact with the camera. "You've already been told about the threats that have been received by my office . . . threats directed against my family."

He gestured to his right. "These sharp and talented men and women of the Secret Service, and those of the Metro Police have all assured me that my family and I will be protected around the clock from now until these threats can be eliminated."

"By eliminated, do you think he means sanctioned executions?" Cyan asked.

"No," I said, "I think he means until the bad guys are caught."

"*Shh,*" Bucky said from over my other shoulder.

"I know you've been given vague details. Today I come before you to share specifics."

President Hyden was positioned just behind Quinones, with Ethan Nagy to his left and Tom to his right. Next to Tom was the White House press secretary. Not one of them cringed or reacted to Quinones's promise of specifics. Part of the script.

"You may remember that my wife and I addressed you a few short days ago when her father was found safe after having wandered away from our family home. We can now share with you that my father-in-law did not wander off. We believe he was abducted." Pausing long enough for that information to sink in, he added, "Abducted by the very same people who are threatening me."

We couldn't see the reporters react, but we could hear the onslaught of questions. Quinones held up a hand. "Let me continue. I'll take questions afterward."

The reporters settled down and Quinones gripped the lectern again.

"As you all know, the White House — and indeed all of us here — suffered a devastating blow last week with the murders of Mark Cawley and Patty Woodruff." Quinones clenched his eyes for an extended moment, and when he opened them he said, "I knew them. Both of them." He took another moment to compose himself. "We now believe that whoever killed those two good souls may also be behind these threats to my family."

From the TV, I heard the reporters gasp. From next to me I heard Cyan and Bucky gasp.

Bucky turned to me, "You already knew that, didn't you?"

"I suspected."

"How?" Cyan asked.

Bucky gave me a shrewd look but didn't say anything.

"Am I frightened?" Quinones was answering a question from the audience. "Of course. Who wouldn't be? But I repeat, I have ultimate faith in our Secret Service and in our police department." When he stared up at the camera again, his expression was grim. "Whoever you are," he said in a low voice, "you will be caught. You will pay for your actions. Bet on it."

After answering a few more questions, Quinones stepped away and the press secretary took over.

We logged off.

"Never a dull moment around here," Bucky said.

Once the kitchen was put back in order and lunch delivered, I set out for the West Wing. This time I didn't tell Bucky and Cyan where I was going. I knew they wouldn't approve.

I knocked at Sargeant's office door and he called for me to enter. As I did, I noticed for the first time that the room had no windows. How dull, and more than a little sad.

"Peter?"

"Come in. You've made quite an impression on Milton," he said as I took a seat.

"He's a lost soul," I said, "and he's been very nice to me."

Sargeant chose not to comment. He folded his hands on his desk. "What can I do for you, Ms. Paras?"

"First of all, I want to thank you again for talking to Milton on my behalf."

"The last thing I need is for one of my relatives to get arrested for being a peeping Tom. I did it primarily for myself."

Bucky's and Cyan's warnings about not helping Sargeant jostled around in my brain. I understood their reluctance to help him. I might even agree with their position, but having the man fired or even reprimanded for something he didn't do wasn't right.

"Was there something else, Ms. Paras?" he asked as though bored to tears by my very presence.

Decision time: help him, or not?

Stalling always worked when I wasn't sure what to do next. "Why do you say that I made an impression on Milton? Have you spoken with him again?"

"Thanks to you, I've had the pleasure" — Sargeant rolled his eyes in the exaggerated way only he could — "of a constant barrage of phone calls from my wayward nephew." He held up a finger. "That's not counting the personal visits."

"It's only Monday," I said. "How many times could he have contacted you in the past two days?"

"You have the Secret Service guarding your apartment again, yes?" he asked as though he already knew the answer. "And an armed escort back and forth every day? Am I right?"

"I do."

"Do you know how I know that?"

"Milton told you?"

His face crinkled into a nasty smile. "Exactly. Seems you've inspired him to go play detective on your behalf."

"I never encouraged —"

"You didn't need to. To him you're a damsel in distress, and although you and I both know you're anything but helpless, assisting you appeals to Milton's romantic streak. The fool."

"I should talk with him —"

"Oh sure, go ahead."

Sargeant's reaction surprised me.

"Why not?" he said. "Go. Talk with him. Take him home and clean him up and give him a cozy little corner to sleep in and maybe take him out for a walk now and then."

"Peter, there's no reason to —"

"He'll be happy to be appreciated. You'll be happy to have a pet to take care of. A match made in heaven."

Sargeant was an unpleasant man. Probably the least pleasant man I'd ever encountered, but this particular spew was his harshest yet.

When he finished, he stared as though daring me to fight back. But something else lurked behind his eyes. He wanted me to fight because he didn't want to talk. He didn't want to open up. Milton had hurt him in the past — that much I knew. From the fear that wriggled behind Sargeant's eyes, I knew that Milton's connection to me was more than the little man could handle.

"I talked with Lynn," I said, "the calligrapher."

The shift in his expression was so sudden it almost set me back. "What did she say?" Before I could answer, he leaned forward. "Does she have any idea who sent her the incorrect list?"

"You generally forward guest lists to Emily in the calligraphy department, right?"

"Yes, yes . . ." Even seated, he danced with impatience.

"They were ready to use the wrong copy until Lynn's 'guardian angel' intervened." I went on to explain what Lynn had told me about the sticky note.

Sargeant wasn't buying it. "If one of her coworkers knew there was a mistake, why didn't that person correct it himself . . . or herself? Her story makes no sense."

"It makes plenty of sense if someone is trying to make you look bad."

I watched him digest that. "But I barely know anyone in the calligraphy office."

"That's why I don't believe the problem originated there. Whoever left the note is probably the same person who sent the erroneous file in the first place. Who has it in for you? Any ideas?"

"Here? At the White House?" he asked. "Besides you?"

I almost laughed. "For the record, it wasn't me."

He stared away, concentrating. "Of course not. That isn't your style. You don't creep around in the background trying to undermine people. You undermine them straight to their faces."

"Is that a compliment?"

When he looked up at me I could have sworn I saw the faintest bit of humor flash across his features. "What do we do now?"

"*We* still have quite a bit of work ahead of us on the secretary of state's party —" I began.

"I mean about this sabotage."

I knew what he meant. "Not much," I said. "We've hit a brick wall. Unless we can find out who left that sticky note . . ."

"We could question the staff. Methodically. Draw up a list of everyone with access to the White House. Ask who was near the calligraphers' office the day the sticky note showed up. Ask who was near my office that day — who might have snuck in to send the e-mail in the first place — and then we'll have our guilty party."

"Do you have any idea how impossible that is?"

"If you and I —"

I waved my hand, taking a tiny bit of pleasure in cutting him off for a change. "Count me out. Interrogating every single person who might, maybe, possibly, have seen someone who could have, perhaps, been in both those places at those specific times is ludicrous. Needles and haystacks don't begin to describe it." I couldn't believe he even considered such a foolish idea. "I mean, poking around and seeing if anything pops is one thing. But turning this into a full-scale investigation would do you more harm than good."

He pounced. "Will you?"

"Will I what?"

"Poke around? See if anything pops?"

"I didn't mean —"

"As much as it pains me to say so" — his eyes regained their familiar, unpleasant gleam — "you have proven adept at uncovering conspiracies."

"Two compliments in one day?" I sat back. "Peter, you're losing your edge."

"If I'm not careful, I risk losing a great deal more than that. This isn't the first unexplained issue that's come up in recent months. But it is the first one I can track down." With an expression so brittle I was afraid his face would crack if he moved, he added, "That is, with your help."

Truth was, I was desperate to know what was going on — not just for Sargeant's sake but for my own. There was something rotten roiling just below the surface. Framing our sensitivity director — no matter how appealing the prospect was — just wasn't right. Whatever or whoever was behind it needed to be stopped, even if doing so resulted in Sargeant benefiting from my efforts. "No guarantees I'll find anything."

He tried to mask his reaction to my response. Surprised, clearly. And pleased. "Let me know if you need my assistance."

"There is one thing," I said.

He nodded in a "Go ahead" gesture.

"Be a little nicer to Milton."

The fuming little squirrel of a man was back in a heartbeat. He rearranged his mouth several times, as though fighting to keep caustic words from blurting out on their own. "I appreciate your help in this matter," he said finally. "Now, I believe we have another visit to Jean-Luc's to discuss . . ."

CHAPTER 18

I was back at my apartment that night, after yet another conversation-less drive with Agent Scorroco. Tonight, however, when he'd asked his perfunctory question about needing to pick up anything along the way, I'd surprised him by requesting a stop. There was something I needed tonight, and I needed it badly.

A quart of Baskin-Robbins ice cream sat on my lap as I sat on the couch, enjoying spoonful after cold, creamy spoonful. My favorite flavor, mint chocolate chip. A second quart, same flavor, waited in the freezer. At the rate I was going, I might even crack it open tonight.

Dipping in again, I savored the creamy mint and told myself for the millionth time that no one made this flavor better than Baskin-Robbins did. I also told myself that drowning my sorrows in this softening vat of ice cream was better than melting down myself.

The TV stayed off, the room was dark, and only minimal light came through the split in the curtains that covered my balcony doors. Gav had told me to keep them closed and I did. Quiet tonight. Peaceful. No bad guys breaking in. An armed guard outside.

I dug out another helping.

I didn't usually sit around feeling sorry for myself. Truth be told, I wasn't even doing so right now. What I was doing was giving myself breathing space. As I popped in another minty bite, I amended that thought. Eating space, too.

The whole Sargeant situation had me puzzled. I didn't know what I thought I might uncover regarding the mystery of how the wrong list got sent to the calligraphers, but I took small comfort in the fact that for the first time in a while, the person in trouble wasn't me.

I pictured Bucky and Cyan reminding me that when I had been in trouble, Sargeant had been the first in line to gloat. He'd sooner use his precious, perfect handkerchief to mop up after the First Dog than lift a finger to help me. Yet here I was, helping him out.

We each have to be true to our own nature, I thought. I took another mouthful, letting the ice cream ooze onto my tongue.

With the spoon still in my mouth, I ticked off everything that had gone wrong lately: my apartment had been broken into, probably by the same people who had targeted Secretary of State Quinones. Probably by the same people who had killed Chief of Staff Cawley and Patty Woodruff.

Reason enough to polish off an entire quart of ice cream, if you asked me.

But I wasn't finished listing.

As much as I appreciated the security an armed guard provided, having them covering my every move put a serious crimp in my life. Not to mention bringing whatever relationship Gav and I were beginning to a screeching halt.

Gav. He got a tick on the list all to himself.

I held another finger up. Possibly worst of all, I was in charge of acting as liaison to this massive birthday party with Sargeant as a partner. Could there be a worse combination?

Oh wait. I couldn't forget Virgil.

I was fast running out of fingers.

The Diplomatic Reception Room, an oval-shaped beauty on the ground floor, was where — as the name suggested — diplomats were often received during official visits. With its south-facing outer doors, the room also served as an entrance to the White House for the First Family. We staffers didn't use it as frequently, but today, with an armed escort waiting at my beck and call, it was a convenient exit. Tuesday morning, Sargeant and I met there at nine. "How many more times do we have to visit Jean-Luc's?" Sargeant asked as we made our way to the waiting car.

"As many times as it takes," I said, taking a moment to appreciate the clear day. I took a deep breath of the air that was finally beginning to warm up. "It's a shame we can't walk today." As we approached, our Secret Service agent was adjusting his official pin. They must have just gotten new ones. This was a rectangular-shaped green one, with the Secret Service star prominent at its center. Agents changed pins regularly as a security precaution to prevent criminal infiltration. When guarding the president, these pins were sometimes changed on an hourly basis.

"You can't walk," Sargeant said. "I could if I wanted to." Without even a passing glance at the Secret Service agent holding the back door of the car open for him, he added, "But I don't want to."

"Thank you," I said to the agent as I got in.

He shut the door and got into the driver's seat. "My name is Agent Edgar," he said into the rearview mirror. "If there is anything you need, please let me know."

Sargeant jammed himself into the far corner. I sat right behind Agent Edgar. "Thank you," I said again.

The ride was short and quiet. Just as we arrived at Jean-Luc's, Agent Edgar broke the silence. "My orders are to come pick you up when you're ready to leave." He handed two business cards over the seat and we took them. "Just let me know."

"Yes," Sargeant said as he got out. The moment his feet hit the pavement, I heard him groan.

I stepped out and saw the reason for his reaction. "Hello, Wyatt," I said to the young man waiting for us. "I didn't know you'd be here."

He pointed to his wrist. "You know how it is when you can't do your real work. You just have to find something to keep busy. I heard you were both coming here today, and I knew I could be a big help."

"How did you know we would be here?" Sargeant asked.

Wyatt pointed in the general direction of

the White House. "Doug," he said as though Sargeant was an idiot for asking. Pointing now at the departing car, he asked, "What's with the escort? How did you two rank a ride?"

"Long story," I said, effectively shutting up Sargeant, who looked ready to explain. "What about you, did you walk?"

"Yeah. Do you mind if I bum a ride back when we're done here?"

Sargeant made that growling noise again, then coughed to cover it. "I'm sorry, but we will be making a stop on the way back."

Wyatt looked about to ask what it was.

"A personal stop," Sargeant said, cutting him off. "Ms. Paras and I are meeting someone privately."

This was news to me.

Wyatt said, "Sure, no problem," and loped up the stairs.

I whispered to Sargeant on the way up. "That wasn't very nice. No need to lie. We could have easily given him a ride back."

"It wasn't a lie." He leaned in closer. "Milton called again. I told him we would talk with him on one condition."

"And that is?"

"This is the last time either of us hear from him unless *we* initiate contact."

"You're so generous, Peter."

He missed my sarcasm.

Armed with a list of to-dos, Sargeant and I hit the ground running and within two hours had a significant chunk of the list completed. Wyatt tagged behind as we measured the overall space as well as the dance floor.

"I'm an impressive dancer, if I do say so myself," Wyatt said.

We'd been treated to more of these Wyatt-tidbits than any human being should ever have to endure. I hadn't exploded yet, but only because I'd been running interference, trying to keep Sargeant from biting the guy's head off. Part of me almost wished he would. Wyatt could be so tedious.

I hadn't told him not to go on, so Wyatt assumed he should. "My girlfriend says I'm the best dancer she's ever met."

Sargeant glanced up. "*You* have a girl-friend?"

Wyatt either missed the sarcasm or chose to ignore it. "Beverly Bronson. Isn't that a perfect name? If we ever get married, she won't even have to change her initials."

The old rhyme came to mind: *Change the name but not the letter, marry for worse instead of better,* but I kept that to myself.

"You thinking about getting married?" I asked. From what I understood, social aides were always single. Maybe this was a way to ease him out.

"Nah. Not yet at least. I like to play the field."

"Does your girlfriend know that?"

He shrugged. "It's not like I'm actually seeing anybody else. But I do have a spare on the side. Just in case. You never want to be caught flat at the side of the road without a spare, you know."

Had he really just compared girlfriends to tires? I vowed to stop asking him anything else about himself. Not that I expected him to keep quiet. This guy never shut up.

Trying our best to ignore his trivial musings, Sargeant and I took copious notes regarding the room's colors. We also took plenty of pictures so that Kendra, our florist, would have a basic idea of how to plan. She would eventually make a trip out here herself, but this would give her a good start.

"Shouldn't you have workers do this grunt work?" Wyatt asked.

"Maybe," I said as I took a closer look at the banquet tables lined up along the room's far end. "But until they assign our replacement, I'd like to be as thorough as possible. These are ten-tops, by the way." I'd expected to find eight-top tables here.

We had planned to seat eight guests per table. "This could give everyone more elbow room. How about we take one down and decide?"

Wyatt held up his injured wrist. "Sorry."

Sargeant came to stand next to me. "Lot of help he is," he said under his breath as we rolled a round table out from the pile and set it up.

We gave it a critical glance. "Two possibilities," I said. "This could be perfect because each group of eight guests has extra elbow room, or it will be terrible because they're spread too far apart for conversation."

"I would prefer ten guests per table," Wyatt said. "Did you know that Mrs. Pittala, of the New Jersey Pittalas, always crammed guests together as tightly as possible? She said it made for good friends and better conversation."

I had no idea who the New Jersey Pittalas were, so I ignored him.

Sargeant said, "Let's make a note. By the time the First Lady's assistants are ready to assign seats, the decision as to how many to place per table will be taken out of our hands."

In other words, avoid the problem. Sargeant had been hanging around with Wyatt too long. His influence was beginning to rub off.

"Did you know that the Pittala family raised championship beagles?"

"No, I didn't," I said, hoping my tone of voice would express my disinterest. He'd been spewing useless drivel the entire time we'd been working here. "You know," I said, pretending the thought had just occurred to me, "I think we've gotten almost everything done here for today. Why don't you head back, Wyatt?"

He looked disappointed.

Sargeant tapped our notes. "We will bring this information to the various departments, and they in turn will have more questions. In fact, Ms. Paras has a number of kitchen issues we still need to work out."

"Today?" Wyatt asked helpfully.

"Another day," I lied. Anything to get him to leave. His manner, his personality, even his voice caused shivers of revulsion up the back of my neck.

"Okay, I guess I'll see you around. Let me know when you need me back here. Although Doug will probably let me know."

"I'm sure you're right," I said.

Sargeant was shooting daggers with his eyes.

When we finished up for the day, I called Agent Edgar while Sargeant pulled out his cell phone to dial Milton. "I have no idea if he'll still be able to meet us," he said to me. "I didn't give him a specific time."

Shortly thereafter, we made our way out to the car, where Agent Edgar opened the back door for us. As we climbed in, I said, "Looks like we have a stop along the way."

Sargeant rattled off an address. Edgar turned around. "That's not a great area."

Sargeant sighed heavily. "It's where my nephew lives." Looking out the window, he added, "Pathetic."

Edgar didn't offer any further comment.

We pulled up to a three-story frame apartment building crammed cheek to jowl between identical neighbors. Every house on the block had cement stairs in various stages of disrepair, leading up to a barricaded front door. Milton's building was white with a brown pitched roof. All homes on the block sported ornate iron bars across ground-floor windows. A couple of the miniature front yards were fenced in, some with upholstered furniture that had obviously been outside all winter. Correct that: several winters.

"I'll call for backup," Edgar said. "I'm not comfortable with you going in there."

"Are you crazy, man?" Sargeant asked as he dialed his cell phone. "I wouldn't step foot in one of those buildings. He'll meet us out here."

Moments later, Milton emerged from the top of the stairs. He waved hello as he made his way down and over to the car, which Edgar had been obliged to double park. Milton climbed into the backseat, causing Sargeant to scooch closer to me. "Why didn't you just get in the front?" Sargeant asked. "I don't appreciate being smashed like a sardine."

Milton gave Edgar an exaggerated glance as he whispered, "Can we talk in front of this guy?"

"Is all this just a ridiculous game, Milton?" Sargeant asked. "This isn't a spy novel or a government conspiracy. The gentleman behind the wheel is an armed Secret Service agent. We agreed to talk to you. So talk."

With another wary glance at Edgar, Milton began, "Okay, so remember I told you I saw those two guys together with a big-shot political guy?"

Sargeant rolled his eyes. "Don't tell me you brought us all the way here to rehash that?"

I wanted to tell Sargeant to quit interrupting. The sooner we let Milton talk, the sooner we could be on our way. Our government-issue vehicle was generating no small amount of interest from people on the street. "Agent Edgar?" I asked. "Do you think we could just drive around a little?"

"I was just about to suggest that," he said. Seconds later we were gliding away from Milton's neighborhood, able to talk without distraction.

I had my back to the door, sitting as far from Sargeant as I could. "I'm not rehashing," Milton said. "I'm here to tell you that I've been following them."

"You can't," I said. "Please don't. If by some chance you *are* right about that guy being the one who bumped us —"

"I am. I'm sure of it now."

"Then you could be putting yourself in danger."

Sargeant was in a snit. "Not only that, you could be putting *all* of us in danger. Did you ever think of that?"

Milton had his back to his door. That left Sargeant in the middle, with the only really plum position in the backseat. "Of course I thought of that," Milton said. Little white bubbles of spittle gathered at the corners of his mouth as his voice rose. "That's why I've been extra careful. They have no idea I've been following them. No idea I saw them with their government friend."

"We're taking you back right now,"

Sargeant said, sitting forward, "Agent Edgar —"

"Wait, please. You have to hear what happened next."

Sargeant sat back and consulted his watch. "You have two minutes. Not a moment more."

"The guy they met. I figured out who he is."

"Who is he, then?" Sargeant asked.

"I don't have his name —"

"Then why the blazes are you wasting our time?"

Milton sat back, almost as if slapped. "You guys have to know him. I can describe him to you. He was just on TV. The other day at that news conference."

"Which news conference?" I asked.

Milton wiped his mouth. "The one with the secretary of state."

"Milton." Sargeant's voice was low, trembling with anger. "If you've wasted our time here —"

"Wait." I addressed Milton. "Which one was he?"

"He's tall. Very fair. Really light blond. You'd probably think he was handsome."

"Ethan Nagy?" I asked. Sargeant's head snapped around and he stared at me.

"Are you actually buying into this foolishness? He probably saw the news conference and made all this up just to feel important. That's what you do, isn't it, Milton? Make up stories so you feel like you matter."

"No, Petey. This is true. I swear."

"But this is not the first time you've 'sworn' something is true, is it? Your two minutes are up." He tapped the back of Agent Edgar's seat. "Let's turn around now. It's time to take my nephew home."

I wasn't satisfied. "You're saying that the two men you followed met with Ethan Nagy — the secretary of state's assistant?"

"I don't know the guy's name or what he does. I can just tell you that he's the guy I saw with the other two. For sure."

Sargeant crossed his arms. "I don't believe you."

Milton's tone was plaintive. "Why would I lie about this?"

"Because you see what a success I am and you want it. You want to be part of my life and you'll say anything to get into my good graces."

Milton's face went red and his bottom lip went slack as he looked away. We rode for a very silent, very tense block before he set his jaw and spoke again. "Maybe that's true. Maybe I do want to be part of your life again, Petey. Like we were as kids. But what

I'm telling you really happened." To me, he said, "I don't care if you don't get me a job at the White House. I just care that my uncle and you stay safe."

We dropped him back off at home. The moment the car door closed behind him, Sargeant scooted as far away from me as he could get. I knew he wouldn't want to discuss this, but there was too much at stake. "I believe him," I said.

"That's your problem."

"I think it's *our* problem."

"Not anymore. We held up our end of the bargain. Now he won't contact us again." Sargeant faced me. The hard glint in his eyes was back, full force. "Mission accomplished."

CHAPTER 19

"Let's go talk to Tom," I said to Sargeant when we arrived back at the White House.

"MacKenzie? The head of the PPD? Are you out of your mind?"

"Milton said —"

"Milton is delusional. He invents stories to bolster his self-esteem. Unfortunately, he believes the nonsense he makes up."

"Peter —"

He held both hands up. "I will not be part of this. Milton tried to ruin me once, I won't let that happen again. If the head of our Secret Service even sniffs that my nephew is trouble, do you know what will happen to me? I will be bounced out without a second thought. All because of Milton and his outlandish lies."

I stopped in the center of the Diplomatic Reception Room. "What if he's right?"

"Go talk to your old boyfriend. Tell him your conspiracy theories. Let him know you heard it from a lowlife busboy who's traipsing around the city like he's Sherlock Holmes." He held a finger close to my nose. "But do not involve me. Why? Because I'll tell you exactly what Agent MacKenzie's reaction will be. He's going to tell you you're nuts."

"No —"

"Yes. Now, you will excuse me," he said and huffed away.

I hesitated for several minutes before making my way over to the West Wing to talk with Tom. The main reason for my delay was so that I wouldn't have to walk with Sargeant. The other reason was because I thought this warranted a call to Gav. I dialed his number, disappointed when my call went to voicemail. I left him a cryptic message about needing to talk and stressing that it wasn't personal. This was important. I could feel it. And it couldn't wait.

"Again, Ollie?" Tom said from behind his desk. He hadn't offered me a seat. "You're bringing this to me . . . why? Do you want me to nab the secretary of state's assistant and haul him in for questioning? Have you really lost it this time?"

"Milton said —"

"Milton is a nobody. Don't you get that?

Even if he swore that Ethan Nagy came to him and confessed to both murders and to abducting Secretary Quinones's father-in-law, I wouldn't believe it. This subject is closed. Now. Permanently. Got it?"

"Tom —"

He stood. "Ollie, I'm going to ask you to please let this go. There's a lot going on behind the scenes that you're not aware of. Nor should you be. By repeatedly meeting with this Milton Folgate, you're stirring up trouble you can't possibly understand."

"How can Milton cause you any trouble?"

"It's not him. It's you. Have you forgotten? Every single place you go, we're with you. We're guarding you. Taking one of my agents on a joyride just to satisfy your amateur sleuth cravings is not a good use of my department's time. Do you understand?"

His voice had grown louder with each syllable.

But *what if?* I wanted to say. What if Milton really did see Ethan Nagy with the two alleged killers? What if?

The look on Tom's face was murderous. Angrier than I'd seen him in a very long time.

"I understand," I said. "I'll be in the kitchen if you change your mind."

■ ■ ■ ■

That night, after Agent Scorroco dropped me off at my apartment, I said hello to a new agent — another female — who met me at the door and accompanied me upstairs where her partner was already standing guard. "If you get frightened during the night — if you hear a sound, or just need reassurance — I'll be right here. Don't hesitate."

Clearly, she thought I was a wimp. "Thanks," I said.

Inside, I opened my freezer, staring at the ice cream container until my nose got cold, fighting the temptation to finish the rest of it off tonight. If I polished it off now, I reasoned, it wouldn't be there to tempt me tomorrow. Ah, the logic of the infuriated brain. Eventually I shut the freezer door to fix myself a much more healthy option. When I was home alone, I ate just the way I liked to eat. No standing on ceremony. No need to make the food look pretty. I steamed cauliflower in a saucepan for a side dish while I put together a quesadilla. Easy-peasy.

I sat down to enjoy my dinner and thought about what was really bugging me: Gav.

After he and I had first met and we'd seen the White House through a significant threat, he'd taken off for parts unknown. We'd kept in contact a little bit, but at that point I hadn't considered our relationship anything beyond friendship. If I didn't hear from him for two months, or three, or even six, it wasn't a big deal. But now it was.

I took a bite of my quesadilla and marveled at how delicious something this easy could be. Two tortillas, a heaping scoop of grilled veggies, and a sprinkling of cheese. A few minutes in a hot panini maker and . . . voila!

Gav was a serious man. More intense and staid than I would have ever imagined my being attracted to. But there it was. You don't pick who you fall in love with, you just do. Was I in love with Gav?

I took another bite, wishing everything in my life was as easy as cooking.

"Hey, Ollie," Bucky said when I walked in the next morning. "That special agent was in here looking for you."

"What special agent?"

"This one." I turned to see Gav in the doorway. "Good morning, Ms. Paras," he said. "Mr. Reed is right. I was looking for you."

I so seldom thought of Bucky as Mr. Reed that it took me a moment to comprehend. Or maybe it was Gav standing five feet away from me that had me discomposed. "Good morning, Special Agent. What can I do for you?"

As always when we were among other White House personnel, his face was without expression, but the rock hard look in his eyes I remembered from that first class he taught was back. "A moment of your time?"

Bucky made the oddest face as Gav led me out of the room.

"Not the China Room, please," I said, remembering all the terse conversations I'd had in there over the years.

His voice was a growl. "I know. This way." He passed the China Room and turned left into the Library, allowing me to enter first. "I just have a few minutes, but I need to talk to you before things get worse."

"What happened?"

He shut the door behind us, so softly it barely made a sound. "You talked with Tom yesterday." It wasn't a question.

"Is there a problem? All I did was tell him what Milton —"

"I know what you told him. I've been briefed."

I waited.

Gav ran a hand up his forehead and through his hair. "I admire the fact that you don't go off investigating on your own, that you always keep the Secret Service in the loop . . ." He rubbed his eyes, keeping his hand there, squeezing.

"Did I do something wrong?"

"Of course not."

"Then why do you look like you're ready to fire me?"

His hand dropped. "Fortunately for you that's not my department."

"Are you trying to be funny?"

"Tom and I have a basic disagreement," he said, ignoring my question. "He believes in playing his cards close to his chest. In most instances I would agree with him. But every once in a while you encounter an aberration."

"An aberration?" I repeated.

"You."

I opened my mouth but it took several seconds to come up with something to say. "I don't know how to take that."

"Tom sees it as a problem. I see it as an asset. You know that." Gav began to pace the room. "You brought Tom intelligence that places Ethan Nagy in conversation with the two suspects in the double murder and

Mr. Bettencourt's abduction."

"I wouldn't call it intelligence. Milton just —"

He stopped pacing. "Ethan Nagy is under investigation."

"Because of what I —"

"No. He's been under investigation for the past several days. For reasons I can't get into right now. But this is extremely hush-hush. Only the highest levels of the Secret Service are aware. A handful of us are investigating, working behind the scenes. Can you imagine what would happen if it got out that we were investigating the secretary of state's right-hand man?"

"Oh."

"Then you pop into Tom's office and announce that Nagy might be a suspect. Do you have any idea how much trouble that could have caused?"

"I didn't know . . ."

He tried to smile. "I know you didn't. I know you did what you thought was best —"

"Agent Edgar!" I said. "The driver overheard everything. If he wasn't originally one of your handful, I think there may be a security leak."

"Already taken care of. Edgar is a good agent. We've brought him in on the investi-

336

gation — reluctantly, of course — but he sees it as enhancing his career to be trusted with the information, so I think we'll be safe from that end. What I need from you is a promise that you won't breathe a word of this to anyone."

"I never would."

"I didn't think so. Tom said he ordered you to let it go. But ordering you to do something without explaining why? If I know you . . ." This time the smile was genuine.

"Sure seems like you do."

"It would be wrong of me to ask you to come to me first, rather than go to Tom in the future, because chain of command is very important. But because —"

"Because I'm an aberration?"

He gave me a wry look. "Yes. That changes things."

"I tried getting in touch with you first. I just thought this was important enough to mention right away."

"I'm sorry I didn't answer. I couldn't."

"I understand."

"Do you?"

I took a deep breath. "I'm trying my best."

For a split second I thought he might close the distance between us and pull me into his arms. But we were in the White House and there was no telling who might dash in here at any given moment. "We'll talk soon, Ollie."

I'd vowed not to push him. I'd vowed to wait. With that in mind I veered back to the topic at hand. "What motive would Nagy have for killing Cawley or Patty? Or for abducting Mr. Bettencourt?" I asked.

"That's the biggest hurdle. Nagy had a shady past growing up, but he turned himself around and has proven himself to be quite the catalyst around D. C. Everybody is convinced Quinones is lucky to have him. *Especially* Quinones. But until we can come up with a motive, none of this makes sense."

"Could he be working for someone else?"

Gav stepped closer and lowered his voice. "You're good. That's another hypothesis we're exploring. But Quinones doesn't seem to have very many enemies. We're coming up empty there, too."

"Thanks for being honest with me."

"Always. I promise."

By the time I left that night, a spring storm had rolled in, lashing the city in a high-pressure torrent. I scooted into the backseat of the car, running out from the Diplomatic Reception Room with Agent Scorroco holding an umbrella over both of us. As soon as he was seated behind the wheel, he turned to ask if there was anywhere I needed to stop on the way home. "Run out of ice cream yet?"

"Agent Scorroco, is that a little bit of personality I detect under that deadpan exterior of yours?"

"No, ma'am," he said, "but I take pride in knowing my subject's habits."

"Thanks, but no. Anyway, it's raining. Not worth stopping. Even for ice cream."

"Yes, ma'am."

We traveled in silence for the short jaunt.

Just as we got off I-395, exiting toward the Pentagon, a loud *pop* lurched the car out of control. "Whoa, hey," Agent Scorroco shouted as he fought the steering wheel to keep the car on the roadway. Even wearing my seat belt, I tumbled sideways.

I righted myself to see Scorroco's face in a tight grimace. He gripped the wheel with both hands as we half-pulled, half-skidded, onto the shoulder.

When the car stopped and Agent Scorroco lowered his hands, I asked, "What happened?"

"Tire blowout, I think," he said. "Wait inside, I need to check."

"But it's pouring out there."

"Tire's not going to fix itself."

"Can't you call for help?"

"I intend to. But before I do anything, I need to assess the situation."

"I thought these cars had tires that didn't go flat."

Meeting my eyes in the rearview mirror, he looked annoyed at me for continuing the conversation. "This isn't one of those."

The loud *shush* of rain made me cringe when he opened the door. Even though he popped the umbrella over his head before getting out, I knew he'd be soaked in mere seconds. At this time of year and this time of day, with the sun beginning to set, he had to be icy cold. Scorroco ran around the front of the vehicle past the driver's-side headlamp to take a look at the front passenger tire. I felt guilty staying warm and dry as Scorroco made his assessment. Within seconds he was back in his seat, dripping wet, calling for assistance. "Looks like a tire blowout," he said to whoever was on the other end of the phone. "I can't see so well. Visibility is bad and there's no light here. Send another car ASAP." He gave our location and hung up.

Oh great. Just what I wanted. Alone time with Agent Closed-Mouth.

"How did this happen?"

"Unknown."

"How long until a new car gets here?"

"Unknown."

Rain pounded the car's roof, a sound that warped me back to my childhood, when I used to sit in the rear seat like this, back when I felt safe and warm and protected. A glimpse of memory — no more than that — had my dad at the wheel, my mom in the passenger seat. I tried to pull more but couldn't. As hard as I tried, I could never conjure up a clear memory of my father. It was always like this — a hint of memory, a sense of him. That seemed to be the closest I would ever get.

"Do you hear that?" I asked Scorroco.

He must have because he held up a finger and faced the passenger side. There was an unmistakable tapping against the side of the car that beat a rhythm out of sync with our slapping windshield wipers. It seemed to be coming from the blown-out front tire. "Sounds like something's ticking," I said, "but it isn't an even tempo. It's . . . haphazard."

"Stay here," Scorroco said. He pulled up his umbrella, opened the door, and got out, slamming it behind himself before the rain drenched his seat. Again, he ran around the front of the vehicle.

Although the headlights were on, our warning flashers were not. Scorroco should have turned them on, but must have forgotten. Short as I am, I couldn't quite reach the controls, so I unbuckled and eased myself over the middle to try to find the button, one leg in the front, one in the back. Before he returned to catch me in such an unladylike position, I shifted all my weight to the front leg, and searched the dashboard for the flashers. As soon as I hit them, I started back over the seat.

Just as I did so, I heard a sickening thump and the car rocked sideways. "Scorroco?" I couldn't see him. Another thud.

The back passenger door opened. "Scorroco?"

Not Scorroco.

I screamed.

The man with a black face mask held an enormous gun pointed exactly where I'd been seated moments before. He leaned in, taking less than two heartbeats to find me in the front seat. I took advantage of those two heartbeats. As he shifted his aim, I kicked a foot at his gun hand.

To my surprise — and his, too, apparently — it fell to the seat. I slammed myself forward as he grappled for the gun, but I'd landed on top of it. I could feel the hard, cold shape under my awkwardly folded leg, and I used his few moments of confusion again to my advantage. I grabbed at his face mask, intent on pulling it off, but he yanked away from me. All I managed to do was twist it enough for me to get a good look at his jawline.

At that moment Scorroco appeared behind him, looking dazed. But not dazed enough. He socked the masked guy in the face. The would-be attacker grunted, fending off Scorroco's fists as he righted his mask.

Why didn't Scorroco pull out his gun?

Why didn't I grab the one I was sitting on?

Feeling stupid, I started to pull it up, frightened to use it, frightened not to. Just as I got a good grip, the assailant ran off, Scorroco in pursuit.

My hands shook as I dialed my cell phone. "Gav," I said the moment he answered, "we've been attacked."

CHAPTER 20

Gav and I were seated in the back of one of five government-issue cars that had pulled up at the side of the road after my call for help. A sea of agents examined Scorroco's car and the surrounding area for evidence. From what I'd gleaned so far, after shooting out the tire to disable our vehicle, the attacker had hit my agent-driver over the head, disarmed him, and then taken Scorroco's weapon. The staff scouring the ground had come up empty finding it. The rain had not let up, rendering the agents' flashlights almost invisible in the dark. Warm and dry, I watched them through wet windows.

"This wasn't a random attack, was it?" I asked.

"With the tire shot out like that? No." Gav worked his jaw. "They're getting bolder."

I sucked in a breath. With the danger past, my entire body trembled with relief. As hard as I tried, I couldn't make it stop.

"What can I do?" I asked, hating the way my voice wavered. "I haven't been doing any investigation. I haven't even gotten involved this time."

"You saw Brad. We know he's involved. You might have seen the killer — the one you call 'bump guy.' To them it doesn't matter if you're poking your nose in or not. They're afraid you can identify them. That's all the reason they need."

"Great."

He stared straight ahead. "What would you think about going to visit your mom? Just for a week or so? I'm sure if I talk to the chief usher I can convince him . . ."

"Can you guarantee they won't come after me in Chicago?"

He shook his head. "And if Ethan Nagy is involved — I hope to God he's not — he has government resources at his disposal. He could probably find you, and quickly. Forget it. It was a bad idea."

"Let's not even go there," I said. "I'm safer here. Safer around you."

He turned to me. "You saved yourself. Again. Your instincts saved you. Always trust your gut. It serves you well."

Gav's door opened. "Yes?" he said to the agent waiting out in the rain.

"Finished here, sir. Agent Scorroco is being taken back to the office. I'm assigned to drive Ms. Paras home."

"Very good." To me, Gav said, "I may have more questions for you, Ms. Paras. Agent Lawrence will see you safely home. Good night."

I was surprised to see Agent Scorroco the next morning when he came to pick me up. For some reason I expected he might have been replaced. The Secret Service pins were purple today. Round.

"How are you today?" I asked after we were settled and he began to drive.

"I'm well. And you?"

"The weather's better than yesterday. By far." Clear skies, and temperatures more suited to the spring.

"Yes, ma'am."

"Did you see a doctor yesterday?"

"I did and you need not be concerned. I'm fit for duty."

"I'm more worried that you're okay in general." He didn't respond, so I added, "Thank you for all you did for me yesterday."

He met my eyes in the rearview mirror. "You weren't so bad yourself."

■ ■ ■ ■

"What happened now?" Bucky asked when I got in.

"Why do you ask? What did you hear?" He had the newspaper open in front of him on the countertop. I came around to read over his shoulder. "I can't believe it was in the paper."

"Whoa," he said, "nothing in the paper. This isn't even today's. I've been saving food sections for the past few days and I'm trying to catch up." Turning to face me, he asked, "Something really did happen, didn't it? Spill."

This wasn't making sense. "Why did you ask if you didn't read anything?"

"An agent stopped by twice this morning to talk with you. Wanted you to know there will be a meeting at nine. Your presence is required."

"Oh." I pulled up a stool and sat.

"Are you going to tell me what's going on?"

I thought about it. As long as I didn't mention Ethan Nagy or the investigation itself, I could give Bucky the basics. So I did.

His eyes were wide by the time I finished.

"Please," I said, "don't —"

"I know. Don't say a word." He put a finger over his lips. "Got it."

I pointed to the paper. "I was terrified that the media had gotten hold of the story."

He gave me a skeptical stare. "Terrified? Really? Terrified is what you should have been last night. This morning, if it had gotten into the paper, you should be angry, annoyed, infuriated. We need to work on your response levels. Your flight-or-fight kicked in for you last night. Don't abuse it."

He was poking fun, but there was weight to his words. "Got it, Buckster."

"Hey, by the way, does any of this have to do with Sargeant?"

"Why do you ask?"

"Sargeant called in sick today."

"So?"

"So the agent looking for you said that sick or not, they're bringing Sargeant in for this meeting, too."

"Huh," I said. "No idea what that's about."

With breakfast to be made and parties to plan, I did my best to take my mind off matters, that is, until nine o'clock rolled around and Agent Edgar came to collect me. "We're meeting in the Red Room," he said.

"Seriously?" I asked. One of the State

reception rooms, it was rarely used for staff business. "Any particular reason?"

"Agent MacKenzie ordered it."

"Good enough, then," I said. Agent Edgar was a lumbering guy, wider than most of the agents I knew. I followed him up the stairs. "Any idea what this is about?"

He spoke quietly. "The matter from the other day," he said with a meaningful look.

The meeting with Milton. "Got it."

We continued without further comment but I could tell from the way he squared his shoulders before ushering me into the Red Room that he was very proud to have been brought in as part of this clandestine operation. He grasped the handle, ready to close the door behind me. "You're not coming in?" I asked.

"I'm on duty out here."

Alone in the Red Room, I wandered past the fireplace to stare out the window. I hadn't gotten more than a passing glimpse at the stunning southern view when the door opened again and Tom strode in. "Ollie," he said by way of greeting, "you've heard, then?"

"Heard what?"

He didn't get a chance to answer. Again the door opened, this time admitting two people: an agent I didn't know, and Peter

Everett Sargeant, who looked like death warmed over. For the first time I saw him in something other than a thousand-dollar suit. Sargeant was wearing brown corduroy slacks and a cream-colored sweatshirt. He looked vulnerable and weak.

"Mr. Sargeant," Tom said, "please have a seat."

He didn't have to be asked twice. The agent who had escorted him in gave a brief nod and left the room.

I sat on the red empire couch next to Sargeant. "Are you okay?"

The man was a wreck. Wringing his hands in his lap, he stared up at Tom with wild eyes and shook his head. "What is happening?"

"You aren't sick," I said, realization dawning. "You're terrified." Bucky's words reverberated in my brain. "What happened?"

His voice was hoarse. "They came to my house. They tried to kill me."

"Who?" I asked. "Who?"

Tom stood in front of us. "We're getting ahead of ourselves here. Let's not begin until everyone arrives."

"Are you kidding?" I asked. "Look at him." For the first time in my life, I felt the urge to put an arm around Sargeant, but he still managed enough of a steely reserve that

I held back.

Agents Scorroco and Rosenow — the woman who'd been guarding my apartment the day Milton came to visit — entered the room. Gav followed seconds later.

"We're all here," Tom said.

Before anyone could take control, I said, "I want to hear what happened to Peter."

Tom nodded acquiescence. "We all need to hear this."

"A man came to my apartment last night," he began. "I don't know how he got past the doorman, but he knocked at my actual door. I thought perhaps it was one of my neighbors, so I opened without looking and he barged right in. Told me to be quiet. But I shouted for him to get out. That's when he pulled the gun."

I gasped.

"Yes," Sargeant said, his whole body shaking in the retelling. I could relate. "He pointed it at my face! I'm just lucky that one of my real neighbors heard me and came over to investigate."

"And?"

"The guy ran out. I live on the first floor. He bolted out the back."

"I'm so sorry this happened to you, Peter."

"The minute he got into my apartment he

351

said, 'You just had to find those bodies, didn't you?' "

I turned to Tom.

"And now you know why I called this meeting," Tom said. "I want everyone in this room to take a look around. These faces are the only ones to trust with all further information regarding this investigation."

Tom explained everything I'd already learned about Brad, bump guy, and the abduction of Mr. Bettencourt. He conveniently left out any mention of Ethan Nagy, which didn't surprise me. This meeting was called, no doubt, for my benefit and for Sargeant's. I was sure this group of agents had already held their own meeting, deciding how much to share with the hired help.

"At this point, neither you, Ms. Paras, nor you, Mr. Sargeant, are to be left unguarded outside the White House. You will both have Secret Service agents assigned to you around the clock. Don't be afraid if you don't recognize your daily guard. Because there are two of you, and so few of us, we will be augmenting with other trusted agents. They may not know the specifics, but they are there for your protection. I will also ask" — at this he shot a pointed look at me — "that you do not seek to circumvent this protection."

Yeah, like I would.

"Of course not," Sargeant said. His voice was getting a little stronger.

"How did they find Peter?" I asked. "I mean, I know I've been targeted since my run-in with Brad, but why Peter? Why now?"

The four agents exchanged a look I didn't understand. "There was a leak," Tom said. "Your esteemed colleague Virgil talked to a reporter about what it's like working for an executive chef who also fancies herself an amateur sleuth."

"What?" I was beside myself. *What?*

"He embellished by providing details the press hadn't gotten hold of."

My shoulders slumped. I rubbed my head.

"I always knew you'd get me into trouble with your nosing around," Sargeant said.

I didn't have the energy to bite back.

"Pointing fingers doesn't help anyone," Tom said in a rare display of support. "We have to play the hand we're dealt. We have to assume that ever since the story hit they've been following you both. Think about that. Is there anything you might have said or done that could impact this investigation?"

I started to shake my head. Sargeant did, too. At the same moment, we looked at each other. "Milton," I said. "We met with him

Tuesday. Do you think they were following us then? When did the news article hit?" Another thought occurred to me. "Has anyone spoken to Virgil about keeping his mouth shut?"

Tom answered. "Short answer? Yes. Long answer," he sighed, "because there is precedent set to overlook transgressions by certain members of the kitchen staff" — another pointed look at me — "he's getting off with a warning."

"Even though lives are at stake."

Tom's face was dark. "This wouldn't be the first time."

Gav interrupted. "We'd like to get in touch with this Milton. It's entirely possible Ms. Paras has been followed for days, and he's in danger now, too. Mr. Sargeant, do you have a number where he can be reached?"

CHAPTER 21

"I'm surprised you didn't go home for the day," I said as Sargeant and I seated ourselves in the Library. A long folding table had been brought in; two workmen were in the process of setting it up.

"That was my intention, but I think I'm safer here. I don't want to leave. Not for anything."

"You'll have to go home sometime."

Two agents carried in armloads of mugshot books and set them on the newly placed table in front of us. "Take your time, folks," the first one said. "If anyone looks familiar, even a little bit, let us know."

I gauged the pile of books they'd brought in. "Not too bad. We should be through these in an hour, don't you think?"

"Oh, there's more, ma'am. They're still coming."

Sargeant blanched. "This is like looking for a needle in a pile of needles."

The agent blinked. "Isn't that supposed to be 'haystack?' "

"Haystacks are innocent," Sargeant sniffed. "We're looking for a guilty, harmful, painful needle among others of his ilk."

The agent raised his eyebrows but didn't comment. "I'll be back with more in a minute."

Left alone to sort through the piles, we decided to each take a book, then trade, then move on to two more books. The process would have been ideal except for the fact that I went through the photos a lot faster than Sargeant did.

"You're skimming," he said. "How on earth do you think you'll find these villains if you're racing through like that?"

"I look at every face. Recognition hits at a gut level. Not one has hit yet."

We were silent a little longer, the only sounds in the room the flipping of pages.

The agent in charge came back to check on us. "You doing okay? Want to take a break?"

"Not yet," I said.

"Not until these dastardly criminals are identified," Sargeant added.

"All right then," he said. "I'll be right outside."

"Have you gotten in touch with Milton

yet?" I asked as soon as we were alone.

"Secret Service said they would do that."

Appalled, I pushed the issue. "Don't you want to know, yourself, that he's okay? Don't you want to make sure?"

Sargeant didn't look up as he turned the page. He frowned. "I called him."

"And?"

"He said he's fine."

This was like pulling teeth. "Did you at least warn him?"

Sargeant ran his tongue around the inside of his mouth. "I did. He said not to tell you, but that he followed one of the men again. The bump guy."

"Why didn't he want you to tell me? Did he find out more?"

"He didn't want you to be worried for him, but he thinks the bump guy spotted him."

I stood up. "Oh, no! Did you tell Tom?"

Sargeant gave me a look of disdain. "Sit down. Yes, I did. You aren't the only one around here with smarts. I told Milton to be careful and I informed the Secret Service. Do you know what Milton said when I warned him?"

"What?"

"He said he would be sure to lay low." Sargeant snorted as he turned another page.

"He should have said 'lie.' Lie low. You see why he's such a deadbeat? Can't even choose the correct form of a verb."

"And to think I always considered you a priss."

He didn't react.

"Did the Secret Service say they'd keep an eye on him?" I asked.

"They were on their way out after the meeting. With the two of us here safe, they can spend time watching Milton." He waved a hand as though it was nothing to be worried about. "He'll be fine. Somehow he always lands on his feet."

Hours later, I returned to the kitchen, my eyes pulsing and out of focus from poring over thousands of pictures. Not one reminded me of Brad, and I had no idea what my roadside attacker looked like, so I was no help there. Sargeant had come up empty-handed, too. During our limited conversation, I'd asked him about the man who'd broken into his apartment the night before. Though Sargeant's description was sketchy and I couldn't be sure, I thought it sounded like Brad. In a strange way, that made me feel better. If there were only two of them, and not an army of bad guys, we stood a chance. Maybe.

"How'd it go?" Cyan asked. "Bucky told me where you were."

"No luck." I was about to ask how lunch preparations had gone when Virgil came around the corner from the refrigeration area. "You're back?"

He glared. "Don't throw a party or anything."

"What has you so angry?" I asked. I was the one with a right to be angry. He had shared privileged information with the media — information that had almost cost me and Sargeant our lives. Although I'd promised myself I would strive to better include him in all things kitchen related, I wasn't about to take any of his guff. "Don't you start with attitude with me. Not after —"

He zinged an arm out, pointing at Bucky. "Then call off your pit bull."

"Time out," I said, making the hand signal. "You will start at the beginning. And you will do so with respect." Cyan's eye were bright blue and super wide. She bit her bottom lip and took a step back.

Still pointing, Virgil's voice rose. "He came at me the minute I got back here. He attacked me."

Bucky was not one to stay silent when accused. He whipped a newspaper out from the side of the computer and held it up. "Did you know our prima donna chef here named you and Peter Everett Sargeant as witnesses to the double murder?"

I closed my eyes for a count of three. "I just heard."

Virgil grabbed a pot from overhead and banged it onto the countertop with an ear-splitting clang. "Doug already told me I shouldn't have said that, okay? The reporter asked if I knew any scoop." He lifted the pot again and waved it around in emphasis. "Everybody always wants to know what you're up to. They forget this is a kitchen, not a private eye's office, and they keep asking what exciting things you're doing. Like that has anything to do with running a kitchen. They forget it's important to be a good chef. They want to find out what trouble you're in this time!"

"And you told them."

He shrugged. "What harm is there?"

"Oh, I don't know," I said, my anger building with sweet, delicious fury, "maybe your scoop is what got me attacked last night. Maybe it has something to do with the man who tried to kill Peter Everett Sargeant yesterday. You think?"

The kitchen went deathly silent.

I lowered my voice. "I know you've been

reprimanded. I know that's as far as they're taking it — this time." I advanced on him. "I warn you: Speak to the media one more time without permission and I will take you down. Permanently. That's a promise."

He banged the pot down again, turned, and walked out.

"Whoa, Ollie," Bucky said. He high-fived Cyan. He knew better than to high-five me. As much as Virgil deserved it, I never derived pleasure taking someone to task like that. I wasn't proud of myself, but I wasn't ashamed, either. It had to be done. I did it effectively. Time to move on.

I waited until my breathing slowed to ask Bucky, "How come you didn't show me the article before you went after Virgil with it?"

There was no remorse in his expression. "I found it this morning while you were busy. And," he cocked an eyebrow, "if I *would* have told you first, you would have handled it yourself. What he did was wrong and I needed to take him down a peg."

"Feel good?"

"I do."

I took a breath. "Thank you, Bucky. Thanks for sticking up for me. But next time, it would be better if you let me handle him."

He nodded acknowledgment but with a

glint of triumph in his eye.

The rest of the afternoon moved quickly. Too quickly. I was beginning to feel the way Sargeant had earlier — I didn't want to leave tonight. It was safe here. If he and I stayed within the confines of the White House, that freed up more Secret Service agents to keep an eye on Milton.

Virgil had returned, and not another word was said about his offense. Didn't matter. The tension in the room was so thick you could taste it. Except for necessary conversation, we worked in silence. Four of us preparing a single dinner meant we were way overstaffed. "Why don't you go home," I said to Cyan. "You too, Bucky. Tomorrow is your day off, anyway; why not get an early start?"

"If you're sure," he said. Cyan mumbled a similar comment.

"Yeah, go ahead. We can handle this — right, Virgil?"

"Whatever you say."

Now there was resounding support.

The minute they were gone he looked up at me. "Go ahead. You want to ream me out again. I can feel it. Let's get it all out in the open."

I sliced a carrot into thirds. "I have no intention of reaming you out."

He barked a laugh.

"I did want to ask you about the interview the other day. That came just as the news hit about the murders. How is it that they held that privileged information for so many days? From what I know of the media, if it bleeds, it leads. Your feature came out . . . how many days later?"

He didn't answer.

"Why the delay?"

Without looking at me, he pulled two onions from the nearby bin and sliced their ends off. "I didn't tell them about that originally. It was part of their follow-up."

"They didn't get the whole story while they were here?"

He cut the onions in half. "It was a zoo here that day."

"I remember being surprised you got clearance for the cameras."

"I pulled a few strings."

"Sargeant?" I prompted. I seemed to recall that's who he'd said had greased the wheels.

"Yeah. He gave the okay."

"I'm surprised. I would have expected him to know better. How did you convince him?"

"I didn't have to. One of those social aides overheard and said he'd take care of it. He talked with Sargeant and got it all worked out for me."

I stopped what I was doing. "A social aide handled this?"

"He cleared it through Sargeant. Said he had an in with him."

"What's the social aide's name?"

Virgil sliced again. "I never caught it. He's working here a lot these days nursing a broken wrist." He shrugged. "Looked fine to me."

"Huh," I said.

"Why? What's wrong with that, now?"

I didn't want to say anything, but a thought ticked in my brain. Changing the subject back to my original question, I asked, "It's just the two of us here. You can tell me. Why did the newspaper really call you for a follow-up? Was it about my involvement in the murder?"

He sliced the onions hard. "No."

I waited.

"They were going to pull the story. They told me there wasn't enough interest right now. Too much going on behind the scenes at the White House that was newsworthy. The timing wouldn't be right to do a feature on me."

Little pieces clicked into place. "By giving them that tidbit you made your story more relevant. Is that it?"

He made eye contact. "I deserve more attention than you. I'm better at what I do."

"You may be right," I said, "but I'm better at what I do."

He glared.

I smiled. "Let's not forget that."

CHAPTER 22

Thank goodness for uneventful trips home. Agent Scorroco dropped me off at my apartment, where Agent Rosenow waited at the door. She and I said hello to the elderly man at the desk — whose name I still didn't know — and took the elevator to my apartment, where a second agent again stood guard. Mrs. Wentworth opened her door to greet us and ensure that all was well; Agent Rosenow said good night, and let me know that her relief would be on duty after three.

And just like that, I was alone.

After fixing myself a quick dinner and reading a few chapters in the latest mystery novel I'd picked up, I decided that tomorrow would be better. Tomorrow would dawn a new day. I hit the sack before ten, and fell into a dreamless sleep almost immediately.

Banging at my door startled me awake. I glanced at my clock and saw that it was 2:30. I shouted that I was coming and hurried to the door.

Gav stood there. "Your phone is turned off."

I rubbed my face. "I shut it off to charge and reboot. You're supposed to do that sometimes."

Rosenow hovered behind him. There I was in my pajama pants and T-shirt — no bra — with half my face sleep-smashed and my hair in complete bedhead mode, standing before two agents who were dressed like it was the middle of the afternoon. My brain was still back in my room. "You came by because I didn't answer?"

"No. May I come in?"

Rosenow averted her eyes in a way that made me uncomfortable. Not like she was eavesdropping on a private conversation. More like she knew what Gav was here for and she didn't want me to know she knew.

"What happened?"

"Can I come in?" he said again.

"Sorry, yes." I held the door open. "I'm still half-asleep."

As he brushed past me, I ran my hands over my hair, hoping to make myself look presentable, knowing it was a useless endeavor. He wasn't making eye contact.

"Something's wrong," I said. "What is it?"

Hands curled into fists, he glanced over to

make sure I'd shut the door. Wide awake now, my heart was speed-beating, waiting to hear the bad news. From the look on Gav's face, it could be nothing else.

He finally made eye contact. Fear, anger, frustration stared back at me. Now my hands fisted. "Just tell me," I said. "As long as you're here and you're okay, it can't be that bad."

If I hadn't known him so well, I might have missed the flash of softness in his eyes when I said that. It was gone before I could react.

"Sit down," he said.

"I'd rather stand."

We were facing each other, six feet apart, in the center of my living room, the only light coming from my small hallway, where I'd flicked on the lights before answering the door. It provided enough for me to see the pain in Gav's expression.

"Please," I said. "I can't take this another minute."

"Milton is dead."

The room spun out of control as my focus lasered in on Gav. I reached out to grab the arm of my sofa, half to steady myself, half to check if this was real. The nubby fabric didn't dissolve beneath my fingers.

"How?" I asked, fighting for control of my

emotions, my brain, logic.

"Please, sit."

I did.

Gav remained standing. He clasped his hands together. "I have no words. I'm very sorry."

"How?" I asked again. This had to be a dream. A nightmare. It had to be. Milton had just —

"Police originally thought it was a break-in gone bad. He was shot in the head from behind."

"Execution style? Just like Cawley?"

Gav nodded. "His place had been ransacked, but it's hard to determine if anything's missing. The only reason Metro Police called us was because we'd put that alert on him."

"No one was watching his house?"

Gav flinched. "He wasn't being covered the way you and Sargeant are. Our agents were simply told to keep an eye on him. Once he was in for the night, their job was done. We didn't know he was vulnerable."

I clenched my hands and stared down at them. "More vulnerable than you realized."

"What can I do for you, Ollie?"

Looking up at him now would just cause me to go weak. I couldn't risk it. I had to stay strong. I had to fight. I was in this now until the end, and there was no way I could let my guard down. Not for one minute. I couldn't rely on Gav because he would make me feel safe. That was far too dangerous, because I was anything but.

"Does Sargeant know?" I asked.

"Tom is talking to him right now."

"Okay," I said. "Thank you for letting me know."

Maybe he sensed what I was feeling, because he didn't move closer. He wanted me to look up — I could feel it — but I just stared at my fingers, twisting themselves as though they belonged to someone else. "Ollie, please. Tell me what I can do for you."

I finally looked up. "There's nothing." I could feel heat building behind my eyes, but I blinked it back. "I need time. I need to be alone."

I could tell he wanted to say more — wanted to do more. But he respected my wish and left without another word. I heard the door click shut behind him.

Would this be how it always was between us? Keeping each other at arm's length when we were sad, or scared, or confused? I was as guilty as he was at avoiding closeness when I most feared exposing weaknesses. And I was feeling very weak right now.

Milton. Poor Milton. He'd just been trying to help.

I sat on the couch staring at nothing until it was time to get ready for work.

Cyan came up behind me. "What's wrong?"

I was washing dishes when she'd come in. Pots, actually. We hadn't used these for at least a week, and I thought they might have gathered dust. Keeping my hands plunged in the hot soapy water and scrubbing stainless steel pots that really didn't need attention kept me busy while my brain worked overtime.

She walked around to my left side, where she could see my face. One side of it, at least. "We have people to do our dishes. Why are you doing them? What's wrong?"

I didn't answer right away. What could I say? That I was mourning a man I barely knew? That, despite the fact that I'd warned Milton — repeatedly — to back away from this investigation, I felt responsible for his death? It wasn't a job at the White House he was after. Ultimately, all he'd wanted was respect. He'd wanted someone to care about him. Now that it was too late, he'd never know I had cared. "Rough night."

Cyan crossed her arms. "Spill it."

I turned the pot in the sink and ran the dishcloth along its smooth inside. "Can't," I said, "not yet."

She shifted her weight. "Whatever it is, Ollie, you know we're behind you."

Who had been behind Milton? No one. "I know that." I tried to smile, but I couldn't. Part of me wished Bucky was here today instead of Cyan. Prickly and persnickety as he was, he understood when I needed to be left alone. "Means a lot to me."

She scrutinized me a moment longer before loosening her arms and backing off. "Just let me know what you need. Okay?"

"You got it."

Virgil took care of the president's meals with nary a peep. Whether it was because he read my mood or because of our prior conversation, I didn't know. Nor did I care. As long as the kitchen ran smoothly, I could get through this day.

Sargeant wasn't in. Of course not. Would my calling to offer condolences make things worse for our sensitivity director? Would he see my gesture as an intrusion, or would he see it for what it was — a sharing of sadness? Though I barely knew Milton, he'd left his mark on my life.

I argued back and forth with myself for hours until I realized why I *had* to make the call. Because that was who I was. I couldn't worry about what Sargeant might read into it. I had to do it because I couldn't live with myself if I didn't.

"I'll be in the China Room," I said to Cyan.

She looked at me quizzically.

"Unless it's an emergency," I continued, "I'd appreciate being left alone."

"Understood."

I dialed Sargeant's cell and waited three rings before he picked up. "I was wondering if I would hear from you," he said.

"How are you?" I asked.

"Keeping busy. Making arrangements. Did you know Milton wanted to be cremated?"

"Peter," I began, "I'm very sorry —"

"Milton prepared a list of what he wanted done if he ever . . ." Sargeant's voice caught. "He's had this planned for years. Can you believe it? Who spends time planning his own funeral?"

A person who isn't sure anyone knows him well enough to get it right, I thought. "I'm sure he's lucky to have you in charge."

"As his closest living relative, I have no choice."

"I'm very sorry," I said.

Sargeant said nothing.

I hesitated, not knowing what else to say. "If there's anything you need . . ."

"Yes, thank you," he said. "Good-bye."

I closed my phone and headed back to work.

"Ms. Paras?"

I looked up to see Gav in the doorway. So deep was I in musings, in replaying scenarios in my mind while I washed dishes that didn't need cleaning, that it took me a half-second to realize it was him. "Special Agent Gavin," I said without inflection.

Cyan and Virgil looked up. They must have read the expression on his face because they didn't stop what they were doing. Didn't even say hello.

"I have an update for you."

I dried my pruned hands on a towel and followed him out of the kitchen. He headed for the Library, but I pointed to the China Room. "It's bad enough already. Choice of room doesn't really matter, does it?"

He led the way in and shut the door behind us. "How are you holding up?" he asked.

"I called Sargeant. He's making arrangements." I didn't want to talk about my feelings right now. "You mentioned an update?"

"Ethan Nagy is coming up clean."

That wasn't much of an update, that was more of a dead end. "That's it?"

"I wanted to see you."

This would be the moment where two people in a new relationship would come together, embrace, profess their undying love, and decide to work together to solve all their problems. We remained apart.

"I'm hurting, Gav," I said, "more than you can imagine."

"It's not your fault. Not even a little bit."

"Yes, it is."

He started to argue but I stopped him. "Tell me more about Ethan Nagy. You're sure he's clear?"

"We're missing a piece of this puzzle. I can feel it."

"Do the police have any leads on Milton's killer?"

He didn't have to answer. I could see it on his face. "Ollie —"

I felt myself holding back, holding tight. Afraid. "Last night, after you left, I asked myself if you and I would always be like this. If we would always push each other away when times get tough. Because they do get tough for us. Maybe you and I are destined to be friends who support each other, but who can't get past all the obstacles — the murders, conspiracies, and constant threat of danger — in our lives."

He stared at me with a look I couldn't

parse. "Tough times," he repeated, "you're right." He studied the fireplace for a moment, and seemed to find an answer there before looking at me again. "I promise you, Ollie. We will talk. Soon. In the meantime, do not hesitate to call me. For anything."

Instead of heading directly back to the kitchen, I decided to take a detour to the East Wing. Sargeant had more to deal with than he should. Despite my personal feelings for the man, I felt the need to try to lend a hand with the one problem where I might do some good. My gut told me that Lynn the calligrapher was not the type to seek me out with an update on her sticky note–leaving guardian angel. If she had any news, she would wait for me to come talk to her.

She was alone in the calligraphy office when I stopped by, hunched over her slant-top desk, light bright on the project in front of her. "Lynn?"

She spun in her seat. "Ms. Paras," she said, "are you looking for Emily? She's at lunch right now." As though noticing the office empty for the first time, she added, "I guess everyone else is, too."

"You don't eat?"

When she smiled, her pale face lit up. She

376

was prettier than I'd realized. "I have a date," she said. Her gaze skittered over to the room's clock and as she continued, her hands came up to pat down her already poker-straight hair. "He's coming by in about five minutes."

Another budding romance in the White House. "I won't keep you, then. I was just wondering if you'd heard anything more about who might have left that sticky note on your lamp. You remember? The one about the guest list?"

She remembered, all right. Her eyes grew big and her cheeks flushed deep pink. Looking like a tow-headed toddler who'd just grabbed another child's toy, she shook her head. "No, nothing at all. Nothing."

Her discomfort spurred me to push. "Did you ask around, like we talked about?"

"Yeah, I did. Sure. I mentioned it around to a lot of people. But nobody said anything that I thought would help."

"But you heard something? Even if you don't think so, it might be more help than you imagine. Who did you talk to?"

Her attention suddenly shifted to right over my shoulder. I twisted to see Wyatt Becker in the doorway. He was smiling — at least until I turned around — and then his face fell faster than one of Virgil's soufflés. Wyatt was evidently just as startled to see me as I was to see him.

He raised a hand in greeting. "Um . . . I was just looking for . . . I guess I'm in the wrong room. Sorry." He ducked out before I could say a word.

I turned back to Lynn, whose own expression was as easily read as if she had a neon pink sign painted across her nose. Disappointment, confusion, shock.

"Wyatt is your lunch date?" I asked.

"Yeah, he . . ." The question had come too quickly for her to lie. "Why did he leave?"

I had a guess. "Was it Wyatt who left you the sticky note?"

Her scarlet face answered that question. "I don't know. Really, I don't. He teased me about my guardian angel —"

"But *you* believe he left the note, don't you?"

"I don't know." Her denial bordered on shrill. "Maybe he wanted to help me out or something. There's nothing wrong with that, is there?"

"Not at all," I said, keeping my voice low and soothing. Her eyes darted to the doorway, as though she expected Wyatt to return any moment. "You know what, Lynn? Forget I asked."

Still suspicious, she quieted. "I didn't do anything wrong."

"I never said you did."

"Then why do I feel like this?"

I had no answer. "Thanks for talking with me. I hope he comes back. Have you two been dating very long?"

"Not long . . ." She thought about it. "Just over a week."

They'd started dating just about the same time Wyatt had been assigned to help us with the birthday party. Coincidence?

I stepped out of the calligraphers' office to start back to the kitchen. At the first corner — surprise, surprise — Wyatt was there, ready to pounce.

"And how are you this lovely afternoon?" I asked.

"You're probably wondering why I want to take her to lunch."

"I think I know why."

He looked at me shrewdly. "Oh?"

I scratched my temple, and glanced back to make sure Lynn hadn't followed me. "Didn't you mention a girlfriend? That one with the perfect name? What was it again?" Thank goodness for my memory. "Beverly Bronson?" He didn't answer, so I pointed back toward the calligraphers' office. "Lynn is that spare you mentioned, isn't she?"

"What of it? I'm a guy. Can I help it if I'm lucky where ladies are concerned? She's got a crush on me, is all. I'm just taking her out to give the kid a little fun."

"You left that sticky note on Lynn's lamp."

Panic jumped into his eyes, but he tamped it down. "I don't know what you're talking about."

"Sure you do. You fiddled with that guest list but made sure it was corrected in time. All to make Sargeant look bad."

Wyatt affected a bored look. "Sargeant doesn't need my help to look bad."

"You didn't answer my question."

"I told you I didn't know what you were talking about and I don't. Don't try to blame one of Sargeant's screw-ups on me."

"Then why did you wait here for me?"

"I promised a young lady I would take her to lunch. I wanted to make sure you didn't spill the beans."

"You mean tell her about your real girl-friend."

He smiled. "I made no promises to either, so no harm done. But that doesn't mean I want her feelings hurt, you understand. Just wanted to be sure you kept my confidence."

"Illicit secrets are never safe with me," I said, "or haven't you heard?"

I walked away without giving him a chance

to reply. Poor Lynn. She was clearly smitten with this buffoon. I thought back to when I was her age and I wondered if I would have listened to anyone who tried to talk me out of a boy I liked. Not a chance. With Wyatt being in the military and all spiffed out as he often was in official regalia, he cut a dashing figure. At least until he opened his mouth.

Until I could make a case against Wyatt, there was not much else I could do to save Lynn from the broken heart I knew she was in for. And until I had solid evidence, I couldn't bring my suspicions to Wyatt's camping buddy, Doug. But I was determined to dig. Reasons aplenty were piling up to get to the bottom of Sargeant's problem.

CHAPTER 23

Cyan, Virgil, and I were wrapping up after dinner when Doug called, asking me to come upstairs. "Again?" Cyan asked. "You've been called to the principal's office more times in the past few days than you have the entire time I've known you. What does he want this time?"

I had no idea. "I'll find out, I guess. Will you two be okay here alone until I get back?" I glanced at the clock. "It's getting late. Don't wait for me."

"We won't," Virgil said over his shoulder.

Cyan rolled her eyes. "If you're not back by the time I leave, enjoy your day off tomorrow."

"Thanks, I plan on getting a lot done. It's been too long since I've had time to myself."

I untied my apron, threw it in the laundry, and headed upstairs. Even though it had been a long day, I wasn't tired. Rather, I was antsy, jumpy, and wired. Like I wanted to run, though I had no destination in mind.

I knocked at Doug's door and he called for me to come in.

"Peter?" I said when I saw Sargeant sitting there, dressed for work. "Why are you in today?" To Doug, I asked, "What happened now?"

"Sit down, Ollie. Nothing happened. Nothing's wrong. Other than what's already happened, that is."

I sat. "Why are you here, Peter? I thought you were taking a few days off."

Sargeant waved my question away.

"There's been a change in plans," Doug said. "Fortunately for both of you, Mrs. Hyden's team has finally assigned a member to take over the secretary of state's birthday party preparations."

"Excellent," I said, clapping my hands. "That means we're permanently off the hook?"

"Not yet," he said. "The new assistant in charge wanted to meet you both at Jean-Luc's on Monday morning to go over all the preparation you've done up until this point."

I waited for the "But . . ."

"But," Doug said, "Peter's nephew's memorial is scheduled for Monday morning. With that in mind, the assistant has agreed to come in on Sunday instead."

"Sunday," I repeated. To Sargeant I said, "You and I will need to coordinate our notes before we hand them over. If you like, you can give me whatever you have and I'll put together a report for her."

Doug shook his head. "This isn't a hand-a-report-over situation. She plans to meet with you both and go over the entire affair — as much as you've been able to organize, that is — step by step."

"We have dinner planned for forty people Sunday afternoon."

"I'm aware of that," Doug said, "which is why I called Peter in today. The two of you still have a lot of loose ends to tie up. I suggest you do that tonight and get it over with. This way you can get in and out of Jean-Luc's early on Sunday, allowing you to be here to oversee the dinner."

I was digesting this when he went in for the kill. "There's another wrinkle," Doug said. "Mrs. Quinones hasn't been able to work with you up until now. This is, after all, a party for her husband. She's available this evening and I strongly urge you both to meet with her at Jean-Luc's."

"When did this all come about?" I asked.

Doug had been talking to us with his hands clasped on the desk. Now he opened them. "I got word about the change in organizational duties this morning, but I only got word of Mrs. Quinones's availability about an hour ago." He cast a pitying look at Sargeant. "I'm very sorry to have called you in like this."

Up until now, Sargeant had sat so quietly, so immobile, staring at the window behind Doug that I wondered if he even heard any of the conversation. Evidently he had. "I'm not doing anything constructive at home. I might as well be here."

"Wyatt will join you," Doug said.

Oh joy of joys.

No reaction from Sargeant.

"Tomorrow is my day off . . ." I began.

Doug looked at me as if to say, "So?"

"Wouldn't it be better if Peter and I met with Mrs. Quinones in the morning? I can make time."

Doug was shaking his head before I could get the question all the way out. "Mrs. Quinones has a commitment tomorrow. No, it's tonight or not at all."

"Why not have the secretary's wife meet with Mrs. Hyden's assistant after she takes over? Wouldn't that be more efficient?" I asked.

Sargeant was staring out the window again. Still as a statue.

Doug's patience began to wane. "Ms. Paras," he said, "in case you haven't noticed, I'm juggling your availability as well as Mr. Sargeant's, Mr. Becker's and, most important, Mrs. Quinones's. If I have to order you to work tonight at Jean-Luc's, I will."

I bit my lips tight, wanting to argue. Knowing I'd already lost.

Doug didn't have to continue explaining, but he blathered on anyway. "This birthday party will be the first one under my watch. Coming off of such tragedies as we are, this event will have to be picture-perfect. You and Mr. Sargeant have been at the forefront of planning this from the start. Mrs. Quinones requested this meeting, and I will not disappoint her. Do I make myself clear?"

Cyan and Virgil were gone by the time I got back to the kitchen. Not that it mattered. I pulled up my notes on the computer and set to work, ensuring I'd covered everything before printing it out to take with me to Jean-Luc's. Doug was right to have the two of us go over the list one more time before we handed it over to a new organizer, I just didn't like the way he went about it.

Twenty minutes later, I was ready to go. I grabbed my notes and coat, and headed out. Sargeant, for all his bluster, wore the ravages of his loss on his sleeve. He met me in the Diplomatic Reception Room, moving and reacting like an automaton. No life behind his eyes.

"Time to go," I said. He followed me outside, saying nothing. I tried again, as we got into the back of the sedan. "We have a new driver today, I see." When the agent got into the driver's seat, I asked his name.

"Frederick," he said. "It will be a few minutes before we leave. We're waiting on Agent Millcourt."

"Two guards?" I asked.

"Two subjects to protect."

Just as he said the words, Agent Millcourt trotted out from the back door and got into our car. "Evening," he said without warmth. The two of them stared straight ahead. Sargeant stared out the backseat passenger window. I stared out from my side.

The two agents guarding us tonight weren't part of the "trusted few" Tom had indicated, so I didn't feel comfortable talking in front of them. But they were both wearing today's golden rectangle pins. "Are you dropping us off at Jean-Luc's, or are you staying there until we're done?" I asked them.

"Staying," said Millcourt. "We will be monitoring the door, making sure no one enters without authorization."

"Who is authorized?"

Millcourt consulted notes. "You, Mr. Sargeant, Social Aide Wyatt Becker." He rattled off several other names and explained they were Jean-Luc's workers on duty at the site. "And Mrs. Quinones, of course."

We arrived at Jean-Luc's without incident, and I was struck by how different the place looked at night. Spotlights, strategically placed around the front, gave the building a sexy, warm glow. Very inviting, very chic. With these lights throwing attention at the lines and curves of the building, it was almost impossible to notice the structure's unsightly neighbors. The adjacent dank alley had been rendered nearly invisible. I decided my initial misgivings were unwarranted. This would be a most beautiful place to host a gala birthday party with a sparkling guest list and top-notch entertainment.

"What time will Wyatt be here?" I asked Millcourt when I got out. Sargeant had alighted before me. He stared up at the building as though seeing it for the first time.

"He should be here already," he said. "Let me escort you in to make certain the venue is secure."

Sargeant followed me as Millcourt led us up the stairs. Agent Frederick followed. Once they'd seen us safely into the banquet area where Wyatt was chatting up the staff, they departed.

"Look who's here," Wyatt said with forced joviality. "I understand this is our last time working together."

Sargeant stood behind me, saying nothing. "Guess so," I said, "and the sooner we get started, the quicker we'll be done." I didn't mention Mrs. Quinones's visit. She was due to arrive in about a half hour. With any luck we might be able to dump Wyatt before she arrived.

"What's left to be done?" Wyatt asked. "I thought we were very thorough last time."

"Mr. Sargeant and I need to combine our lists and go over them, step by step, to make sure nothing's been overlooked, nothing forgotten. I would appreciate any notes you have. Just in case we missed anything."

Sargeant wandered away. I let him go.

"What's wrong with him?" Wyatt asked in a stage-whisper. Then, as realization dawned, he said, "Oh that's right. That nephew of his died, didn't he?"

Wyatt was not one of our trusted confidants, nor did I like him very much. "How was your lunch with Lynn?"

He had the decency to avert his eyes, though only for a second. "Unfortunately, I was called away on another duty. I haven't spoken with her at all. Beverly has been keeping me busy."

"Too bad," I said. "I think Lynn sees you as her guardian angel."

He faked a smile.

"Your notes?" I asked again. "I assume you brought them."

He tapped the side of his head. "I rely on my brainpower, not notes that can be lost or stolen. I prefer to keep all pertinent information here. And I do a fine job of it, if I do say so myself. I can't think of anyone with a better memory than mine."

"Let's get started then, shall we?" I looked around. "Peter?"

Sargeant came around the corner. "Yes, I'm ready."

Forty minutes later, we'd gone over every detail twice. I'd made notes about kitchen equipment we needed to have brought in from the White House. Although this place was well-equipped, there were a few items I relied on regularly — the jumbo immersion blender, for one. My knives, of course. Those would need to be escorted in via Secret Service. There was no way I'd be able to walk into this setting with my arms full of super-sharp blades.

Sargeant had a list of non-food-related preferences on his version of the guest list. The location was disabled-accessible, so no worries there, but he'd worked enough with guests' requirements in the past that when he pointed out the need to replace the orange linens with blue, I didn't argue.

So intent were we in our activity, I'd almost forgotten about Mrs. Quinones's visit to finalize plans, until she showed up.

"Hello?" she called into the wide warehouse-sized ballroom. "Which one of you is Olivia Paras?"

I glanced up and waved. "That would be me. I'll be right there."

Wyatt grinned when he saw her. "One of my favorite ladies," he said. "Did you know she and I went to school together? She's way younger than Mr. Quinones. Maiden name was Bettencourt. We were in the same class lots of times."

I started across the dance floor, hoping Wyatt would stay back with Sargeant. No such luck; they both followed me. Mrs. Quinones pointed off to her right, indicating she'd meet me out there.

"She's here to talk about the party," I said.

Wyatt was unfazed by my hint to shut up. "She studied ballet as a little girl. Did you know that?"

"A lot of girls do."

Sargeant shuffled behind Wyatt, saying nothing at all.

"Yes, but she was supposed to go to Juilliard. Full-ride scholarship. But her parents refused to let her move away. Thought it would corrupt her. Shame."

I figured if I kept quiet he might, too. We were about fifteen steps before exiting the ballroom into the vestibule, when he added, "Poor little Mandy."

I stopped. The two men stopped with me. "Her name is Cecelia," I said.

"First name, yeah," Wyatt smirked, "but she always preferred her middle name. Cecelia Amanda. Went by Mandy to her friends growing up. Her parents hated it, of course, and once she was out of high school, they insisted she go by Cecelia. I think Quinones likes that better, too. Sounds way more classy, don't you think?"

"Mandy?" I said. "Are you sure?"

He gave me a look like, "Am I ever wrong?"

The ringtone on Cawley's cell phone had been playing the opening notes to "Mandy" when we found him. That information had not leaked to the press and no one, other than those present at the scene, and those investigating the double murder, would know that. I studied Wyatt's face. He wasn't making this up. Could this just be a weird coincidence?

"She's waiting," he said, breaking into my thoughts. "I thought you wanted to get out of here."

"I do," I said, "I do. Peter, come with me. Wyatt, stay here."

Wyatt was obviously put out by my tone. He folded his arms across his chest. "Fine. But I think she would want to at least say hello to me. It's been years since we've had a chance to talk."

"Later," I snapped. "Why don't you go home? We're just about done here now."

Sargeant followed me out of the ballroom into the expansive lobby area. Carpeted, plush, and high-ceilinged, it made Mrs. Quinones, waiting by a distant pillar, look tiny. Her Secret Service guard nodded as we approached. He then stepped away to give us a modicum of privacy. I hurried over, glad to have Sargeant with me.

This was the first time I'd met Mrs. Quinones up close. She was a pretty woman, easily twenty years younger than the secretary of state, with a smooth, pale complexion, and enormous brown eyes perfectly set off by the longest eyelashes I'd ever seen.

She didn't smile.

"Mrs. Quinones," I said, "I'm sorry to not have come out to greet you. I thought the Secret Service would alert me when you got here."

She waved away my apology. "We used the side entrance," she said, pointing to her escort. "He couldn't find a parking spot out front."

So much for our security. I launched into the reason for her visit. "I know you're here to talk about your husband's birthday party, but —"

"No, I'm here to talk to you. It's important."

"About the party —"

"Forget the party," she said. Eyeing her Secret Service escort, who studied the doors as though expecting terrorists to storm in any minute, she stepped closer and whispered close to my ear. "This is about the murders. The two murders at Lexington Place."

I backed up. Stared at her. "You're Mandy, aren't you?"

Out of the corner of my eye, I'd been watching Sargeant. Close enough to listen in, he'd blinked at the mention of the murders. "What's going on here?" he asked.

Mrs. Quinones started to tremble. "It's

bigger than me. Much bigger. I need to talk with you where it's private. Not here." She tilted her head toward her guard. "He promises to give us privacy in the car. Would you come outside with me so I can tell you what's going on?"

"No," I said, "not a chance. We can talk here. He's far enough away."

She glanced at her agent again. "But I don't want to take any chances. It's important. And he can't know what I'm about to tell you."

Tingles ran up and down the back of my neck. She had the answers. I could see it, feel it. The agent accompanying her was not one of the "trusted few," so I wouldn't want him to hear what she had to say, either. I desperately wanted to know what she wanted to tell me, but I wasn't about to follow her outside without the protection of a Secret Service agent. Or two.

She looked ready to cry. "Agent Sanker," she called. He half-turned, never taking his eyes off the door. "Would you give us some privacy?"

"I'm sorry, ma'am," he said, "my orders are to keep you within reach at all times. I am already farther away than I should be."

She obviously ranked higher than Sargeant and I did. We'd been allowed to work here while our escorts waited outside. But then again, even though we'd all been threatened one way or another, Secretary of State Quinones ranked a whole lot higher than a chef and a sensitivity director did.

Mrs. Quinones asked, "Please?"

Sargeant turned to me. "Would you feel better if we asked our escorts to join us?"

For once he had a decent idea. "That would work."

Mrs. Quinones sighed with relief. "Good. Agent Sanker, would you please alert the agents in charge of Ms. Paras and Mr. Sargeant?"

He asked their names, which Sargeant had forgotten, but I'd remembered: Frederick and Millcourt. Sanker spoke in low tones into his microphone and nodded at whatever response he received. "They'll meet us at the car," he said. "It's parked on the side of the building."

Mrs. Quinones turned to me. "Okay now?"

I had one more question. "Why are you here? I have questions for you, sure, but why in the world would you need to talk to me?"

Her eyes clouded and she leaned close to whisper. "I need to talk with *both* of you. That's why this meeting was arranged.

You're both in more danger than you realize."

Ethan Nagy, I thought. "Danger from whom?"

She widened her eyes and tilted her head toward the agent. "Not here."

We followed Agent Sanker in silence. He led us out of the lobby toward the side door and held it open. I wished I'd brought my coat. "I'd rather not get into the car until Millcourt and Frederick get here," I said, pulling my arms tight around myself. Where was the car? Light spilled out from the warm Jean-Luc's into the empty alley and I wrinkled my nose at the smell.

As I walked past Sanker into the dark passage I took notice of his Secret Service lapel pin.

It was a red square.

Not a golden rectangle.

Stifling a yelp, I grabbed Sargeant's arm. He recoiled. "What on earth?"

I shushed him. "Hang on," I said with forced calm. "I forgot my notes. Give me a minute to run back." I didn't know how to alert Mrs. Quinones that Agent Sanker was not who he pretended to be. We had to get away.

But Sanker had seen my reaction. He grabbed me. As I opened my mouth to scream, one of his big hands smashed me silent, the other wrapped around my middle, immobilizing my flailing arms. I struggled, trying to make as much noise as I could, vaguely aware of the horrified look on Sargeant's face. Sanker's partner emerged from the building across the alleyway. Mrs. Quinones held her face in her hands and wept.

It was obvious Millcourt and Frederick weren't coming. Still positioned at the front of the building, they were too far away to hear our scuffles. Only screams and shouts might bring them running. Sargeant was frozen silent.

I fought Sanker, kicking him wildly. Fighting back, he managed to reach over, grab the handkerchief out of Sargeant's breast pocket, and shove it into my mouth while pushing me to the ground. My cheek skidded against the rough pavement, and the air was knocked out of me long enough to render me helpless. Sanker tied my hands behind my back. As I wriggled, feeling like a worm ready to be speared with a hook, the partner came close enough for me to see his face.

Brad.

He'd dyed his hair, but there was no mistaking that cleft chin, that insouciant expression. He grabbed Sargeant, dragging him across the alleyway into an open doorway. Why wasn't Mrs. Quinones screaming? Why wasn't she running for help?

Sanker hauled me up and dragged me, kicking, into the dark building behind Brad and Sargeant. I tried to see around Sanker, hoping to catch Mrs. Quinones's eye, hoping to inspire her to wake up and call for help.

To my utter astonishment, she followed us in.

"Shut up," Sanker said, using both hands now to carry me, arms tight around my legs and arms. I was no more than a squealing lump, trying to squirm out of his grip. He was too tall, too strong, too prepared for me to fight. He'd planned well. I'd been stupid. I'd walked straight into this trap.

Behind us, a metal door clanged shut.

There was just enough ambient light from high windows to allow them to navigate around old furniture to the back end of this floor. My eyes adjusted quickly — until we passed through a thick doorway leading to a darker, narrow room with what looked like small rectangles decorating the walls. Just ahead of us Brad dropped Sargeant, where he landed in a sad thump. His voice was plaintive. "What are you doing? What's going on?"

Sanker dropped me next to him. I landed on my stomach and rolled to my back. With my hands tied, I couldn't easily right myself. In a moment of brilliance, Sargeant yanked his handkerchief out of my mouth. I screamed as loudly as I could.

"Won't make a difference," Brad said. "You're in an old bank vault. And" — he turned and pointed to where Mrs. Quinones stood — "no one can hear you from here. We aren't making any mistakes this time." He gave a soft chuckle. "Once that door closes, there's no opening it from the inside. You'll be locked in. And nobody will know you're here."

Mrs. Quinones gasped.

"Don't worry," Brad said to her, "at that point, you won't really care."

I scooted toward Sargeant and backed my hands up to him. He untied me. Brad and Sanker didn't seem bothered. This made no sense at all. "Why?" I asked Mrs. Quinones. "Why?"

She wasn't paying attention to me. She'd run to the far end of the vault. As my eyes became accustomed to the darkness, I noticed another person in our little group. Mr. Bettencourt. Pieces began to click into place. She helped her father to his feet.

"What's wrong, honey?" he asked her. Bettencourt patted his daughter's hand as she led him forward. "What happened? Why are you so sad?"

Mrs. Quinones faced Sanker. "I did what you wanted. Can we go now?"

He ignored her and pulled out a gun. Pointing it at us, he said, "Hand over your cell phones. Drop them to the floor."

"But you said we could go once you had these two," she said. "You promised you wouldn't hurt anyone."

"I lied. Cell phones. All of you. Now."

We complied.

Brad made us step back before he gathered them up, stuffing them into his pockets. When he got to mine, he looked up and grinned. "They can be traced, you know," I said.

"Not if they're disabled."

"Is that what you did with Patty Woodruff's phone?" I asked. "Disable it? What was it to you, just a trophy?"

Sargeant jabbed me with his elbow. "Stop. You're just making them angry."

"So what, Peter? Do you think that if we behave like nice little captives they will let us go? Who cares if they're angry?" My voice rose as I advanced on Brad. "*I'm* angry."

Sargeant grabbed my arms, pulling me back.

Brad laughed, but Sanker was all business. "No screw ups this time, Brad. You ready?"

Brad pulled out a gun. "As I'll ever be."

He pointed it at me.

Chapter 24

Soundproof. Empty. There was no one coming for us in this vault. No one riding to our rescue. Our Secret Service agent escorts were waiting for us out in front of Jean-Luc's. I'd even sent Wyatt home. No one would miss us except Frederick and Millcourt. By the time they came to look, it would be too late.

All this rushed through my brain as I stared into the barrel pointed at my face.

A combination of bravery, fear, and down-to-my-toes realization that I was facing death made me wrench out of Sargeant's grip to launch myself at Brad.

"What the —"

I jumped straight at him, banging his gun arm. The weapon skittered across the floor as I dug into his face with my fingernails. "Grab the gun," I shouted.

No one heard me.

Sargeant was shrieking. Mrs. Quinones

sobbing.

Sanker roared as he pulled me off Brad. I twisted in his grip and started punching his face, hoping to land one of those nose-to-the-brain shots. My adrenaline gave me power I didn't know I possessed as I kicked and dug my fingers into anything that would give. "My eye," he shouted, thrusting me off of him. He must have holstered his gun when he'd pulled me off Brad because both hands held his injured face. He swore and staggered backward.

Brad grabbed me tight, placing the barrel of his gun against my temple. "What do I do, Luis?" he shouted. "What do I do?"

Sanker grimaced as he doubled over in pain. I'd gotten him good, but I couldn't take time to congratulate myself. We had to take advantage of the moment. As Brad dragged me closer to Sanker, asking again for direction, I turned to Sargeant.

"Run," I mouthed. "Go. Run. Get help."

For the first time in his life, Sargeant listened to me.

Mrs. Quinones tried to follow, pulling her father along. She was too slow, too late. Brad spun just as Sargeant cleared the vault door. "Go," I screamed to him. "They're coming."

"Get back," Brad shouted as he threw me

to the ground. "Luis! We have to get him before he gets away."

Sanker shouted expletives as he followed Brad out. Brad took a moment to glare at me. "You're going to die anyway. You still lose."

The vault door shut with a whisper. I heard metal turning, then all was silent. Cave dark. Like they tell you on tours . . . stay in long enough and your eyesight will atrophy.

"I'm so sorry," Mrs. Quinones said from behind me.

I put my hands against the metal door. I guessed it to be at least two feet thick and the only way out was with a key, or via a mechanism put in place to save people who might inadvertently lock themselves in.

"You don't understand," she went on, "they told me they would kill my father. They said they would torture him if I didn't bring you here."

"And we see how well that plan worked."

I wanted to ignore her, but my anger had built such steam I was afraid my head might pop off the top of my shoulders.

"You don't understand —"

I spun to face her, despite the fact that I couldn't even see. "I *do* understand. You had an affair with Chief of Staff Cawley.

You got caught, and now he's dead. What I don't understand is who cares about your sordid business enough to kill him. Enough to kill Patty, too. What sense does that make?"

Even as the words tumbled out, I began to see a pattern emerge. Secretary of State Quinones had Secret Service agents watching his family around the clock. But the two who had captured us were not real agents. Could it be . . . ? No, I thought. Too far-fetched.

But if he'd been jealous of his wife's affair . . .

"You know what?" I said, turning back to the door, "I don't care right now. There has to be a safety latch. There has to be."

"They said there wasn't a way out."

I spoke over my shoulder through clenched teeth. "At what point do you intend to stop believing everything they tell you?"

I was being short with her, but she deserved it. My mind was on Sargeant. Where was he? Please let him have gotten away. If they caught up with him, I knew they'd kill him. Would they bring him back here first?

According to the doorman, this building had housed a bank in the nineteenth century. That meant this safe was old. Possibly too old to incorporate any safety features, but there had to have been a retro-fit at some point, right? Wasn't that what the Occupational Safety and Health Administration was for? "Hey," I said, as my fingers found an uneven bump between the door and its cold metal jamb. "I might have found something."

Her hands were next to mine in seconds, confusing my sense of touch. "Back up," I said. "I'll let you know if this works."

She did. I heard her murmur to her father as I pressed, tapped, and rubbed the uneven section. My fingers fanned out from it in concentric circles, looking for any mechanism, any moving pieces. There had to be a way out.

"Can we get a bite to eat?" Bettencourt said. "I'm hungry."

Mrs. Quinones was sobbing again. "I'm so sorry, Dad."

"It's okay, honey, I can wait. I might have a peppermint in my pocket. Would you like it?"

The woman was falling apart by inches, yet I had no urge to console her. My mind was on escape, on Sargeant. By my best guess, we'd been alone here for no more than five minutes, but it felt like a lifetime.

I went over every square inch of the door's

edge, skimming, hoping a latch would make itself known, but came up empty. Starting from the bottom, I tried again, slower this time, my hopes dissolving with each brush of my fingers against steel.

"All this time," I said to Mrs. Quinones, "I thought Ethan Nagy was calling the shots. He was just doing your husband's dirty work, wasn't he?"

She didn't answer, but from the sound of her sobs, I'd hit it square on.

"What about Patty? I don't understand. Why kill her?"

Mrs. Quinones took two deep, hiccupping breaths before answering. "My husband thought my affair would make him a laughingstock. I wanted a divorce, but he wouldn't give it to me. Said he'd see me dead first. I was supposed to meet Mark Cawley that day at Lexington Place. I think I was supposed to die, too."

"That doesn't answer my question."

"They . . . killed him."

A fresh burst of sobs. I was really getting tired of this woman.

"Yeah, I got that. What about Patty?"

"I threw off the plan because I couldn't make it to Lexington Place that day. They left Cawley there to come back to kidnap my dad. My husband wanted to prove a point to me. To let me know there was no escape. By the time the two men went back to pick up Cawley's body later, that other girl, Patty, was there. They didn't know what to do. So they killed her. They might have gotten away with it, but then you showed up."

Her tone made it sound as though it was all my fault. "Yeah, well, next time tell them not to leave their dead bodies where people can find them."

"You don't understand —"

My fingers were going numb from the constant pressure of skin against metal. "You keep saying that," I said into the darkness. "You're right. I don't understand. People have been killed. Not just Cawley, not just Patty, but a friend of mine, Milton." I swallowed back the heat in my throat. "They're dead and you don't care."

"But I do care. I loved Mark. I wanted —"

"I don't care what you wanted." I turned again — pointless, but I had to. "You know what I want? I want to keep on living. Because of you, I may not get to do that. Because of you, we may all be stuck here until we die of starvation or lack of air. You'd better hope . . ." I pressed my ear to the edge.

"What?" she asked.

"Be quiet."

"Do you hear something?"

"Be quiet."

Mr. Bettencourt sneezed. I heard him wipe his nose. "Dusty in here," he said.

Whatever I thought I'd heard was gone. Probably just my brain playing wishful tricks on me.

"Be safe, Sargeant," I whispered against the cold steel. "Be safe."

CHAPTER 25

"What's going to happen to us?" Mrs. Quinones asked. Her father had been pestering her about being hungry, and now expressed the need to perform another human function.

"Where's the lights around here, anyway?" he asked. "Somebody turn on the lights."

She whispered to him — why, I have no idea, there was no one else around to hear — "Just a little longer, Dad. You're okay, right?"

I'd given up my search for a safety latch. There wasn't one. I wished I had one of those light-up watches so I'd know how much time we'd spent here. Of course, maybe I was happier not knowing.

I'd been hoping that Sargeant had gotten away, that help would come. If he had, shouldn't they be here by now? It wouldn't take long for him to run around the front of the building to alert our Secret Service guards. It wouldn't take long to swing open the door to set us free.

No, I thought as I slid down to the floor with my back against the confounding metal. They must have caught up with him. They might even have killed him by now. Even if they hadn't — if they'd taken him prisoner and disappeared — it was obvious they weren't coming back for us.

Agents Millcourt and Frederick would eventually grow suspicious as the hours wore on and Sargeant and I failed to emerge. I expected them to investigate, but if Sanker and Brad had planned this well enough to scope out this vault ahead of time, I had to bet they'd also found a way to blur their trail. Eventually the Secret Service would burst in here looking for clues. But would that be too late for us?

"It's getting hard to breathe," Mrs. Quinones said. "Have you noticed?"

I had, but I'd chalked it up to paranoia. More brain tricks. This one designed to induce panic. If my mind believed we'd run out of air, my body would respond sympathetically. Like a psychosomatic terror. "Then let's not talk, so we don't use up whatever oxygen we have left."

"No talking?" Bettencourt asked. "Whenever our mother told us no talking, we would sing instead. Do you want to sing?"

"Dad, no."

"A hundred bottles of beer on the wall . . ."

"Mr. Bettencourt," I said, "how about we play a game?"

"I like games."

"Great. Let's play . . ." I scrambled to come up with something, "what's that in the dark?"

"I don't know that one."

"We all have to sit very silently until we hear whatever the leader calls. I'll start, so I'll be the leader. If you hear it first, then it will be your turn."

"Okay."

"I call . . . a bird singing. Whoever hears a bird singing first should call it out. Then you'll win."

He sounded excited to play. Thank goodness. Maybe the concentration would put him to sleep. People took up less oxygen when they slept, didn't they?

We were quiet for all of two minutes, when Mr. Bettencourt said, "I don't hear anything at all."

"Just a little longer," I said. "You know there has to be a bird out there somewhere."

This time when he went quiet I suspected he had, indeed, fallen asleep. Eventually he began to snore. Rumbles at regular intervals. Except . . . the noises came from behind me.

"What's that?" Mrs. Quinones asked.

I'd already scrambled to my feet and pressed my ear to the metal. I couldn't hear anything. "Maybe it was a big truck going by —"

There it was again.

"Someone is out there." I began pounding at the door with both fists, both arms.

Mrs. Quinones was at my side seconds later, trying to pull me away from the door. "What if they came back? What if it's them?"

Shaking her off, I said, "*You* are why women in distress get a bad name." I resumed pounding. "In here! In here!"

For at least fifteen minutes there was little change. The occasional rumbling, followed by silence. Mrs. Quinones started to cry again. "It's got to be a machine making that noise. There's no one out there."

Her attitude was jaw-droppingly underwhelming, but the same thought had occurred to me. What if this was nothing? What if I'd wasted precious oxygen on shouting for help to an empty room? "We can't think like that," I said, "so don't."

"But —"

Mr. Bettencourt stirred. "Cecelia, honey,

when can we go home?"

"Soon, Dad. Very soon."

"You keep saying that, but . . ."

Whatever he said next was lost to me. The rumbling was back. This time louder. Closer. Maybe? "Hello!" I shouted. "In here!"

This time the rumbling didn't stop. It grew louder and stronger. So strong that I stepped back from the door and covered my ears against the shrill screech of metal against metal.

When the door finally swung open, I blinked against all the light. My hands flew to cover my eyes. "Who is it?" I shouted. "Who's there?"

The first voice I heard was Sargeant's. "They didn't kill you!"

The rest was a blur until we all got outside, shuttled into waiting cars, and driven with lights and sirens back to the White House.

Mrs. Quinones and her father were taken to the doctor's office on the ground floor so that Mr. Bettencourt could be checked out. I suspected he would be fine, but it never hurt to be sure.

Sargeant and I had been brought up to the Red Room again, where we took the same seats on the couch we'd occupied before. The group gathered this time, however, was much larger. Doug was present, as were more Secret Service agents in one room than I'd seen in a long time. I didn't recognize most of them. But I did recognize the golden rectangle on each of their lapels. I hadn't noticed Mrs. Quinones's guard's pin when they first showed up because Sanker had kept his back to us most of the time. While I'd believed he was giving us privacy, he was actually protecting his cover.

My biggest mistake was in trusting Mrs. Quinones. She'd sold us out — something I could never have imagined. Even doing so to protect her father wasn't a good enough reason.

Tom strode in to take charge of the meeting. As he made his way to the front of the group, I leaned closer to Sargeant. "Thank you," I said, "for saving my life."

Sargeant didn't look at me. "I couldn't save Milton's."

I patted his hand. He didn't pull away.

Tom cleared his throat. "Everyone, we've all had another exciting night and we have a lot of information to cover. I will appreciate your attention while we sort through what we know, what we don't, and where we go from here."

I couldn't wait to hear everything. The agents in the car had been close-mouthed. All I knew was that Sargeant had alerted them and that it had taken considerable time to find a drill that would cut through the vault door.

"Here's where we stand," he said. "Mr. Sargeant was able to provide us with important information that led to the release of Ms. Paras, Mrs. Quinones, and Mrs. Quinones's father from confinement. The Metro Police have issued an all-points bulletin for the two men who abducted them in the first place. We don't have a make and model for a car, but we do have other agents working a different angle." He turned to me. "Ms. Paras, please share with us what Mrs. Quinones told you while you were in captivity."

I hadn't expected to be put on the spot. I explained what she'd told me, implicating her husband and his assistant, Nagy, in the process.

When I was finished, Tom continued. "Special Agent in Charge Gavin is currently bringing Mr. Nagy and Secretary Quinones to headquarters for questioning. We will keep you all informed."

He explained a few more details about the night, details I hadn't heard before. Sargeant

— at least twenty years older than Sanker and Brad — had known he couldn't outrun the two men, so he'd hidden under a desk until they left the building looking for him. When he believed the coast was clear, he'd run directly to Millcourt and Frederick. They'd leaped to action, and as the APB went out, the rescue efforts began.

When the meeting broke up, Tom pulled me aside. "There was some doubt as to whether you were alive inside that vault. You couldn't hear us, and we couldn't hear you."

I took a deep breath. "Thank goodness you came when you did. I was starting to lose hope."

"You?" Tom asked. "Never." He whispered close to my ear. "There's one more thing you ought to know. He would be furious if he knew I told you, but your buddy Sargeant was panic-stricken out there. I think he was the most excited guy in the room when you came out safe."

"Sargeant?" I said. "There's got to be a mistake."

"Speak of the devil," Tom said as Sargeant approached. "See you later."

"How are you holding up, Peter?" I asked.

"Fair enough. Did you hear we still get guarded until they pick up those two thugs?"

"Makes sense."

The agents had all dispersed and it was just me and Sargeant making our way to the stairs. "How did you do it?" he asked. "How did you stay so calm, so focused when they were ready to kill us?"

"Calm? Focused?" I almost laughed. "Me? Not even close."

"You fought them. How did you do that?"

I thought back to that moment, to springing at Brad in the face of a gun pointed straight at me. "When you have nothing to lose, Peter, you have everything to gain."

CHAPTER 26

I got back to my apartment courtesy of Agent Scorroco. "Sorry it's so late, Ms. Paras," he said as we pulled up to my apartment building's front door.

Shocked that he'd initiated conversation, I smiled. "Could be worse," I said.

"That it could. I heard about this evening's trouble," he said. "I'll be here in the morning in case you need to go out anywhere."

"I'll be going in to the White House again," I said. "Just not so early. What's good for you? Nine o'clock? Or would later be better?"

"Isn't tomorrow your day off?"

"I have to talk with Doug about something pressing. It can't wait."

"Yes, ma'am," he said. "Nine o'clock will be fine."

Agent Rosenow met me at the car door. "Everything safe and secure," she said. "I bet you're happy to be home."

"I am," I said, and I was. There was an emptiness I'd felt since I'd departed the White House tonight. Even though I'd been surrounded by people who were thrilled that I was safe, I wanted to talk with Gav. I needed to. But he was out catching bad guys, and I had a guard on duty all night. There was little chance of our seeing each other. All I could hope for was a phone call. But who knew when that might come. If it came at all.

After Rosenow ensured my apartment was secure, I said good night and settled in. Hours later, still no word from Gav, I shut off the light and tried to sleep.

As promised, Agent Scorroco was at the building's front door at 9:00. We drove in without conversation, which, for today at least, was fine with me. I'd made an appointment to see Doug at ten. I knocked at his door right on the dot.

"Good morning, Ollie. I was surprised to get your message. How are you feeling?" He gestured to one of the chairs opposite his desk, and I took the one closer to the wall.

"Much better this morning," I said. "By the way, I've asked a couple of other people to join us. Tom MacKenzie should be here any —"

"I'm here now," he said.

Doug gave me a funny smile. "What's going on? Is there more I don't know about? Do we have a problem?"

"We do," I said, "and his name is Wyatt."

Doug's face closed. I'd expected it would, which is exactly why I'd asked Tom to be present. There would be no protecting of friends here. Not when so much was at stake.

"I have reason to believe Wyatt has compromised White House security," I said.

"Wyatt? The social aide? You've got to be kidding."

"I know he's one of your buddies," I said as though he hadn't interrupted, "but I have reason to believe he changed the guest list to eliminate the Baumgartners from it, then left a note for Lynn, the calligrapher, to catch the omission."

Doug sat back, dumbfounded. "Why would he do such a thing?"

"He hates Sargeant," I said. "Simple as that. He's trying to discredit him. Did you know that he approved Virgil's interview — the one that eventually resulted in Virgil telling the world that Sargeant and I had discovered Patty's and Cawley's murders?"

I didn't give him a chance to respond. "Do you realize that article could have cost us our lives?"

Doug shook his head. "Sargeant approved that."

"Check again," I said.

Tom sat forward. "Ollie asked me to look into this. We've found multiple instances where Wyatt Becker overstepped his authority. All using Peter Sargeant's name or access codes. Yes, we will be talking with Mr. Sargeant about protecting his personal information, but the fact is, Wyatt Becker is a security risk."

Doug stammered, "But . . . but . . . are you sure?"

"The investigation is ongoing, but yes. We have enough information now to press charges. There has been no real harm done at this point — except to Mr. Sargeant's reputation. Once we have it all complete, we will need access to files to see what damage has been attributed to Mr. Sargeant that was actually Mr. Becker's doing."

"Did you know Wyatt was doing this?" I asked.

"Of course not," Doug said.

Tom tilted his head. "You should have. Paul should have. I understand he's been worried about his wife, and perhaps he slacked off these past weeks. We will be taking a look at all your procedures."

"Of course," Doug said, his always-pink cheeks glowing red. "I apologize."

At that moment, Lynn knocked on the door. "You wanted to see me?"

Doug looked confused. I took control. "Yes we did, Lynn. It's about that sticky note again. Do you like working at the White House?"

She took a step back as her hand flew to her throat. "I do. I love it here. What's wrong?"

"All we ask is that you be completely honest with us."

She nodded vigorously.

Out of the corner of my eye, I thought I saw Tom smirk.

"Did Wyatt Becker have anything to do with that sticky note you found, alerting you to the incorrect guest list?"

Loyalties waged war across the young girl's face. "He did," she said finally, her face crumpling. "He told me not to tell anyone. He said it would be our secret." She looked up at us with tear-filled eyes. "Are you going to fire me?"

Doug assured her that since she'd told the truth, her job was secure. "Just remember," he said as we sent her back to her office, "no secrets in the White House."

After further discussion, Tom accompanied me out. "Nice detective work, Ollie."

"Aren't you going to chastise me for butting in where I don't belong?"

"Not this time. This was a wrong in our midst. You righted it. Best of all, you didn't have to put yourself in danger to do so." He thought about that for a minute, then turned to me. "Did you really just save Sargeant's job?"

I laughed. "I guess I did."

"Then I take back what I said about putting yourself in danger."

After a brief stop in the kitchen to bring Bucky and Cyan up to speed, I called for Scorroco to drive me home. But when I hurried out the back door, it was Gav who waited for me.

"You're done," he said.

"What do you mean?"

"They're all in custody. Your buddy Brad, his friend Luis Sanker — we're betting he's your 'bump guy' — Ethan Nagy, and the secretary of state. You really aim high, don't you?"

"They're all arrested?" I asked. "You mean, no more guards?"

"You're free again."

I dropped my head back to stare up at the

sky. Clear blue and bright. Just like spring should be. "I love it."

"Let's celebrate. Where do you want to go?"

Although there was a chill in the air, the sun was out, so I suggested we leave the car and walk up 17th Street and grab something from a local vendor. "I'm starved."

We strolled past Connie in her tent across Pennsylvania, taking our goodies to a bench just inside Lafayette Park. "I first ran into bump guy . . . what's his name?"

"Luis Sanker."

"Here. I thought he was reading Connie's posters. After all that's happened, I realize he was waiting for me."

"I talked with Brad. He spilled his guts in exchange for a lighter sentence. Once they realized you had seen Luis — the 'bump' — when Milton shouted at him — they reported in to Nagy. Bettencourt had already been kidnapped and Brad was supposed to leave him to wander in the city with the thought that some good Samaritan would eventually help him out."

"The abduction of Bettencourt was to send Cecelia a message, right?"

"A warning for her to cooperate. Behave like a good wife. What kind of a guy does that?" Gav took an angry bite of his hot dog.

"Did Brad just happen to run into me at the Metro?"

Gav swallowed. "Nope. Seems your kind-hearted tendencies are well known. We can thank the media for that. Brad waited for you at the station with Bettencourt. They'd hatched a plan to use the older man to find out how much you'd seen at the murder site."

"Stupid plan," I said. "Whose idea was it?"

"Does it matter? And it might sound stupid, but it almost worked." He took a breath, then said, "It gets worse. You remember that gift — the pen Ethan Nagy gave you?"

"Yeah?"

"Inside was a tiny tracking device. So they could keep tabs on where you were."

"But I left it at home the night you and I went to dinner," I said. "I guess I thwarted them again, without even knowing it."

"You have the knack." He said it lightly, but the fact that I'd been followed bothered me more than I cared to admit. I didn't want to think about that.

"So what now?" I asked.

"The media will go nuts when all this breaks. Quinones was beloved around here. A genius in foreign affairs."

"Too bad he wasn't better at his domestic ones."

"Sad to say, but true. You can bet there will be a full investigation into all his dealings."

I'd taken a couple more bites of my hot dog, but my appetite suddenly waned. Gav's apparently had, too. We both got up and threw our remainders in the nearby trash can.

"I've been thinking," he said, "about us."

"So have I."

"You asked a question the other day," he said. "You asked if we would always push each other away when times got tough."

I waited.

"That made me think. You and I met under fire — almost literally — and we've both faced more than our share of danger. I signed on for that sort of thing. You didn't."

Here it comes, I thought. He'd never berated me for getting involved in matters far beyond my control. In fact, he always supported me. This time, however, I could feel a lecture brewing.

Instead, he chuckled. "You should have, you know."

"Should have what?"

"Joined the Secret Service, the FBI, or the CIA. Like I said, you've got the knack." He sobered. "I've been on this job a long time. I'm quite a bit older than you are."

"Seven years is not so much."

"I feel older. I'm used to a world where I pick and choose what I do and what to share. I order people around and I call the shots. But you . . ."

"I mess things up for you?"

His eyes were bright, focused. "You do. You've messed up my tidy world. I don't know how to deal with that. My paradigms have shifted. Are shifting."

"Is that a bad thing?"

"The other night, you didn't want me to help you, comfort you . . . anything. You wanted to deal with your grief over Milton's death on your own. Why is that?"

"Because . . ." I had to think for a moment. ". . . because I'm not used to sharing like that. Because I've learned to rely on myself."

He nodded as I talked. "You and I are very much alike."

"Are we having that talk you promised?"

He smiled. "Yeah."

"I'd come to the conclusion that maybe you and I can only be friends. Good friends," I added hastily, "but nothing more."

"Is that what you want?"

I looked away again. Tiny green shoots were popping out all over. The smell of spring was in the air. The smell of hope, of new beginnings. The temptation to allow such promise to sway me was great. Making eye contact with him again, I said, "I want to be able to share my life — fully — with someone, and have that someone share his life fully with me. For a time, I thought that was you."

"And now?"

"I'm not sure."

He nodded. "I understand."

We were silent then, listening to the birds chirp. A cheerful sound. I turned to look at Gav and my heart gave a little lurch when I did. Handsome, confident, with just enough life experience in those eyes to make for one alluring package. He was different than anyone I'd ever known and I'd fallen for him, hard. I wasn't quite sure I was ready to give him up yet, nor sure I'd ever get over him if I did.

"Let me throw something at you," Gav said. He stared away, his jaw tightening ever so slightly. I recognized that look. Whatever he was about to say would be hard for him. No doubt hard for me to hear, too.

"Go ahead."

He twisted his body to face me, taking

both my hands in his. They were warm, comforting, strong. The look in his eyes was warmer still. "Ollie, it's simple. I want you in my life. When I saw you sitting there the other night, alone, I knew I wanted to be the one to see you through the hard times. To share the good times. I want to be the person you fully share your life with."

I held my breath. This was not what I'd expected.

"I realized as I watched you," he continued, "that you would never share your life with me until I learned to open up to you."

I blinked. Yes. Exactly.

He winced. "I've been holding back from you. I know I have. I asked you to wait, to give me time and space, but I never really intended to let you in. Not fully."

"I was afraid of that."

"Because if I did, I was afraid I'd lose you."

He didn't have to explain. I remembered what he'd told me months ago about the two women he'd been engaged to. "I'm pretty good at saving my own skin," I said. "Or haven't you noticed?"

"I noticed."

I grinned. "Of course, this time I needed Sargeant's help. He'll probably never let me live that down."

"So what? You're here. You're safe, and you've got another wild adventure to tell our grandkids someday."

"Grandkids? Aren't we getting a little ahead of ourselves here?"

"Maybe." He brushed hair out of my eyes. "I've been a fool to not let you know how crazy I am about you."

My heart was practically jumping out of my chest. "Am I daydreaming again?"

"Only if we both are." He cleared his throat and sat back. "Speaking of daydreaming . . ."

I waited.

"When I checked your apartment out that first time, I saw the oddest notes on your kitchen table."

My heart dropped to my stomach. "You saw those?"

"My name, your name . . . a bunch of numbers."

"And you want to know what they were?"

"No, I know exactly what they were. And since I'm feeling like a teenager myself right about now, I guess we should make the big leap."

"What do you mean?"

"Ollie, will you go out with me? Be my girlfriend?" He snugged me close. "I'll even put it as my Facebook status."

432

I laughed. "You don't have Facebook."

"How do you know?"

"I do my detective work."

Staring into my eyes with a look I'd never seen before, he tipped my chin up. "That's my girl," he whispered, and kissed me softly on the lips.

CHAPTER 27

Sargeant stood alone in the funeral parlor, hands clasped behind him, staring at the maroon urn that had been placed atop a marble stand. The soft tones of a solitary harp filtered in through the sound system as I walked to the front of the chapel. Even though there was just one floral display, the scent of roses hit me the moment I'd entered. I suppose it was one of those smells that so permeated the place it never went away.

I touched his shoulder. "Peter," I said, "I'm very sorry."

His didn't look at me. "This funeral home has a backlog on cremations," he said. "They moved Milton up to the top of the list because of my White House connections."

"That was nice of them."

He still didn't avert his gaze from the urn. "I don't really know what to do with the ashes, but I think I'll keep them until I figure it all out. I might like to scatter some in the Rose Garden. Just a handful. Do you think Doug would allow that?"

"I think," I said, "this might be one of those times when it's better to ask forgiveness than permission."

His mouth twitched. "Bad habits I'm learning from you."

"They come in handy."

"Yes," he said.

I took a closer look at the sole floral arrangement. A traditional display of carnations, roses, lilies, and chrysanthemums. A wide ribbon crossed the front with gold letters spelling, beloved nephew.

Sargeant seemed to want to talk. "Once my sister died, we only had each other. I should have done more for him."

I had nothing to say to that.

"I never forgave him."

I watched as Sargeant bit the insides of his lip. I think he wanted to tell me. If he didn't now, he never would. "What did he do?" I asked softly.

"Seems so silly."

I waited.

"He got me kicked off the wrestling team in college. Told them I'd gotten drunk." He turned to face me. "I hadn't. The club had a strict, zero-tolerance policy and I would never have broken it."

My mind was trying to grasp the image of Sargeant as a wrestler. "I believe you."

"My girlfriend didn't. One thing about Milton, he was always an entertaining liar. Embellished like you wouldn't believe. Made for great stories, but the truth was unrecognizable. He told the team I'd been out all night carousing. Womanizing. They believed him. And because everybody at school had a crush on Jenny, they made sure she heard, too."

I kept silent, listening.

"Just like that, she broke up with me." He gave a soft, sad laugh. "Everybody at school wondered how I'd landed such a gorgeous girl. What on earth she saw in me. Maybe she'd been looking for an excuse to dump me all along. Maybe it was inevitable." He sighed. "Never met anyone quite like her since." He turned to me and seemed about to say something further. Instead, he shook his head.

"What?"

"She was strong-minded, strong-willed. A real pistol." He frowned, then gave me a wry smile. "Absurdly enough, the same could be said about you."

I didn't know how to take that, but he'd

turned back to staring at the urn. "All these years later, it still hurts like it was yesterday." He shook his head again. "Milton did that to me. And I've been trying to hurt him back ever since."

"I understand."

He turned to me again. "Do you?"

"For what it's worth, I think he was sorry."

Sargeant nodded. "Yes."

"What now?" I gestured with my head. "Are you taking Milton home?"

"I have a better idea."

After ensuring that Milton's urn would be kept safe until he came back for it, Sargeant asked the funeral director for a resealable plastic bag. From the man's smile and unquestioning cooperation, I had a feeling he got that request a lot.

We waited until he left the room for Sargeant to tilt the urn while I held the bag. Once we had it filled about half full with ashes, we zipped the bag shut, righted the urn, and were on our way.

An hour later, the two of us stood in the Rose Garden.

"It's a gorgeous day," I said, "finally starting to warm up."

"Milton would appreciate this."

"The clear sky? The weather?"

Sargeant reached into the bag. "No," he

said. As he scattered the ashes, he said, "Here you go, Milton. You're finally part of the White House after all."

When we were finished, I invited Sargeant to the kitchen to grab something to eat. "You must be starving," I said.

He admitted he was.

I guess I should have been prepared for the looks of incredulity on Cyan's and Bucky's faces when we walked in together. They knew I'd taken the morning off, but they didn't know why.

As I started to put together lunch for the two of us, Cyan hurried to my side. "Need any help?" Under her breath, she asked, "Since when are you and Sargeant so chummy?"

"Shared experience makes unusual bedfellows."

Her eyebrows shot way up.

"I don't mean that literally. Sargeant just needs a friend today —"

Virgil's voice pierced the kitchen's tranquility. "All I'm saying is that no matter what I do around here, no matter how much better a chef I am than she is," pointing at me, "everybody just goes on and on about what an asset she is to the White House. Doesn't anyone notice that she spends more time catching criminals than she does creating menus?"

"Hold your tongue!"

We all spun at Sargeant's directive. He advanced on Virgil. "If you know what's good for you, you will take that contemptible attitude of yours and hide it where no one can see it. Do you know what this young lady did? She saved our lives. Saved my job. And she doesn't even *like* me. If I were you, I'd do my best to get on her good side. Or are you too dull-witted to comprehend such a thing?"

Cyan's mouth had dropped open. As had Bucky's. As had mine.

Sargeant turned to face us. "Yes, well," he said. Recovering his composure and adopting the persnickety expression he usually wore around me, he stepped close and wagged a finger in my face. "Don't let this go to your head, Ms. Paras." His eyes narrowed. "I'm still watching you."

FUN WITH PUFF PASTRY

Needless to say, the White House has its share of formal events. Some come with multi-course dinners and rounds of dessert. Others are more free-form, with an array of hors d'oeuvres beautifully displayed in the various public rooms of the mansion. In either case, the stars of the show are frequently formed with that magical substance, puff pastry.

Puff pastry is both breathtakingly simple and amazingly difficult. It's made of flour, butter, salt, and water. In theory, a four-ingredient recipe should be simple enough. But in practice, puff pastry is one of the most fiendishly difficult recipes to master. It involves taking a simple pastry dough, folding it over and over again and rolling it out again and again, sandwiching layers of chilled butter into the flaky pastry dough with each rolling until the pastry is microscopically thin and sandwiched by equally thin layers of cold butter. If the dough isn't perfectly handled and kept at just the right temperature, the layers disintegrate and the chef ends up with a gelatinous, fatty mess.

When finished, puff pastry looks like ordinary pastry — until you cook it. At that point, the ultra-thin layers of butter and pastry separate, and the pastry cooks up light as a cloud, gently browned, flaky, and delicious. It's a very traditional preparation by classically trained chefs that separates expert pastry workers from mere poseurs. . . .

. . . Until it became possible to buy puff pastry in the freezer section of most grocery stores. Now anybody can have fun with puff pastry. Use it, and you can impress your friends and wow your enemies — who will still eat your treats. Puff pastry is deliciously irresistible. A warning for those of you who are having health issues: It's also chock-full of butterfat — so be sure to limit consumption for those with cardiac issues.

As I'm sure you know, the White House pastry chef handles most of the following items, but as you also know, I'm curious and hate to think there's anything I can't do. The recipes that follow are adapted for home preparation, using the store-bought pastry I talked about above. They are all surprisingly easy to make, meltingly decadent, and delicious. They are a perfect addition to your next New Year's party, bridge brunch, or family gathering. Puff pastry isn't appropriate for everyday consumption, unless you want your waist to vanish and your life to be shortened. But for special occasions, nothing is tastier, more impressive, or easier to use.

You can see the "Classical French Chef" nature of puff pastry in the French lineage of several of the names of the recipes that follow.

A couple of important notes on working with puff pastry:

- Thaw the dough slightly before using. Remove it from the freezer about thirty to forty minutes before you want to use it.
- Keep it cool. Thaw the dough just enough to make it workable. If it gets too warm, the layers lose their integrity and the pastry won't puff up properly.
- Cut it with the sharpest implements you own, and don't twist or shift the implements as you make your cuts.

Cut straight down. If you don't use sharp knives or cutters to work with the dough, you'll glue the edges together by mashing down on the pastry to cut it, and the pastry won't puff.

- Chill your working implements, if possible. Put your rolling pin, your knives or cutters, and your pan into the freezer about thirty minutes before you start working with your dough — the same time you take the pastry out to thaw. Having them cool keeps the dough from sticking and disintegrating.

- Roll the thawed puff pastry dough out again after you get it out from the package, just a little. This will iron out the creases resulting from folding the dough into the box and give you a smooth surface to work with as you make your own puff pastry masterpieces. Sprinkle a little flour on your work surface to keep the dough from sticking, and a bit more on the top of the pastry before you roll it to keep the rolling pin from sticking. A few passes across the top with a rolling pin will give you a nice, smooth dough sheet.

RECIPES

Cranberry Pecan Brie En Croûte

Makes 8 appetizer portions

1 (16–20-oz.) package puff pastry
2 8-oz. Brie rounds
8 ounces whole pecans, shelled and picked over to remove any shell pieces
4 ounces craisins
1/4 cup good maple syrup
1 egg
1 tablespoon water

Preheat oven to 400 degrees F.

Roll out the thawed sheets of puff pastry. Place an unwrapped round of Brie cheese in the center of each sheet of puff pastry. Top each round with half the pecans, half the craisins, and half the maple syrup. Fold the puff pastry around the Brie, trimming off extra pastry as needed.

Place the egg and water in a bowl, and whisk to mix.

Use the egg mixture to cement the pastry folds closed.

Place the pastry-wrapped rounds on an ungreased baking sheet, seam sides down. Brush all over with the egg wash. If desired use the leftover puff pastry to make decorations for the top of the Brie rounds, and cement them onto the pastry with the egg wash.

Place the prepared rounds in the oven until the pastry is golden brown and cooked through, roughly 25 minutes.

Let cool for 20 minutes before serving to let the cheese inside the pastry equalize in temperature and melt. Cut each round into quarters with a sharp knife, and serve warm.

BEEF WELLINGTON

This recipe is actually very easy to make, but you'll need about three hours to get it on the dinner table from start to finish, so plan your schedule accordingly.

Serves 8

1 2-lb. beef tenderloin
1 tablespoon steak seasoning
1 egg
1 tablespoon water
2 tablespoons canola or olive oil
1 small onion, peeled and minced
8 ounces fresh mushrooms, cleaned and finely chopped
1 (16–20-oz.) package puff pastry

Preheat oven to 425 degrees F.

Rub the tenderloin with the steak seasoning. Grease a roasting pan, place the meat in it, and place in the oven for 40 minutes. Remove the meat from the oven, and place it in the refrigerator for an hour. (This will distribute the meat juices throughout the piece and tenderize it.) Keep oven on.

While the meat is chilling, whisk the egg and the water together in a small bowl and set aside.

Place the oil in a skillet over medium heat. Stirring often, sauté the onion until it is clear, then add the mushrooms and sauté until the liquid that comes from the mushrooms has evaporated, leaving the mushrooms and onion cooked through and tender, about 3 minutes.

Roll out the puff pastry sheets. Use the egg wash as a glue to paste the two puff pastry sheets together on their long edges to give you enough pastry to work with. Overlap the sheets together by an inch, after painting the joined edges with egg wash to seal the joint. Make sure that after you roll it out, the finished puff pastry sheet is at least 6 inches longer than the tenderloin piece and 5 inches wider than it needs to be to wrap all the way around the tenderloin.

Spoon the onion/ mushroom mixture down the center of the puff pastry. Remove the chilled meat from the refrigerator and place it over the mounded mushroom mixture in the middle of the puff pastry. Fold the pastry up and around the tenderloin, sealing the edges with egg wash.

Place the wrapped tenderloin seam-side down on a roasting pan or rimmed baking sheet, and brush with egg wash.

Place the wrapped tenderloin in the 425 degree oven. (I cook my side dishes in it during the interval — or you can reheat it, as you prefer.) Bake 25 minutes for medium rare, or 32 minutes for medium.

Remove from oven. Let rest for 5 minutes

to let the juices equalize inside the pastry. Slice and serve warm.

PASTRY-WRAPPED ASPARAGUS SPEARS WITH PROSCIUTTO
Makes 24–30 appetizer portions

1 1/2 pounds asparagus
1 (16–20-oz.) package puff pastry
1 (3-oz.) package herbed or garden vegetable cream cheese, well softened
1/2 pound prosciutto or good deli ham, very thinly sliced

Preheat oven to 400 degrees F.

Wash the asparagus and trim off the tough stems at the bottom. Lay the vegetables on a towel to dry.

Gently roll out the puff pastry sheets to smooth them. Spoon half the softened cream cheese onto each sheet, and spread evenly across the pastry. Divide the prosciutto evenly and place half on each piece of puff pastry, covering the cream cheese in a thin layer.

Cut the puff pastry into long, thin strips, approximately 1 inch wide.

Starting at the base of the spear, wrap the pastry strips — prosciutto and cheese side inward — snugly around the asparagus in a spiral, like stripes on a candy cane.

Place the wrapped asparagus spears on ungreased baking sheets. (You'll likely need two baking sheets.)

Bake until pastry is golden brown and the asparagus is tender, roughly 15 minutes.

Serve hot.

SUMMER TOMATO TART

When beautiful heirloom tomatoes show up at the farmers' markets, this is a nice way to showcase them.

Makes 16 appetizer portions

1 (16–20-oz.) package puff pastry
4 tomatoes at the peak of summer ripeness, washed and sliced thin
One small onion, sliced thin and separated into rings
2 tablespoons olive oil
1 tablespoon herbes de' Provence
1/2 teaspoon salt (I prefer kosher salt)
1 tablespoon balsamic vinegar

1 oz. Parmigiano Reggiano cheese, grated

Preheat oven to 375 degrees F.

Lay out each sheet of thawed, rolled puff pastry on a baking sheet. Leaving a 1-inch border all around each sheet (this will puff up and form a raised crust), prick the remainder of each pastry with a fork every inch or so.

On the forked portions of the pastry, lay out the tomato slices in a pretty overlapping arrangement.

Top with the onion rings.

Wisk together the olive oil, herbs, salt, and vinegar. Paint the tomatoes and onions with the mixture. Sprinkle the tomato tarts with the grated cheese.

Place the tarts into the oven for 25 minutes, until the pastry is golden, the tomatoes and onions are cooked, and the cheese is browned and bubbly.

Cut each tart into 8 portions, and serve warm.

VOL-AU-VENT

A *vol-au-vent* is a very traditional application of puff pastry. Essentially you make a case of puff pastry with a lid, in which you can serve all sorts of sweet and savory fillings, everything from creamed shrimp to lobster thermidor to chocolate sauce to fresh berries. You can make small cases for individual servings, or large cases for a multi-serving entrée or dessert. Once you've mastered the technique, you've got a base for an amazing variety of fancy appetizers, main courses, and desserts.

And, with frozen puff pastry, it couldn't be simpler. In fact, you can often find appetizer-sized *vol-au-vent* casings premade in the freezer section of the grocery store. But I like making my own.

Individual *Vol-au-vents*
1 (16–20-oz.) package puff pastry
1 egg
1 tablespoon water

Preheat oven to 375 degrees F.

Roll the pastry sheets a couple of times to smooth them out. Using a 3-inch biscuit cutter or cutting around a wide-mouthed glass with a sharp knife, cut out as many perfect circles as you can from the sheets.

Arrange half of the circles on a baking sheet and set them aside.

Using a 2-inch biscuit cutter or by running a sharp knife around a small juice glass, cut small circles out of the middles of the remaining half of the puff pastry rounds.

Whisk the egg and water together in a small bowl.

Paint the whole circles on the baking sheet with the egg wash. Gently separate the inner circles from the outer rings of the other puff pastry rounds. Place the rings on the whole puff pastry circles so that you form a cylinder with a central depression. Paint the rims of the rings with the egg wash. Place the small rings on the baking sheet or a separate baking sheet if there is not enough room. These will be your lids. The cylinders will be your containers.

Place all rounds in the oven and bake until brown and crispy, about 20–25 minutes.

Set aside to cool.

Fill with the filling of your choice.

Possible Fillings:
Berry-Filled *Vol-au-vents*
1 pint fresh strawberries, rinsed and picked over

1 cup fresh blueberries, rinsed and picked over

2 tablespoons confectioners' (powdered) sugar, divided

1 drop almond extract

Prepared *vol-au-vent* casings and lids

Sweetened whipped cream and fresh mint sprigs to garnish (optional)

Slice the strawberries into a medium bowl. Add the blueberries. Sprinkle with 1 tablespoon sugar, add the almond extract, and mix well.

Spoon the berries equally into the vol-au-vent casings. Top with the lids.

Sprinkle with remaining tablespoon of sugar.

Serve each on a dessert dish with a side spoonful of whipped cream topped with a mint sprig, if desired.

Chocolate Sundae *Vol-au-vents*

1 pint good vanilla ice cream (or some vanilla/chocolate variant like cookies and cream, turtle, fudge ribbon, or other personal favorite)

2 ounces chopped pecans

1/4 cup maple syrup

Prepared *vol-au-vent* casings and lids
1 cup chocolate fudge sauce

The prep work for this should be done in advance, the desserts assembled at the last minute, and served in a jiffy.

Clear out space in the freezer to accommodate a couple of pie plates or a cookie sheet.

Scoop out the ice cream into individual balls that will fit into the *vol-au-vent* shells. Place the scoops into the pie plates or cookie sheet that fits in your freezer. Freeze solid.

Place the pecans into a skillet over medium heat and toss to toast them — this is fast work and you have to watch to make sure the pecans don't scorch. Add the maple syrup and stir. Set aside. (You'll warm the mixture again right before you serve these.)

To assemble, place an ice cream ball inside each *vol-au-vent*. Top with warm pecan/maple syrup mixture. Place *vol-au-vent* top on the ice cream. Drizzle heavily with chocolate sauce.

Serve immediately.

Warm and Savory *Vol-au-vents*

All you have to do is make a nice cream sauce, add the meat and cooked vegetable of your choice, possibly some wine or sherry, and maybe some melted cheese. Pour the resulting mixture warm into the *vol-au-vent* and serve. The following recipe can be tweaked to provide endless variations.

2 tablespoons butter
1 tablespoon flour
1 cup milk (or cream, if you want to live dangerously)
1/2 teaspoon salt
Fresh ground pepper, to taste
1/4 cup sherry or white wine
6 ounces cleaned frozen cocktail shrimp, thawed and rinsed (fresh shrimp are great, too, but this is a LOT faster)
4 fresh mushrooms, cleaned and very thinly sliced
1/2 cup frozen peas, thawed
Prepared *vol-au-vent* casings
Fresh parsley to garnish (optional)

Melt the butter in a large saucepan over medium heat. Whisk in the flour until it forms a smooth paste. Very gradually whisk in the milk, until it is smooth. Bring the sauce slowly to nearly a boil, whisking constantly until it thickens. Turn down the heat to a low simmer. Add salt and pepper, to taste.

(At this point you've just made a classic French béchamel sauce. From here on in you're just seasoning it to your taste.)

Whisk in the sherry. Add the shrimp, mushrooms, and peas. Stir until the additions are warmed through.

Place each *vol-au-vent* on a plate. Carefully fill with shrimp-vegetable sauce. Lean the lid at an angle to the *vol-au-vent.* Garnish with fresh parsley, if using. Serve warm.

Other Variations

Use cooked cubed chicken instead of the shrimp.

Use peas and carrots instead of just peas.

Use chunks of lobster tail meat instead of the shrimp.

Use cubed ham instead of the shrimp.

I'm sure you'll think up your own favorites, as well.

APPLE STRUDEL

Makes 12 appetizer portions

4 Granny Smith or other cooking apples (apple varieties can be mixed for richer flavors and textures)
2 tablespoons lemon juice
1/2 cup sugar
1 teaspoon cinnamon
1/4 teaspoon freshly grated nutmeg, or to taste
2 tablespoons flour
1/2 teaspoon salt
1/4 cup raisins
1 (16–20-oz.) package puff pastry
1 egg
1 tablespoon water

Preheat oven to 375 degrees F.

Peel, core, and thinly slice the apples. Place in a large bowl. Add lemon juice and toss — this will prevent the apples from discoloring.

Add the sugar, cinnamon, nutmeg, flour, salt, and raisins. Toss until the apples and raisins are evenly coated with sugar, flour, and spices.

Roll out the puff pastry sheets. Place half

the apple mixture in a line in the center of each sheet. Spread across the pastry, leaving the edges free from apple mixture. Roll the apple mixture up in the pastry, jelly-roll style.

Place the rolled pastry, seam-side down, on a baking sheet.

Whisk the egg and water together in a small bowl. Brush the pastry rolls all over with the egg wash.

Make diagonal slices with a sharp knife into the pastry every two inches down the roll, cutting one-third of the way through the pastry rolls. This lets the fruit filling show through jewel-like in the finished pastry.

Place the pastries in the oven and bake for 35 minutes, or until the pastry is golden brown and puffy.

Remove from oven and serve warm. A side of good ice cream or whipped cream topped with a sprinkle of cinnamon is always good with this.

NAPOLEONS
Makes 12

This is such an easy dessert that it is almost

like cheating when you use frozen puff pastry. The way the pastry is folded into the box actually gives you a perfect template for cutting the dough.

1 (16–20-oz.) package puff pastry
4 tablespoons sugar, divided
2 cups mixed fruit — sliced peaches, berries, sliced pears, and mandarin orange segments are all fine. Pick what is seasonal and beautiful.
1 tablespoon Amaretto liquor (optional)
1 cup cream, whipped and sweetened with 2 tablespoons confectioners' sugar (or you can use the canned stuff or whipped topping, if you're in a hurry)
1/2 cup chocolate sauce
Powdered sugar, to garnish

Preheat oven to 400 degrees F.

Unfold puff pastry and scatter 2 tablespoons sugar across the dough. Using the fold marks to guide your knife, cut each piece of the dough into three pieces. Cut each of the six rectangles into six equal-sized rectangles.

Place the pastry, sugared side up, on baking sheets, and bake until brown and flaky, about 15 minutes.

While the pastry is baking, slice the fruit

into a bowl. Toss with remaining 2 table-spoons sugar and the liquor, if using.

When the pastry is done, remove from oven and let cool.

For each Napoleon, place a bottom layer of cooked puff pastry on a dish. Top with whipped cream and a spoonful of fruit. Repeat this for a second layer. Top with a third layer of puff pastry. Drizzle with the chocolate sauce; sift powdered sugar onto the finished dessert. Serve chilled.

Chocolate Napoleons

To make this variation, add 1 teaspoon cocoa powder to the whipped cream, or buy chocolate whipped cream in a can or chocolate whipped topping.

Use either strawberries or raspberries for the fruit. Proceed as with original recipe.

SPINACH TRIANGLES

This recipe is based on a traditional Greek dish made with phyllo dough called spani-kopita. But making the dish this way is much faster and easier.

Makes 32 appetizer portions

1 (10-oz.) package frozen spinach, thawed

3 eggs, divided

1/2 cup crumbled feta or ricotta cheese

1 small onion, finely diced

1/4 teaspoon fresh grated nutmeg, or to taste

1/4 teaspoon salt

1 small bunch fresh parsley, chopped finely, stems removed

1 tablespoon water

1 (16–20-oz) package puff pastry

Preheat oven to 400 degrees F.

Combine spinach, 2 eggs, cheese, onion, nutmeg, salt, and parsley in a bowl and mix thoroughly. Set aside.

In a small bowl, whisk remaining egg and water.

Roll each puff pastry sheet into a 12-inch square. Cut the squares into 3-inch squares.

Place a scant tablespoon of spinach filling into the middle of each square. Brush around the square with the egg wash. Fold the square into a triangle around the filling. Press the edges of the triangle to seal. Place on a baking sheet. Continue until all the squares of puff pastry are filled and sealed.

Brush the triangle tops with the remaining egg wash. Place the pastries in the oven and bake for 20 minutes or until the pastries are golden brown.

Remove from oven. Serve warm.

INDIVIDUAL CHICKEN POT PIES
Serves 6

4 tablespoons butter
2 tablespoons flour
2 cups chicken broth
1/2 teaspoon salt
Fresh ground pepper, to taste
1/4 cup sherry or white wine
1/2 pound cooked, cubed chicken
8 ounces fresh mushrooms, cleaned and very thinly sliced
1 (10-oz.) bag frozen peas and carrots, thawed
1 (16–20-oz.) package puff pastry

Preheat oven to 375 degrees F.

Melt the butter in a large saucepan over medium heat. Whisk in the flour until it forms a smooth paste. Very gradually whisk in the chicken broth until smooth. Bring the sauce slowly to nearly a boil, whisking constantly until it thickens. Turn down the heat to a low simmer. Add salt and pepper, to taste. Whisk in the sherry. Add the chicken, mushrooms, and peas and carrots. Stir until the additions are warmed through. Leave the sauce to simmer slowly.

Arrange 6 ovenproof bowls, soufflé dishes, or other individual containers on a baking sheet. Spoon the chicken filling into the containers. Top each container with a piece of puff pastry cut to fit.

Place the pies into the oven. Bake until the puff pastry is brown and puffed, about 25–30 minutes.

Serve warm.

The employees of Thorndike Press hope you have enjoyed this Large Print book. All our Thorndike, Wheeler, and Kennebec Large Print titles are designed for easy reading, and all our books are made to last. Other Thorndike Press Large Print books are available at your library, through selected bookstores, or directly from us.

For information about titles, please call:
  (800) 223-1244

or visit our Web site at:
  http://gale.cengage.com/thorndike

To share your comments, please write:
  Publisher
  Thorndike Press
  10 Water St., Suite 310
  Waterville, ME 04901